HEARTSWAP

Flora drinks herbal tea, meditates and believes in the abundance of the universe. Georgie drinks black coffee, drives a car called Flat Eric and believes in hard work. But they agree about a lot of things. They're getting married, they know all men are victims of their own biology, but they're not choosing Hillary Clinton for a role model. Which means they've got the whole biology thing sorted. So when their old boss bets them they can't seduce each other's fiancés, they're up for it. Will it all go horribly wrong? Are men really all the same? Biology is destiny, true or false?

HEARTSWAP

Celia Brayfield

CHIVERS PRESS
BATH

First published 2000
by
Little, Brown and Company
This Large Print edition published by
Chivers Press
by arrangement with
Little, Brown and Company (UK)
2000

ISBN 0 7540 1479 7

British Library Cataloguing in Publication Data available.

Another one for Chloe

CHAPTER ONE

FEBRUARY 7–APRIL 10

To: Georgina.Lambton@winsex.com
From: flora.aromatix@earthnet.co.uk
Monday
Yes yes yes. I love this man. He is so totally the one. Loaded. Mad for me. So, so cute. Why are you in Chicago when I need you?

To: flora.aromatix@earthnet.co.uk
From: Georgina.Lambton@winsex.com
Monday
Who is the one? And have you done it yet or are you twitching the poor bloke's chain? Every morning I ask myself why I am in Chicago so don't you start.

To: Georgina.Lambton@winsex.com
From: flora.aromatix@earthnet.co.uk
Tuesday
Oh, please. Get off my case. Tonight is the night. He doesn't know that. So, so cute.

To: flora.aromatix@earthnet.co.uk
From: Georgina.Lambton@winsex.com
Wednesday
And?

1

To: Georgina.Lambton@winsex.com
From: flora.aromatix@earthnet.co.uk
Wednesday
He wants to get married. Why are you in Chicago?

To: flora.aromatix@earthnet.co.uk
From: Georgina.Lambton@winsex.com
Wednesday
DON'T ASK. Way to go!!!!!!!! Omigod, omigod, omigod. You ultrafox.

To: Georgina.Lambton@winsex.com
From: flora.aromatix@earthnet.co.uk
Wednesday
I said yes. Am I crazy?

To: flora.aromatix@earthnet.co.uk
From: Georgina.Lambton@winsex.com
Thursday
Not necessarily. I don't believe this, so romantic. I may die of jealousy. Wossisname, anyway?

To: Georgina.Lambton@winsex.com
From: flora.aromatix@earthnet.co.uk
Thursday
Dillon. Financial products design. 6ft 2in. Buns of custard but will work on it. Do not die of jealousy, you've been with Felix forever.

2

To: Georgina.Lambton@winsex.com
From: flora.aromatix@earthnet.co.uk
Friday
Hello?

To: flora.aromatix@earthnet.co.uk
From: Georgina.Lambton@winsex.com
Friday
Pleeeeeease—Nikkei went mental last night or didn't you notice? I miss custard. No custard in Chicago. Not with Felix forever, only two years this Sunday. Love him to bits, undo jealousy. Are you really doing this?

To: Georgina.Lambton@winsex.com
From: flora.aromatix@earthnet.co.uk
Friday
Yesssssss.

To: flora.aromatix@earthnet.co.uk
From: Georgina.Lambton@winsex.com
Friday
Way to GO. Our anniversary Sunday. I left my old diary out by juicer to remind him. Is that sad? 6–4 he still forgets?

To: Georgina.Lambton@winsex.com
From: flora.aromatix@earthnet.co.uk
Friday
Evens. Don't be pathetic. You too are ultrafox.

To: flora.aromatix@earthnet.co.uk
From: Georgina.Lambton@winsex.com
Friday
TFI Friday. So have a brilliant romantic weekend. See if I care.

To: flora.aromatix@earthnet.co.uk
From: Georgina.Lambton@winsex.com
Monday
Omigod. Felix has a grant from some London hospital to do his research, we're coming home and WE'RE GETTING MARRIED.

To: Georgina.Lambton@winsex.com
From: flora.aromatix@earthnet.co.uk
Tuesday
How cool is this! Ultrafoxes RV lunch, 1 Lombard, day 1.

To: flora.aromatix@earthnet.co.uk
From: Georgina.Lambton@winsex.com
Tuesday
I'll be there. Must go now, he wants to buy a ring.

To Flora Lovelace and Georgina Lambton, it seemed as if nothing that happened in their lives had really happened until they had told each other about it.

*   *   *

'Sweetheart,' said Felix to Georgina, moving aside a curl of her black hair so he could kiss her neck, 'let me handle this. I'll find us a place to live. I'll take care of all this dreary moving shit, all the packing and the shipping and the paperwork and stuff. You don't have to worry about anything. You can just keep going to work like you always do, one weekend we'll catch a plane, and then you'll go to work in London.'

'Would you really?' she murmured. It was 5 a.m. They were in bed, in the warm damp afterglow of morning sex, Felix's favourite. Dawn was happening. She imagined that the light skidded over the ice on the lake, shot into the city and ricocheted around the edge of the blind and into her bedroom.

' 'Course. I'd say it was the least I could do. You're relocating for my sake, after all.'

'For both our sakes.'

'For us, for me. You're still doing it. I should pull my weight here. The hospital will let me out of a few weeks of my notice period. Just tell me where you want to live and what you'll be making, and I'll work out what we can afford, get on the Net and find us a place to live. Then I'll start packing.'

'Your hospital is in the west, my office is in the east. Everything in the middle's too expensive. It'll be down to transport. Find us something on the Central Line, that's the shortest distance between two suburbs. Oh—

5

they're giving me a relocation package,' she remembered, already wearied by thinking of her new job, her new desk, her new dealing room, and her new business cards. Even newness could not make these things exciting. The only fun in sight was her new car. It seemed that she now qualified for a motor that was almost sexy.

'Well so they should,' he congratulated her, squeezing a fond handful of her backside. 'We can do better than suburbs. Leave it to me.'

Georgie felt a pulse of tension answering his squeeze. 'You're so wonderful,' she sighed. 'I don't deserve you.'

The hospital where Felix worked was content that he was leaving them. Georgie registered that, but did not immediately see the significance of it.

*   *   *

Flora bared her pretty teeth and took a bite into one of Dillon's buttocks. She clenched her delicate jaws. Playfully, she shook her head.

'Argh!' he protested. It was difficult to be more articulate when you were choking with pain and passion simultaneously.

Flora opened her mouth and let the flesh drop. The day was starting. She felt a dirty gleam rise from the surface of the Thames, trickle across the riverside roads and seep under her gauzy curtains.

Her teeth left a circle of red marks on his skin. 'Look at that,' she invited him.

'I can't look at it, how can I look at it?' he mumbled into his pillow. Flora brushed his backbone with her fingertips, just over the fifth chakra, the seat of desire.

'It's disgusting,' she told him. 'It ripples like water. It's pure fat.'

'Mnrgh,' was all he could say. It was hard to be more precise when you were having flash visions of your erection ripping a hole in the sheet.

'Flobber. Blubber. Adipose tissue.' She smacked the spot a little harder than was friendly with her adorably small hand. 'I'm not walking down the aisle looking at that, for God's sake. It's got to go.'

'How?' he demanded. It was impossible to complain when you were unexpectedly shivering with the terror of being outed as a closet sado-masochist.

She gave the offensive flesh a jab with her silver-tipped finger. 'You go to a gym, don't you? Make them do something about it.'

'Right,' he promised, risking a roll over to kiss her.

'Oh no you don't,' she said, sliding quickly off the bed. 'You had yours last night. You'll be moaning that you're late for work in five minutes anyway.'

*   *   *

7

They converged from opposite sides of the Bank of England, two figures moving smoothly through the crowd like currents in water. Their black shoes glided economically over the paving, their matte black legs stepped silently. They were fluid, flexible, future-friendly, multi-skilled, relational, communicative, radiant with intelligence, swift with modesty, aware of their superiority and above competitiveness. Which is to say, they competed only over things that did not matter. It was simple, really: they were women. Tomorrow belonged to them.

As they moved through the ancient alleys they left the others behind, the men who strolled obliviously in twos and threes, men illogically uniformed in dark blue suits with pastel shirts and loud, busy ties, men who were rigid, bloated, wordless, incapable of evolving and stuck in eternal childhood. Tomorrow was a fugitive shadow that glanced back at them with a regretful face. They were loud because they were afraid but they had no words for their fear and so no one heard them. They looked about them but only a few of their neurones could register what was happening. Thus the dinosaurs blundered towards their last grazing grounds.

Time moves fast in the economic acropolis of London. Georgie Lambton crossed the jammed street to reach the restaurant, a

8

deconsecrated temple of commerce whose grey pillars echoed the mercantile classicism of the Stock Exchange, which faced them across the traffic. The *maître d'* was casual and her blue fingernails would not have been appreciated in Chicago. She blanked on Georgie's name. I've been away, Georgie told herself, and settled at their table under the glass-paned rotunda. Other diners were taking seats but she knew none of them.

Flora appeared, to be first-named and waved across the clattery white floor towards her. Friendship instantly burst into flame. They exclaimed, they squealed, they kissed, and they sat down busily to command cucumber soup with caviar and nage of lobster and langoustines. Ten years earlier they had been eager schoolgirls, and the price of today's lunch would have bought them each a complete new outfit for Saturday night. They were not counting the cost now. They were excited to be together and excited also by the passing of time.

'Well,' Flora said. 'How about this?'

'Yes. Takes some getting used to.'

'Give it time, you've only been back two days. You're still jet-lagged.'

'I meant the getting married thing.'

'Oh, I can get used to that. No problem.'

'It's great to be back.'

'And with your Felix. I can't wait to meet him. And you must meet Dillon.'

'Oh, yes,' Georgie agreed, but without urgency. Woman to woman was sweet. It was simple, logical, easy. With a man there were sulk attacks to deflect and an eggshell ego to be coddled, and those long, long fences of pretension to be patrolled. So exhausting. They savoured the luxury of keeping all their energy for their own enjoyment.

'Wow.' Flora suddenly seized Georgie's hand and held it in the pool of light from the glass dome. 'It's beautiful. It's so classic. It's really subtle. It's a ring, for God's sake.' A thick band of pale gold with a diamond buried at the top. Whenever Georgie moved her hand, which she did a lot because she was a hand talker, the sparkle burst out of the surface of the gold like microscopic searchlights.

'Felix is crazy about design. He went off and got it made and never even told me.'

'It was a total surprise?'

'Total.'

'So go on—what, when, how?'

'Sunday morning. I'd just got up and I was putting the washing in. He made me stop and sit down at the table. And my heart hit the floor, you know, because he'd been acting weird for a few days and he was *really* not smiling. I mean, he isn't smiley anyway. He works with families under stress all the time, he has such terrible choices to make, smiley wouldn't be right. But he looked so grim I

10

thought he was going to tell me we had to break up. But instead he said that finally, finally a hospital had offered to fund this research. And I knew he'd been hassling around everywhere, it's something that's only just been discovered, Lightoller's Syndrome . . .'

'Huh?'

'Lightoller's Syndrome.'

'Lightoller?'

'Some German in the twenties. He discovered it but nobody realised what it meant. Nobody before Felix. It's a congenital biochemical deficiency which causes behavioural problems. Felix has shown that it may affect one in every five hundred babies. That's a lot.'

'OK, OK. So then what?'

'Then he said the hospital was in London and then he said when he started thinking it through it'd made him realise that he—well, that he—well . . .'

'Well?'

'He couldn't live without me.'

'That's so beautiful. He actually said that?'

'Uh-huh. And then he put this little box on the table right by my fingers and he took this huge great gulp of air and he said, "Georgina, will you marry me?"'

'You're crying.'

'Well, I'm really not ready for all this, am I?' Georgina groped in her bag for tissues but there were none.

11

The gesture alerted a waiter who sulked to their vicinity and demanded, 'Ladies?'

'We must have the pink champagne,' Flora said.

'Two glasses of pink champagne, please,' ordered Georgie.

'Tssssk. Do they wipe your memory at the city limits in Chicago? There is never any next point ordering champagne by the glass. You end up having ten glasses for the price of two bottles. Bring us a bottle of the Billecart-Salmon Rosé. And some tissues for my friend. She's just had a moving experience.'

The waiter had eyes like cold boiled eggs; he rolled them in Georgie's direction and slouched away.

'Nobody drinks in Chicago.'

'I thought you didn't want to get married,' Flora teased her.

'I thought Felix didn't want to get married. He's so *vocational* about his work.'

'So you didn't want to get married because you thought Felix didn't want to? No, you never wanted to, I remember. Felix changed your mind.'

'On this one street in Chicago there's a sign telling people not to drive agricultural vehicles on the highway.'

'Felix changed your mind, admit it.'

'OK, he changed my mind.'

*   *   *

12

The old Georgie never cried that way, as if she was helpless to stop her feelings oozing out all over everywhere. The old Georgie had laughed, a deep, bosomy laugh which used to reverberate up and down the fund managers' desk at Ardent Holdings. The old Georgie had been able to do anything except find a skirt to fit. The old Georgie had surged through life like a raft on the Zambesi. This was not the old Georgie.

Perhaps, Flora speculated, the old Georgie had started to mutate on the night when The Scumbag Whose Name Shall Be Shit Forever told her he could no longer be seen with a girlfriend who didn't have a trust fund and was still driving a 3-series BMW. Georgie had sat on the end of Flora's bed and cried until she was sick, then dried her tears and rushed off to Chicago to wash that Scumbag right out of her hair.

Now Georgie had the slick, sorted, high-maintenance gloss of a world-beater and she was crying because she was happy. What was that about? Flora asked herself.

*   *   *

'So,' Georgie prompted her, digging into the caviar. 'Let's see yours.'

'Mine's—well, different.' Flora was sitting with her knees together, one hand coyly

13

covering the other, resting on her thigh. Mischief sizzled in her speckled eyes. As Georgie was about to say something reassuring, Flora revealed her left hand. The ring was huge. It was funky. It was a micro-sculpture, with silver claws clasping a blue-white crystal to a chunk of metal.

'Oh my God.' Georgie wondered about the thing. The crystal looked as if it might crumble like a piece of cake.

'Isn't it? It was the biggest one. I had to have it. It's celestite. Full of heavenly energies. And the rest is platinum.'

'Oh, celestite.' Georgie had made a bet with herself that the crystal thing would last six months with Flora.

'It's incredible. Like a modem for the astral world, you know. Brilliant for spirituality, enlightenment, empathy, openness, clear thinking, seeing the truth and keeping a pure heart.'

Georgie acknowledged that her own heart was not pure in this matter; her heart was hazy misgiving and she needed to change the subject. 'I can't believe we're both getting married at the same time! This is just too amazing.'

They had to stand up and hug again, until they noticed the waiter approaching with the bottle, when they disengaged, because in No 1 Lombard Street hugging was not performed. Flora smoothed her hair. Ten-year-old girls in

14

ballet classes had that kind of hair, very long, very straight, very shiny, very brown. Flora's hair made Georgie feel guilty, a non-specific free-floating guilt about the effort she had to put into her life. And guilty about her own hair, a dark, dysfunctional mass that could only be straightened with much effort and was usually twisted into a pleat, clipped back and forgotten.

'There's so much air in here,' she said, looking around. 'Where is everybody?'

'Nobody has time for lunch now. People are so into their health and that's really good. And there's so much movement. Hiring and firing, especially firing.' Flora winked over the rim of her glass, the gesture of a wise woman who had chosen a better life. 'Ever since Asia and everything. Everybody watched Japan like watching a train crash. So they all want to get in the office at six and look good. I'm so glad I'm out of all that.'

'That's me you're talking about. I still have to start downloading the prices from Tokyo at six. Actually I was in at half-five today, since it's my first week. When I left the country I never thought you'd take a flying dive out of the City.'

'Well,' said Flora, and stroked her hair again.

'So?' Georgie prompted her.

*   *   *

She wanted to know how life fell out when you kissed goodbye to a salary and set up a consultancy as a healer of sick buildings. Flora was beautifully unchanged. Nothing random with Flora, nothing unconnected, everything was placed exactly like the stems in a Japanese flower arrangement. Flora was still a dancing child who skipped smiling through life with the pure-hearted belief that the world would provide. Her smile was for herself. Flora's smile never vanished, even on the day when she had lost 25 million dollars somewhere in the system at Ardent Holdings and the IT director himself had to come down from the fifty-third floor to find it. Flora smiled as if she knew a secret. She believed she knew many secrets: health, serenity, and a pure heart. Georgie wanted to believe that they really were enough to support a life.

*   *   *

'How was it?' Georgie prompted.

'It was incredible. Really. I mean, looking back, I must have been crazy. I just got these cards printed.' Flora dipped into her bag and produced a card. Handmade, with something like rice grains pressed into the edge. Flora Lovelace, Environmental Consultant. 'The last month at work I went to every party and just passed them around. And Donna was great.'

'Donna? Donna the Prima donna?' When Flora and Georgie sat side by side at Ardent Holdings, Donna dominated their lives from her corner office. On Donna, Flora's special charm had been absolutely lost. 'Did I miss something? You're being mentored by *Donna*?'

'She put me on to my first client. National Bank of New Caledonia, opening their first London office, wanting to get everything up to speed.'

'But running a scam, right?'

'Of course they were running a scam but they paid up front and I never looked back.'

'And what exactly . . .'

'I do a basic Feng Shui rundown, very simple, no fishtanks or anything unless they want fishtanks, then I dowse the site with a crystal pendant just to check the energy flow. The celestial service includes the horoscope and numerology analysis of everyone working in the environment. The clearing ceremony gets rid of stagnant energies in a new office and cleanses the space with sound, light and scent for the new owner. I can work with the designer, getting the lighting right, choosing natural materials. Quite simple things can also make a lot of difference, painting a wall a more inspiring colour, moving the furniture to ease the airflow. When everything else is in balance . . .' she dipped into her bag once more and brought out a glass bottle attached

17

to an electric plug '. . . the Environmental Aroma Harmoniser. In this reservoir here, I put an individually blended selection of essential oils whose fragrances are released throughout the day when the balancer is switched on. You can choose the model with a time-clock to release aromas only when you need them, or by changing the reservoir, you can choose to change your scents through the day. I've got this guy working on designing a totally automatic aroma system. People like a reviving blend in the morning, then calming if it's a stressful environment or energy-boosting maybe in the afternoon. It's scientifically proven, you know. A study by the University of Arkansas showed that changing scents in a workplace enhanced productivity. I also blend ambient perfumes for the home. I get the oils from this Australian company that imports only organically grown . . .'

'Flora, you're pitching. You could never pitch.'

Flora's smile glowed. 'Oh, I know. And I know Donna only set me up because she was going to have to fire me and if I resigned it saved Ardent the cost.'

'This was all Donna's idea, wasn't it?'

'Well, in a way. But I never saw what there was to pitch in all that crappy buying and selling. This is something I can get excited about.'

Georgie sipped her champagne. Whatever,

18

her sip said. You are my friend, we walk the path of life together. I accept you as you are. If you can be sincere about dowsing the energy flow in what is actually a high-class money laundry, that is how you are. You could not be sincere about suggesting a pension-fund manager protect the life savings of hundreds of little Mom-and-Pop pension-holders, by moving out of a bad market at the right time, but that was how you were. Whatever.

'It's just so real, Georgie. I feel so connected, so in tune with all the right energies. I feel I'm really, really doing something to keep the world turning, you know. And it works. I have the proof, I have Dillon. When we did it,' she leaned forward and dropped her voice, 'I made this blend of vetiver to relax him, lavender to balance him and a shot of black pepper for hot, hot sex. And I energised my marriage corner with a rose quartz crystal. Voilà. Result.'

'Your MBA is better than my MBA,' Georgie reminded her.

'Dillon is a Harvard MBA,' Flora replied. 'And he is just adorable. I can't wait for you to meet him. By the way, I brought you something to say welcome back.' From her bag she took a rounded package wrapped in ragged red paper and tied with orange silk cord. It was heavy and fitted exactly into Georgie's palm.

'Beautiful paper,' Georgie commented,

19

dipping into her bag for a square black envelope fastened with a bead and a tassel.

'Why thank you. You dear person. Handmade in Nepal, the paper.

They opened their packages. Georgie held a lump of shiny black crystalline mineral with rainbows glinting from its facets. Flora held a floppy disk.

'It's a screensaver,' Georgie explained, 'based on the dream nets of the Hopi Indians. With pipe music.'

'Oh, wow!' Flora caressed the disk tenderly with her clean round fingertips. 'Dillon can install it for me. And yours is a piece of carborundum from Ecuador. Its special energies will stop the bastards grinding you down.' Her eyes crackled at Georgie.

'Just what I need. Thanks a million.'

They giggled. They swapped more kisses. They broke the code and hugged again. They unclinched and flicked their hair back in place and poured out the last of the bottle.

'So why are you living on the other side of the City? I'm never going to see you. I was dying for an excuse to throw Des out, I'm sick of falling over his Absolut in the freezer and his Nikes on the stairs. Isn't Seventeen-A good enough for you now you're almost a married woman?'

After the desk at Ardent Holdings had come the straight and narrow house in Bow Quarter, a dwelling chucked up two hundred years earlier to shelter French immigrant silk-weavers. 17A had a drunken staircase and a sublime eastern light in the front rooms. Georgie had painted the common parts in yellow and her room in mauve. Flora had painted her room in six different shades of white. The Scumbag always claimed he could smell rot in the joists.

'Felix wanted to be near the hospital.'

'Notting Hill? Haute Notting Hill, near Portobello? His hospital is where?'

'Isleworth. I know. He still has a forty-minute journey in.'

'Out. Isleworth is out. *You* have a journey in. It must be forty minutes at least.'

'Over an hour. But his work is brainwork, you know. Not like what I do. He needs his mental energy, he needs to get in fresh and hit the ground running.'

One of Flora's eyebrows lifted in doubt. 'We have to compromise,' Georgie insisted. 'I have to work in the east, he has to work out west. Notting Hill is in the middle.'

'Not in price, exactly. What's it costing you?'

'He likes the area. I like the area. I'm earning really well, Flora. Why not?'

Flora sighed. Men meant conflict. Even talking about men spoiled the harmony of the moment. She decided to move back to the safe subject of bliss. 'Can you believe this? We're both getting married.'

'I was fine as I was, you know.'

'You said.'

Flora thought that Georgie stressed too much. She collected things to make her anxious like a mad millionaire collecting tin soldiers. Georgie liked whole armies of things to worry about. Felix, now. Flora had never met the man but she knew him from the grief he had given Georgie.

The way she had introduced him, Flora recalled, had been just a shade apologetic. Right for me now but not for me in the larger sense, definitely not. Not my type but good therapy. Just part of the Scumbag repair programme. Short term. Transient. A phase I need to go through.

Six months of that, and then there had been a shift. Georgie had started with answers to questions nobody had asked, such as 'Felix needs time' and 'Felix believes in living for today and I respect that' and 'Felix says his research comes first, he must go wherever it takes him'. Now Georgie was planning to marry Felix, and Felix apparently needed to live in the most expensive district on the Central Line. Flora considered asking Georgie if she was sure about marrying this Felix person, but the energy was not right so instead she sighed to herself and said, 'So no more girls' nights out then.'

'No way,' Georgie answered swiftly. 'We can still go out, of course we can. Felix has an evening lecture Wednesdays, we can do it then.'

'Wednesday . . .' Flora was testing the wind. She was smiling as if she knew the answer to every riddle asked since the beginning of human intelligence. 'I kind of like to do my yoga Wednesdays.'

'OK,' Georgie sensed the challenge and picked it up. 'Friday, like it used to be.'

'Friday,' Flora agreed. 'We can start in the Bit Bar.'

'You know,' she added after a moment of thought, 'you're different.'

'Thinner,' Georgie admitted. 'Haircut.'

'No, there's something else. Your energy's changed. You're reckless, that's what you are. Reckless. If I could read auras I could see it, it'd be a red flash just . . . there.' She pointed to the air above her friend's right eyebrow.

'I've done reckless,' Georgie told her. 'It knackered me. I'm grown up now. I can be whatever I want. Wait till you see my car.'

CHAPTER TWO

APRIL 10–14

That night, Felix got home just after nine. Because there was parking at the hospital, and a good Underground connection from their home to the City, they had decided it made more sense for him to take the car. This caused Georgie a pang, because she had been awarded a covetable Audi coupé and she had named him Flat Eric.

'How was Flat Eric?' she asked him once there was a glass of Chardonnay in his hand.

'The car was OK,' he answered. 'But I think the timing is a little out. You could get someone to look at it. How was your friend?' He put a special emphasis on the word 'friend', an accent positioned to tell Georgie that it was fine for her to see her old friends, that he was not jealous, that he approved.

'Flora's just the same,' she said happily.

'That's good. It's good to find that friends haven't changed, isn't it? Enhances the sense of continuity of life.'

'Yes.' Just for a second, she had to struggle with her nerves. 'We fixed to go out in the evening on Friday.'

'Friday? Sweetheart, can you ask me tomorrow when I'm by my diary? I have no idea what my schedule is on Friday . . .'

'Just us. Flora and me. We always used to . . .'

'You mean Flora and I. So you two want to go out by yourselves on Friday?'

'We always used to . . .'

Felix was sitting dead-centre on the sofa, picking through a little bowl of celery sticks and red pepper slices on a bed of ice. Georgie had taken the chair. Since Felix expected to finish work late quite often, they had decided not to eat a big meal in the evening, but to sit together like this, put on some music, talk over their days and share a low-calorie high-vitamin snack of Georgie's devising. Consecrated time, Felix called it. He chose the music, John Coltrane tonight.

'Hum? Who did?'

'Flora and me. No, Flora and I.'

'That's it. That's right. Did what?'

'Flora and I want to go out on Friday. Just us.'

'Terrific.'

'Really?'

'I love you so much, sweetheart.' He reached across the corner of the table and cradled her face. She could smell the pepper juice on his fingers. 'You're so special. You really, really understand me. Quite naturally, you're just following the instinct. You want to go out Friday. That means I can stay at the hospital and keep working without any sense of pressure, any of that feeling of a little

25

woman tapping her feet, waiting for me to get home. I really used to hate that. I'm so lucky to have found you. Come here, let me hold you a moment.'

And he pulled her over to sit beside him. He kissed her neck and then unbuttoned her blouse a little way and started on the upper slopes of her breasts. Not wishing to appear rejecting, Georgie brushed her fingertips over his head. She wondered where this was going. She was tired but Felix had a ravenous libido and thought that a sensitive lover should avoid the banality of always making love in bed.

He murmured from below her ear. 'Interviewing bio-med graduates today, there was one . . . She had this split in her skirt, kind-of off centre. When she crossed her legs there was all this thigh. Gave me a bit of a stiffie. More than a bit, I must admit.'

Looking for longer term anxieties, Georgie wondered also about the other women, the women before her, the little women who had tapped their feet and waited for Felix to come home.

'She was the best qualified,' he murmured in a ho-hum tone. 'So we'll be making her an offer.'

*　　　*　　　*

'Mummy, I'm going to get married,' improvised Flora, talking to herself while she

26

parked in the cracked driveway behind a Christo-like package of polythene and string that was undoubtedly Baby Brother's latest boat. It sounded weak.

'Mum, I've decided to get married,' she tried, stepping around the turd in the side alley that had undoubtedly been left by Middle Brother's dog. It sounded tentative.

'Good news, Mum. I'm planning to get married,' she suggested, opening the back door very quietly so as not to disturb Big Brother, who was undoubtedly working.

She had to hold the door because her mother was bending over the washing machine, stuffing it with her brothers' clothes.

'I didn't know you were coming today,' her mother greeted her. The breasts sloshed about under the sweatshirt as she stood upright. The thighs in the washed-out leggings quivered in sympathy. Her mother's body moved around like one of the fairground rides that flings itself out to each point of the compass in turn. From habit, Flora felt embarrassed and looked down. Feet and paws had left muddy imprints on the vinyl floor covering. Something slithered under the sink. 'It isn't Sunday, is it?' her mother asked.

'No, it's Wednesday,' she confirmed. Time, like everything else, was never disciplined in this house.

'Is something wrong?' her mother demanded, slamming the washing-machine

27

door. 'Because I don't know why you've come to tell me about it if it is. I've got enough trouble here, I don't need any more.'

'Nothing's wrong,' Flora pacified her.

The kitchen door crashed open. She stood back to let the dog through. 'Yo, Wormy,' Middle Brother greeted her. He opened the larder door. For a few seconds the two doors filled the mean room. Flora and her mother retreated to the scullery. The house had been built in the thirties in a new suburb full of hope. Since then, hope had relocated and none of the house's subsequent owners had found the money to remodel it for modern domestic living.

Middle Brother kicked the back door shut, shot a pile of dog meal into a bowl, threw the packet back into the larder and shouldered past them into the house, tipping over the dog's water bowl on the way.

'He sees the probation officer on Friday,' Flora's mother explained. 'It always upsets him but they made it a condition of his parole.' She slammed the larder door as the dog returned to eat. It was mostly a Border Collie. The wagging tail flicked their knees. 'He loves that dog,' Flora's mother observed. 'I suppose we'd better go into the lounge.'

'Wormy! You're here!' enthused Baby Brother in the lounge, where he was kneeling beside a chunk of metal components on the floor. He got up to give her an oily embrace

28

then returned to his work.

'He's going to sail around the world,' her mother told Flora.

'Good for him,' said Flora. The sofa, covered with a rug that was matted with dog hair, was listing backwards into the wall. Or perhaps the wall was holding up the sofa. The prolapsed seats of the chairs were also hairy. Flora could remember when they had lived in a big house with a big garden, and the suite had been new, a mountain range of luxurious pink damask. Her father always sat in the corner of the sofa by the big window that overlooked the lawn. Then he had left, they had moved and her brothers had climbed over everything and broken it.

Flora pulled out a hard chair from the dining table and found a stack of Big Brother's manuscripts. 'Be careful!' her mother yelped. 'That's his symphony.'

Baby Brother snorted and threw down a wrench. Putting the papers on a free corner of the table, Flora turned the chair around and sat down. Her mother stayed standing. Experience had shown her that there was no point in sitting down when you always had things to do.

'I've got to work Sunday,' Flora explained, 'so I thought I'd pop over to see you this evening.'

Her mother's face brightened briefly. 'Have you got a new job?'

'I meant my consultancy work. It's going very well. I've got clients to see this weekend.'

'I wish you had a new job,' said her mother, slumping as her face fell back into shadow.

'I have a job.' Flora deployed what patience she had. 'It's going really well. I have to work this weekend.'

'We're having trouble with your father again.' Her mother advanced this as if it were an argument in her favour. Baby Brother made a noise that was half a curse and half a grunt of effort as he loosened a stubborn nut.

'What's my father got to do with whether I have a new job or not?' Flora demanded.

'He's trying to get out of paying for the boys,' her mother complained. 'We're going back to court next week.'

'Don't look at me,' said Flora immediately. 'I need to be careful while I'm starting the business.'

From the master bedroom above came a *glissando* of electronic screeching. 'That's the third movement, he's calling it *Allegro Febrillato*. He got this recording of parrots from Australia,' said her mother with pride. Baby Brother threw a wrench across the room, just missing the dog as it jumped on the sofa. 'I'm not looking at you,' she told her daughter tartly. 'I know you've never got enough to help us out.'

'I don't see why he should pay for the boys.' Flora knew she was losing control but decided

30

to go with it. She needed to externalise some of her feelings here. 'They're grown up, for heaven's sake. They should be out working. I was at their age.'

'They need to fulfil themselves,' her mother argued, vague but immovable. 'All the problems they've had, only because they've got all this potential that they've never been able to do anything with since their dad left. The school's never helped. I've had to do everything.'

'You shouldn't,' Flora suggested. 'Not any more. It's down to them. They're adults.'

'He's only twenty.' Her mother indicated Baby, now intent upon his socket set.

'That's old enough,' Flora persisted.

'You little cow.' Baby got to his feet, towered over his mother and put his arm around her shoulders. 'How can you take Dad's side? What do you know? You left us the minute you could, you didn't care. You haven't hardly been home since.'

'I went to university,' Flora protested. 'I paid my way, I never asked for anything.'

'You went to university? Well, lucky old you. You only ever come home to make us feel stupid, don't you?'

'I do not! That's not fair!'

'You should think of their feelings,' squealed her mother. 'Boys are sensitive, you know.'

'What do you want, anyway?' honked Baby.

31

'Coming home like this, not telling anybody?'

Boots crashed down the staircase and Big Brother loomed in the doorway. He had his headphones over his ears and was holding their jack plug in one hand. 'Will you all just shut up!' he yelled. 'How can I get any work done with this bloody row going on?'

'It's her, it's your sister.' Her mother stabbed the air under the tip of Flora's nose with her finger.

'What the fuck does she want?' Big Brother demanded.

At this point, Flora lost it completely. As she always did. 'I don't want anything! I never want anything! I just came home to tell you—'

'Well, we don't want to know. You can just fuck off!' Big Brother yelled, crashing back up the stairs.

'You're upsetting them,' her mother accused her. 'You mustn't stay.'

'Yeah, fuck off, Wormy,' echoed Baby.

'My pleasure,' Flora assured them. As she wrenched the front door open, she heard the noise of the dog being sick.

*   *   *

On Friday morning, Flora reached Dillon on his mobile at around eleven. 'Where were you?' she asked him. 'I called earlier. Haven't you picked up your messages?'

'I was with the boss. It's always target review

32

on Friday morning.'

'Look, I'm going out with Georgie tonight. We can catch up tomorrow sometime.'

'Yeah. Sure. Of course.' Dillon was alarmed. Friday? The day that led to Saturday, which led to the weekend, which a woman might be expected to spend with her fiancé doing those thrillingly pointless things that people did when they were in love, like going out for lunch or wandering round Spitalfields market buying little presents or having sex all day. She was going out with another man on Friday. There must be an explanation. He would discover it. 'And George is . . .'

'Georgie. That friend who's just come back from Chicago.'

'Oh, her. Yes, I remember.' A quick rush of relief, followed by a new order of unease. Dillon didn't like the sound of this friend from Chicago. In the transmissions from his beloved so far, she sounded like one of those thrusting power-women who didn't frighten him, exactly; they concerned him. He worried about them. OK, he was frightened. Power-women had big metallic fingernails and they stared.

Flora never stared. When she talked to him, sometimes, she looked down at her plain cropped fingertips in a way that turned his heart to slush. Sweet, creamy melted ice-cream slush. And her hair rippled with beautiful silvery lights when she threw it behind her dear sharp little shoulders in the way she did

33

without any idea how much he loved it.

'Are you still there?'

'Yes, of course I'm still here. Look—um—so when . . .'

'I'll call you tomorrow morning. Love you.'

'Love you too,' he said. She rang off so quickly. It was quite unearthly how fast she could do things. She was a sprite, a nymph, a dragonfly. And she was going to marry him. She would always be there, a hovering, darting presence, like a sunbeam dancing around their home. But his flat! So small, so cold, every lonely hour he'd spent there oozing a sour memory from the walls! The putrid carpet in the bathroom, that hole in the kitchen roof— he didn't want to think about how it had got there. Nor did he want to think about how he came to be living in a sort of tenement by a railway line on Madagascar Basin. When he had bought the place Madagascar Basin was going to be the next Jamaica Wharf, the railway was going to be scrapped and the building was going to be refurbished. None of these things had happened. He could afford better but he had never found the motivation to move. Until Flora refused to go into his kitchen because of the mice. Call the estate agent, put the place on the market!

Where would she like to live? By the water, hadn't she said something about loving the river? A brand new place with a balcony over the water! They would sit out in the sun on

Sunday! The scent of the coffee he would make, the little waves lapping below them, her white, white teeth biting into a croissant! They would laze in French café chairs—no, too uncomfortable, something else, she would know what to buy—they would laze on their balcony in the sun every Sunday, amusing themselves with shiny newspaper supplements with pictures of girls not half as beautiful as Flora . . .

'Dillon, what are you looking at?'

Shit, the boss. Usually she was safely locked up with the head of sales for twenty minutes after target review. 'Looking at?' Automatically, guiltily, his hand reached out for his mouse.

'You've been looking at the wall for five minutes. The wall you're looking at is just a plain white wall, Dillon. Unless there's writing on the wall that I can't see. Is there writing on the wall, Dillon?'

'Ah—I was thinking,' he was blathering—he knew he was blathering but he couldn't stop— 'about what you said. About the pet market. The small-pet market. Conceptualising the small-pet owner and her or his needs. Asking myself whether . . .'

But she had moved on, with one of her acid whinnying noises which people were inclined to mimic, so the whole of the design desk fell into furtive snickering whenever she appeared.

Dillon conceptualised the small-pet owner.

He saw himself aged eight, his hands drowning in his father's rose-cutting gloves, clutching Archibald by the scruff of the neck. Archibald was not a rabbit, he was the spawn of the devil. The idea of designing an insurance policy to cover veterinary bills for the Archibalds of the world was morally offensive to him.

Archibald used to stink if he wasn't cleaned out but he would bite any hand that entered his cage. Eventually he had settled his own fate by savaging the cat from next door, thus proving to the young Dillon that there was a God because his mother said that Archibald might have rabies and had to be put down. Archibald had always been on borrowed time with her. His mother was right about everything, he hated that about her. Flora, with her oils and crystals and New Age moonshine, was adorably wrong, always. And she was going to marry him.

*　　　*　　　*

'It's so-o-o-o nice.' Georgie stirred the red scummy surface of her Seabreeze with the tip of the straw. 'All these things I didn't expect. Thinking of all this getting married stuff. Nice but weird. Weird but nice. Waking up with Felix and knowing you're going to wake up with him every morning always.' She lolled happily against the banquette, groping for the words to tell Flora about the altered state she

36

had been experiencing ever since Felix's proposal, but it was Friday, she was still jetlagged, she had been at work since 5.30 a.m. and vodka never helped her think.

'Always,' said Flora. 'Always and forever. That's the plan, isn't it?'

'And thinking about his parents, and your parents, and wondering how they'll get on and realising that you're really making a whole new layer of family here, you're like extending the dynasty or joining the clan or keeping the race going. I bet your mother was happy.' Georgie had never met Flora's mother. She had a vague idea of a wispy mum in a neat sweater with pearls in a small half-timbered mansion in the Home Counties. She was not far off; if she had been able to retain her husband, Flora's mother would have been just like that.

'Ecstatic.' Flora pasted on a fond smile. 'Now she's hassling us for a church wedding. And Dillon's got this mad idea about us writing our own ceremony and running away to get married on a wild heathery moorland or something.'

Georgie assessed the sense she had of this Dillon person. Flora preferred men who did what she told them, and her mother had always loomed large in her life. 'Eight to one on your mother?' she offered.

'Against my darling boy? Are you crazy?'

'Seven to one, then.'

'OK, you're on. What are we betting?'

37

'Champagne would be appropriate, wouldn't it? The pink stuff again.'

'Right.' Flora dipped into her bag for her Psion and made a note of the bet and so they caught up another thread of their friendship. Georgie seemed to revive; the warmth came back to her smile and the sparkle to her eyes.

Betting on life was something Georgie had learned from her uncle, her father's brother, a priest who had made a lifetime study of innocent pleasures. He gave things nicknames. When he wanted to be emphatic, he said, 'For the love of Mike,' and explained that this was still technically swearing because Mike was the Archangel Michael. Her uncle also explained that betting was not gambling if no money was involved and you bet on things that were not officially sport. When he was posted to Ireland the whole family went to visit and he made bets on the weather with jelly babies. Ever afterwards a bet held out to Georgie the guaranteed happiness of summer holidays in childhood.

'So,' Flora ventured, encouraged to see her friend more cheerful, 'how does it feel, to be a wife-to-be?'

Georgie considered. Bliss? Too pink. Peace? Too political. Safe? Too feeble. Calm? Was that it? Too boring.

'It feels like calm but not boring. And bright like light. And colours, lots of colours. And warm. Calm in neon, maybe. And scary

38

because it's time to grow up now.'

'You were born grown up,' Flora told her, then added, 'so was Dillon. He'll be a great dad. I'm going to leave all that to him.'

'You mean he wants to be a house husband?' She was so tired. Easier not to talk about herself, easier to talk to Flora about Flora. Satisfaction, that was what was coming off Flora. She looked very, very satisfied. And happy, of course. Astonishing she could drink so much and never seem drunk. There she was, still poised like a Japanese flower, while Georgie felt herself getting rumpled and blurry.

'I don't know. Maybe. Dillon's a real golden boy. He's totally brilliant, even Donna says so. If he works like stink for ten years and gets all the bonuses, he'll have made enough money so he never has to work again. Then we're going off to . . . I don't know, Bali or Fiji or somewhere. Somewhere we can have a life.'

'Well, I don't know about Felix. We haven't gone that far yet.' A frown seized her temples and squeezed. Extraordinary that Felix, a master of method, hadn't told her about his plan for children. 'I suppose we'll wait until there's enough in the bank so we can really afford to start a family. It'll be a few years, anyway, until Felix has published at least. Then when he's off lecturing I'll be able to stay home with the children. Yes. That'll be the plan.' The glass was empty now except for the

39

ice, which Georgie swizzled wistfully with her straw.

'You'd hate it,' Flora predicted, 'not working.'

'And I'd get miserable if Felix was away a lot.'

Flora was smiling. 'If Dillon has to be away a lot I'll go with him because I want to know what happens with him, I don't want him falling into another woman's clutches. Like going off to Prague or somewhere with all those raving Natashas just waiting to pounce.'

'Felix wouldn't get into that kind of trouble.'

'Of course he would. Any man would. Look at the Scumbag.' Georgie's eyes became two wounds and Flora realised her friend was still not ready for the whole truth about that subject. She backtracked. 'Look, fact of life. Men are all the same. If they're offered pussy on a plate and they think they can get away with it, they'll be in there, they'll be on it. Whoever they are, they're all the same. Doesn't matter. Only thing to do is keep young and beautiful and never let 'em out of your sight.'

'Felix . . .'

'If you think Felix is any different . . .'

Georgie tried to shake some of the vodka out of her brain and explain. 'Felix knows he's a man, that's what I mean. He knows he has this genetic programming but he believes that personal integrity is very important. And

40

honesty. So he suggested we should be totally open, right from the beginning. We decided to build our relationship on total, complete honesty. Even with what we're thinking.'

'So you're saying he'd do it and then tell you about it? Are you crazy?'

'No, no. You're not getting it. It's about telling each other what's going on with us. So if I fancy another man, I tell him. So it's out in the open and we have complete trust and there's nothing to worry about.'

'What happens when you do that?'

Georgie had fallen into the habit of making false confessions of lust just to keep up with Felix and stop him feeling like some monster of raging testosterone. 'Well, he's hurt. But he'd be more hurt if I weren't honest. That would be the real cheating.'

'And if Felix fancies another woman, he tells you?'

'Absolutely. I mean, he almost never does. It's usually crap, he's embarrassed to own up to it, being such a slave to his hormones. He admits he has these idiotic fantasies about a waitress in a restaurant or someone. Or a flight attendant. He has a thing about air hostess uniforms. It's all about fear, really, isn't it? The fear of flying is displaced and becomes arousal. Women are more highly evolved, that's for sure.'

'So it's all fantasy? He never fancies another woman for real?'

'He doesn't seem to. I mean, we have sex a lot you know. He's a very passionate man.'

Flora noticed that when Georgie confided this her top lip twitched and her eyes grew big and dark. Another problem with Georgie was that she hadn't transcended her physical being. She still wasn't in balance with her sensuality. That, in Flora's opinion, had been what went wrong with the Scumbag. Someone who let herself be a slave to her hormones like that just didn't give out the right energies.

Flora said, 'Dillon is just brilliant at sex.' That one landed. Georgie rallied out of her trance of exhaustion and said, 'Really?'

'Oh, yeah. I think one of his old girlfriends really trained him up. He loves doing all the stuff guys hate, you know. Says it really turns him on.'

'Wow,' breathed Georgie, her eyes now enormous.

Flora was about to elaborate when they sensed a disturbance at the far end of the bar. There was flouncing in the coat-check area and fawning from the manager and a raised voice saying something about taking care with other people's property.

All over the room, people took their attention off their glasses and their companions and looked to see what was happening. Minimal was also the Bit Bar's style, and minimal was the behaviour practised within its smooth beech-clad walls. Most of the

. 42

clientele needed to abuse chemical substances to be capable of more than the animation of a zombie. A raised voice was an event. Slowly, ripples of concern spread around the room.

'Who is that?' Georgie asked, dragging herself upright to get a good view of the action.

'I forget how tall you are,' said Flora. This was another thing which bugged her. Georgie was four inches taller than Flora, so sometimes she slumped to try to look smaller and other times she over-braced her shoulders and flattened her spine too much. Either way, a disaster for her upper vertebrae, inducing tension in the neck, crushing the cervical nerves, blocking the energy flow to her upper chakras. Flora visualised Georgie's third eye firmly closed and her thousand-petalled lotus tightly shut up in a bud. No vision, no enlightenment. Sometimes Flora considered that all the problems Georgie had with spirituality could be traced back to her height. It was karma, of course, the payback for an earlier life.

There was a crescendo of voices at the entrance, then the coat-check girl shot off to the toilets in tears and the cause of the outbreak surged forward, leaving the manager bobbing apologetically in her wake.

'I think that's Donna,' Georgie announced.

'It is really?' Flora whipped around and half-rose to get a look at the new arrival. 'This

43

is just brilliant. That woman is such an icon.'

'I can remember when you said she intimidated you.'

Flora was no longer paying attention. A black-haired figure was powering towards them on legs as thin and smooth as knife blades. Pearl grey suit, white skin, black hair and a violet pashmina streaming over her shoulders.

'Georgina!' throbbed the woman's voice. 'And Flora! Together again! My best babes!'

'Donna!' Flora sprang up and there was kissing. It seemed rude not to do the same, so Georgie lurched to her feet and into the miasma of scent which brought back memories of their rough, nervy, sleep-deprived mornings at Ardent Holdings.

'Look at you,' Donna homed in on Georgie, holding her at arm's length and making her twist to be admired. 'You look terrific now. Chicago's being good to you, huh?'

'You always said Georgie was world class,' Flora put in.

'It's a great city,' was all Georgie could say. The twisting manoeuvre was dangerous. She thought she could feel the vodka sloshing around against the inside of her skull. She was disappointed. In a few more seconds, she identified the cause. Donna was unwinding her shawl and making as if to join them, which was going to move the evening up a couple of levels. End of bonding, no more cosy, no more

44

girly Friday-night downtime.

'I said she was looking fantastic,' Flora went on, smoothing her skirt as she sat.

The waiter arrived like a speeding bullet. 'Just a juice.' Donna took a perch on an empty chair at their table. 'And more of whatever my girls are having. I always knew you were a star, Georgie. A star and a babe. Unbeatable.' She nodded, agreeing with herself, fingering the tooth-like grey pearls of her necklace. Statement jewellery, that was Donna's thing. 'Good to see you, really good. How long are you here?'

'She's come back,' said Flora.

'You're *back*? You mean like back, like for good?' The winged black eyebrows undulated in perplexity. 'You're back from Chicago?'

'Not entirely my decision.' Even through the blanket of vodka Georgie felt the fangs of doubt.

'So where are you?'

'Eon Plc. Still in fund management.'

'But that's good. Good, good. Quite a track record. They're getting a great team together over there. You've probably heard that I moved on from Ardent.' Donna sent a nod to Flora, an inclusive nod which said that this was a person on the inside track with her, a person already trusted with all her material intimacies. 'Into products. I'm at Direct Warranty.'

'New Business Director,' Flora supplied.

'Actually she's Dillon's boss. Did I tell you it was Donna who introduced us? We owe it all to her.'

'He's a bright boy,' Donna shook her head, regretting her mistake. 'Just two hundred pounds of pure top-quality intellectual capital. I didn't know what I was doing. I just thought they'd have some fun, make a great couple. I didn't see her getting quite so carried away with him, our impetuous friend here. But she thinks that's what she's into.' She paused as the waiter arrived and distributed three red drinks around the table. 'Maybe you can talk some sense into her, Georgie.'

'Uh-huh,' Flora giggled, and squeaked and shook her head violently, shaking with it the whole length of her hair. 'Georgie's on my side.'

'You can't be. She's just started a business. She's twenty-eight. It's practically child-rape.' She was not really kidding. One of the first things to learn with Donna was that she was usually most serious when she was joking.

'Georgie's getting married too,' Flora announced.

Donna said nothing. A major nothing. She flicked away the skirt of her jacket—long jackets were her things too, a dandy touch added to the principal-boy legs. She took a sip of her juice. She looked around, she looked at the ceiling. Her unconcern was deafening. Georgie felt fear in the pit of her stomach, another sensation she remembered from morning meetings at Ardent.

'But this calls for champagne,' Donna announced, eventually.

CHAPTER THREE

APRIL 14

'I suppose what I'm afraid of is what it would do to me.' Donna poured out the last of the bottle.

'Not for me,' said Georgie, and put her hand over her glass. She was too late and the champagne splashed her fingers. Donna picked up her own glass and looked into it with a sad face. 'There've been times, you know, with some cute bloke or other, when I've thought it would have been nice. Then I'd get this vision of one of those doo-dahs for storing old plastic bags hanging on the back of the kitchen door. I'd see myself actually wasting thought on a plastic bag. Balling it up and stuffing it in one of those doo-dahs and telling myself I'm being a responsible home-maker and saving the planet.'

She raised her glowing eyes and looked at them. Flora was giggling and swaying like a sapling in a storm. Georgie was licking champagne off her fingers. 'Which is such bullshit, isn't it? What does it matter if a plastic bag gets thrown away now or after spending six months balled up in a doo-dah on the back of my kitchen door?'

Georgie started to laugh in her contralto

range then shot into soprano for a hiccup. Flora's giggles were getting out of control. At nearby tables, people looked over their way. Nothing minimal about this hilarious party. Did they really belong in the Bit Bar?

'Pointless! Total waste of life! When they're storing plutonium waste in leaky rusty old oil drums on the edge of Lake Baikal? I mean, what do all my plastic bags really mean to the planet, actually? And I'd see myself *actually buying* that doo-dah, and they are so naff, all of them.' Flora squawked.

'And I'd see myself actually trailing round shops looking for a doo-dah that was, like, in the *lower echelons* of naffness.' Georgie was laughing like a big cat purring.

'And actually being pleased when I was able to buy a doo-dah that was the least worst doo-dah in all London, a doo-dah I could bear to look at to hang on my kitchen door so I could waste time wadding up old plastic bags and stuffing them in it so I'd have a really good supply of *old plastic bags* when I needed them. I mean, whoever needs an old plastic bag, for God's sake?'

'Nobody!' chortled Flora. 'Never!'

Georgie thought about plastic bags for muddy trainers, which led to small boys in football kit, which led to commercials for washing powder, which led to a vision of herself in a floral pinny pegging a thousand nappies on a washing line in a slum back yard.

'I will be responsible for fifteen million in new business this quarter.' Donna held out her arms as if an angel was getting ready to drop the rational explanation into them. 'They cost my time at a thousand a day. If I kept a doo-dah full of bags in my kitchen I'd see two million in *lost business* every time I looked at it.'

Flora's smile temporarily faded. 'My God, Donna, fifteen million a quarter—that's awesome.'

'Yes it is. Just buying that doo-dah would probably use up half a day, that's five hundred pounds' worth of *prime executive time*. But married women do that kind of thing. That's what they do. When they're married. Even the good ones. The ones like us. So when that happened, when I saw myself doing all that, getting married and giving my life to a plastic bag doo-dah, then I just told them it wasn't for me. Getting married. You girls have more guts than I have. Here's to you.'

Donna raised her glass. Shaky with hilarity, Flora and Georgie found their own glasses and clinked them with hers.

Georgie thought about all the cute blokes Donna had refused to marry. She saw them trudging, love-lorn, through empty lives, despairing of finding a woman foxy enough to erase the memory of the brave, the beautiful, the hilarious Donna. She felt sorry for them. She felt sorry for Donna, single forever, her kitchen pristine, her kitchen door innocent of a doo-dah stuffed with old plastic bags. She felt thirsty and she had a headache. She downed her last drops and pulled a face.

'You're right,' said Donna. 'The fizz in this place is crap. Let's go somewhere decent.'

'What's the time?' asked Georgie.

'That's another thing I'm afraid of.' Majestically, Donna rose to her feet and waved at the waiter. 'Slowing down.'

'Call him,' Flora suggested. 'What time did you say you'd be back?'

Now Georgie saw herself after marriage, a crouching, oppressed little figure, forever scurrying home to a censorious Felix while free women went where they chose and got back when they liked. 'Forget it,' she said. 'He'll be OK.'

'I can't wait for you to meet him,' Georgie said as she shrugged herself into her coat and knocked over a vase of phallic red jungle flowers.

'I can't wait for you to meet Dillon,' answered Flora, catching the vase as it toppled.

Donna masked her face in her shawl and pondered this double revelation in silence.

*   *   *

'I'm a liar,' Donna admitted when they had been in the next bar an hour. 'I'm not really

51

afraid of the bag doo-dah. Not as afraid as all that. I'd take it on, if I got married.'

'It was so sad,' Georgie protested.

'It was so funny,' Flora corrected her.

'But that's not really what gives me the screaming meanies. You want to know what freaks me out about getting married? Why I've never dared to do it and I never will?'

'What?' Georgie thought she might cry. Her eyes were prickling. Maybe it was the bubbles. But it was so tragic. A wonderful, wonderful woman like Donna too scared to get married. Scared! She who had more front than Harrods!

Scared, Flora marvelled, Donna was actually scared. She who was generating new business worth fifteen million a quarter, she was scared of getting married. Of course, this was a precious conversation. Donna was really opening up tonight, she was sharing her significant stuff. Because she knew them, because she trusted them, because the energy was right, Donna felt bonded—yes, she must feel that now, bonded to them. Because of that she was talking about things nobody had any idea she felt. Amazing. Flora felt brushed by the wings of glory.

'What really scares me is the *shame*. The shame, the humiliation. When he'll be running around with the bimbo who's going to be Wife Number Two and I'm the last to know. Or lots of bimbos, even. I couldn't hack that. It would

52

kill me, the shame of being cheated on. I mean, think of *Hilary Clinton.* Looking like a fool in front of all the world. Who'd want that?'

Astral, that was how Flora was feeling. As if on the astral plane. The feeling of being a long way above everything, looking down on the table. She heard herself say, 'Dillon won't cheat on me because he's totally goofy about me. And anyway I'll never give him the chance.'

The waistband of Georgie's skirt was cutting into her like a wire. She reached back under her sweater and released the button. It snapped off and fell somewhere. She eased the zip down a couple of inches. That was better.

Donna let her question trickle out on a drawl. 'You mean you're starting out thinking he's going to cheat? So the answer is you're going to run a surveillance operation on your husband?'

'He'll never know. I'm pretty subtle about it. There are ways, you know.'

'That's so sad,' Donna sighed, swirling the very expensive, very good and very delicious champagne around her glass. 'I suppose I'm just too romantic for marriage, as well as all the rest.'

'Ask her, then.' Defiantly, Flora waved her full glass at Georgie, splashing half the precious nectar on the table. 'If you think I'm unromantic, you ask her about Felix.'

'Felix and me, we just admit that there is a problem with fidelity in a long-term relationship. Especially for men,' Georgie protested, amazed that she was sounding so lucid. 'So we share things with each other.'

'They tell each other everything,' Flora explained. 'If he fancies someone else, if she does, they have these great confession sessions.'

Georgie shook her head. Not a good idea. Her head felt as if it might topple off the top of her spine. 'Not like that. Not a big deal. We just talk about our feelings and get rid of the transgressive thing. So once it stops being forbidden fruit, we stop wanting it.'

'You mean, you've *just got engaged* and you still fancy other people?' enquired Donna with care.

'Not me. Felix. Because he's a man and he's got those hormones and that programming and those instincts.' She was lying, she knew she was lying. She had those instincts. That very morning her eyes had slithered lustfully over the back of the third junior from the end of the desk when he leaned over the terminals to pass someone a note. Great lats. Lovely the way the shirt clung to that little valley down his spine. But it was just lust. She'd tell Felix tomorrow, it'd be OK.

'You mean this Felix has just proposed to you and he is still aware that there are other women *on the planet*?'

'Well, of course,' Georgie said. 'He is a man. We're not denying that.'

'Nor are we,' chipped in Flora.

'So you agree that basically all men are bastards but you think you can stop yours reverting to type?'

'Yes,' Georgie answered in that level, no-shit way which Donna recognised as dangerously confident.

'You really believe you've got this thing taken care of?'

They nodded. 'Yes,' said Georgie, 'we do.'

'I'd put money on it,' said Flora.

'So would I,' affirmed Georgie.

'So you're not a hundred per cent sure, then? It's a probability, not a fact?'

'Well, if you put it that way . . .' Georgie felt her headache returning.

'Who knows why the wind blows?' demanded Flora. 'We can't know the unknowable. This is about human nature.'

Donna picked at the fringe of her shawl as if getting up courage to speak. Then she dropped it and said, 'I have an idea.'

There was some ritual attached to the statement. At Ardent Holdings, whenever Donna said she had an idea, the result was usually a new winning strategy and big bonuses all round. When Donna said, 'I have an idea,' like that, a meeting would freeze and everyone would reach for their pens to make notes. Flora and Georgie leaned forward to listen.

'You're sure you've got your guys handled?' They nodded.

'But it'd be nice to know, right?' They nodded.

'I mean, know for sure. So you can really trust them.' They nodded.

'And you've not met each other's partners, have you?' They shook their heads.

'So they don't know who you are?' Flora nodded. Georgie frowned. 'You know what I mean.' Georgie nodded.

'And you're both gorgeous.' They smiled.

'So why don't you try it on with the other man? The other woman's man? Like, make a play, make a pass, seduce the bastards.'

They looked at each other. Donna continued, 'As I see it, the down side would be that if they fall for it, you'd find out they were a pair of weak, willie-led wallies—which is just what you know already. The up side . . .' And she paused for emphasis, looking deep into the four round and fascinated eyes. 'The up side is that if they don't fall for it, then they're better men than you thought they were, and you can get married in total trust to a man you know can resist temptation even when it's on a plate in front of him in an Agent Provocateur G-string.'

'I hate Agent Provocateur,' Flora complained. 'Their bras are like spinnakers. I think their house model is that creature on *Eurotrash*.'

'The underwear is not the point,' Donna said with severity. 'The point is, you'll be able to trust your guys.'

'It's an idea. But I trust Felix anyway,' said Georgie.

'And I trust Dillon,' said Flora. 'But it is a good idea.'

'Well, then,' said Donna, waving at the waiter for the bill. 'I'll leave it with you.'

Flora gave them a crooked smile and collapsed along the banquette.

'The dear girl,' Donna smiled at Georgie, then glanced at the body, now lying with parallel limbs as neatly as it had been sitting before. 'She shouldn't drink, she can't take it.'

Georgie preened. I can take it, she told herself. Whatever Donna can dream up, I'm way ahead of her.

CHAPTER FOUR

APRIL 15

Too early the next morning, Felix stood at the end of their bed and announced: 'The liver is a forgiving organ, but after the age of twenty-five it becomes increasingly less efficient at processing sugars. Alcohol is a sugar. And a toxin, of course. It is a medical fact that women's livers are less efficient in coping with alcohol than those of men. Early liver damage is indicated by arterial disease, premature dementia, mature-onset diabetes and in extreme cases multi-organ failure leading to death. There really isn't anything you can do to prevent liver damage except not overload the organ by binge drinking.'

'We were not binge drinking. We were having a night out.' Georgie sat up. Bad move. Bad.

'In a country with a public health service, taking care of your health is just good citizenship. I mean, why should people who've always lived right have to pay for the treatment of people who abuse their bodies?'

Georgie put her feet on the floor and looked for something to grab. The table was fashionable and had no real legs. The bed was fashionable and had nothing except a mattress on a platform. Felix was standing too far away. She made a supreme physical effort and stood up without help. The Seven Dwarfs were mining diamonds in the region where her neck joined her head.

'I need coffee,' she said, managing to place one foot in the direction of the door.

'The best thing you can drink in your condition would be water. You need rehydration.'

'Yes,' Georgie agreed, getting the second foot in front of the first. 'I will make the coffee with water.'

'Look, you know that caffeine is a stimulant . . .'

He followed her out of the bedroom and downstairs to the kitchen. It was a sunny morning and the room was bright so she had to snap the venetian blind shut.

'You should at least have some juice,' Felix pleaded, standing in the doorway.

'I will have juice when I have had coffee,' said Georgie, concentrating her entire mind on filling the coffee compartment of the espresso machine with medium-roast Colombian.

'You're just assaulting your liver with that. You should take some plain water, then juice, then a little protein, tofu or some cashew butter on sourdough or something.'

Georgie found the thought of tofu unwelcome. She asked him, 'Do you want some of this?'

59

'No, thank you. I can't watch this. I've got work to do.'

Felix strode to his study and shut the door. The espresso machine started brewing. It was chromed and weighty, and sat farting sulkily on the worktop looking like an evil alien spacecraft. Music started behind the study door. Georgie rubbed her eyes. Eventually the black liquid ejaculated into the tiny cup. When it was done, Georgie disconnected the hot coffee holder, banged it on the side of the waste bin to eject the old grounds in a neat wad, refilled it and started the machine again.

Her espresso skills were impressive. Pulling an espresso reminded her of waitressing when she was a student. Georgie climbed on to a stool at the breakfast bar and started to ingest her coffee. Ten years of pulling coffees. Ten years of wearing shoes that made her feet ache. Ten years of some man standing in the doorway and watching her work. Now she was going to be married and everything would be different. Felix was only trying to be kind, he was concerned about her, that was all.

The espresso machine dribbled and spat and produced a second cup. Georgie identified a sense of dissatisfaction. She realised that she preferred Java to Colombian. In addition, she liked coffee in a big, abundant cafetière, not a mean tight-arsed espresso leaving black scum in its little cup. She also would have preferred anything to the Miles Davis which was trickling out under the closed door of Felix's study. Chopin, actually, she'd really like some nice splurgy Chopin. Her cafetière and her Chopin were with friends in Chicago, because, as Felix had pointed out, it was crazy to keep two sets of everything now that they were going to become one household for good. He was quite right, of course; they didn't need two of everything.

Defiance was not Georgie's way. She moved on from coffee to juice—cranberry, when what she really liked, what she had in fact missed in Chicago, was fresh English single-variety Bramley apple juice. She allowed herself the luxury of some negative thoughts.

To stop going mad, Georgie found she had to organise her mind like a computer screen. She didn't really think she was going mad, it just felt that way. She always had so much to do. Down the side of the screen in her mind was a menu of things she had to do. It was always there, even on a wiped-out Saturday morning. On this menu she noticed a resolution to confess to Felix her lust for Great Lats, the third junior from the end. Well, sod that, Georgie resolved. She would say nothing. That'd fix Felix.

*   *   *

'If you loved me, you would bring me three paracetamol, two capsules of milk-thistle and a

61

towel wrung out in that nice lavender water you've got for ironing your shirts.' Flora said this to Des when he looked around her bedroom door in the early afternoon.

'You're awake,' he observed.

'Of course I'm awake. Are you going to fetch my stuff or stand there being stupid all day?' Under the duvet, she lay as flat as a corpse.

'She's awake,' he confirmed. 'Wouldn't you rather have some nice little slices of cucumber to put on your eyes? The lavender water costs nearly as much as my shirts.'

'You don't love me,' she accused him.

'I thought that was Dillon's job now.'

'It's everybody's job,' said Flora. 'You're not going out, are you? I thought when I was feeling better you could massage my scalp.'

'What else do I have to do with my life?'

'Quite,' Flora agreed.

'Dillon's called three times. And Donna called just now.'

'Donna?' Flora's head left the horizontal plane. 'Why didn't you tell me?'

'She said not to bother you. She said she was going out. She's going to call later.'

'Damn.' Flora's head fell back on the mattress.

'She said she bet you couldn't score some guy.'

'You didn't get it. Not any guy. Georgie's fiancé.'

'I told her she was crazy, she was bound to lose, you were invincible.'

Flora found this opinion a good reason to sit up. 'She wasn't serious.'

'She sounded serious to me.'

'Are you getting my drugs or just leaving me here to die?'

While she was alone, Flora remembered the evening. She remembered it clearly. She remembered Georgie getting pissed in half an hour. She remembered Georgie going all gooey. She remembered her describing that pervy confessional thing she had going with Felix. She remembered Donna making her entrance. God, that woman was amazing. She remembered the expression on Donna's face when they told her Georgie was getting married too. She remembered Donna's idea.

So, Donna was serious. In Flora's mind, there was nothing more to be agreed. She remembered that both of them accepted her challenge. The next thing to do was check in with Georgie and get a line on this Felix. And maybe fix a bet on the outcome.

Des returned with the medicine and a glass of filtered water from the tap. She sent him back for a bottle of Welsh spring water.

'Des,' she said, pulling back her feet so he could sit on the end of the bed. 'If you're with a guy, you know, like in a relationship, like it's love or something. And you fancied somebody else. Would you tell him?'

'Oh yes. That's the whole fun of being with someone. You get jealousy to play with.'

'And if you had sex with somebody else? Would you tell him?'

'Absolutely. If he was into that. What am I saying, even if he wasn't into it.

'What do you mean, into it?'

'Well, a bit of pain makes it more exciting, doesn't it? You can do all the rowing and the screaming and the hitting each other and the waving broken bottles about and then the crying and sobbing and the making it up. I mean, it passes the time, all that. It's great if you can be bothered.'

'I suppose so.'

'What do you mean, you suppose so? You know so, you minx. You do it all the time, I've seen you. Go out to dinner with some poor schmuck and spend the whole evening drooling over another poor schmuck so you can go home with lover-boy and have a row and have loads of crazy sex to make it all up. You do that, Flora, don't lie to me. I know what goes on, I sleep underneath you.'

Flora giggled and hugged her knees. The paracetamol was taking over, her head was throbbing quietly. She pulled aside one of the bedroom curtains to let in some light. Des sat cross-legged on the bed, lolling back a little to be comfortable with his belly-button rings. He had been cursed with clean-cut boyish looks, clear skin, rosy cheeks, and floppy dark brown

64

hair. Monday to Friday, when he was a junior negotiator at the hottest estate agency in the east, the looks were a plus. But on Saturdays he felt challenged to appear degenerate.

'What have you done to your hair?'

He caressed his head. 'D'you like it?'

'What is it? Spots or something?'

'Leopard spots,' he told her, putting on a snarl. The floppy locks were now one inch long and spattered with leopard spots in two shades of silver.

'Nice,' Flora agreed. 'Easier than the spikes.'

'No, they're a drag, it took me hours to spray them on. But everyone's doing spikes now. So, come on . . .' He hugged his ankles in anticipation. 'What am I to tell Donna? Are you pulling this poor pathetic bastard or not?'

'I'm up for it,' she told him. 'But we'll have to make a plan. When my head's sorted I'll call Georgie.'

'So is it, like, reciprocal? Does she have to start prowling around Dillon?'

'That's the whole idea.'

'Wicked,' Des approved. 'That should start a fire in the engine room.

*   *   *

The Sir Rudolph Trippitt Retirement Home for Actors. This stone was laid by Miss Tallulah Bankhead on July 20, 1923. Georgie smiled while she waited for someone to answer the door. Whenever she came in this way with her father, he made an eloquent gesture at the foundation stone with his good arm and chuckled, 'And the stone wasn't all she laid, so the story goes.' Then Georgie would wonder how often the home's secretary heard those words as she struggled with the antiquated but highly polished brass latch on the door.

'He'll be simply ravished to see you,' the secretary promised her.

The primary smell of the Sir Rudolph Trippitt home was of beeswax furniture polish mixed with the scented flowers and rotting stems of the purple stocks in the flower arrangement that sprawled over the hall table. Georgie could only just detect a tang of the antiseptic solution that was used to steam the carpets every week.

'I'm here, Daddy. Wow, it's bright in here.' Her father's room had fresh wallpaper since her last visit. As she kissed him, Georgie registered grandiose flowers which were apparently tumbling from the ceiling.

'My darling! Do you like them? I made them put it on upside down. I thought it was time I was showered with carnations again. Linnet just despises them.'

'They're fantastic, Daddy,' she assured him. Each bloom was the size of a baby's head so she was speaking the truth. 'How is Linnet?'

'Apart from losing some of her joy in

66

vulgarity, Linnet is the same, my darling. Just the same. She was here yesterday. She comes most Fridays.' He blinked in delight. Georgie deduced that Linnet was still his lover. In many ways, the woman made Georgie feel that someone had walked on her grave. At the minimum age of fifty, she wore hoop ear-rings and ankle socks with ballet pumps, looking and sounding like a superannuated member of the cast of *Grease.*

'That's good.' She sank into the visitor's chair, a comfortable neo-Victorian velvet affair with fringes to its mahogany feet.

'As good as it gets at my age,' her father agreed, 'let alone in my state. Probably better than I deserve. I know you don't like her.'

'She makes you happy,' Georgie proposed.

'She makes me come.' He blinked again, several times.

'I don't wish to know that.'

'I thought you were in Chicago, not Kansas, dear.'

'Wherever I was, I'm happy for your private life to stay that way.'

'But can't I be proud of it, dear? Just a little bit?'

'You can be proud without actually telling me.'

'The prudery of the young.'

He smiled at her and blinked again. Any degree of pleasure sent his long eyelashes fluttering. His hair and eyebrows were pure white but the lashes were still dark and hinted at the feline handsomeness that had made his name. He claimed that the blinking mannerism was involuntary but since it had disappeared when he was working, Georgie assumed it was sheer affectation. Her father had worked only once since his accident. There were, he said, a surprising number of parts for old men in wheelchairs but the scripts were all crap.

'God, it's good to see you. Way-hay-hay!' He shifted unsteadily on his inflatable cushion and dropped his half-glasses. Georgie picked them up for him. He was seventy-nine. She was his only child, born when his bachelor days were finally ended by her determined mother, who was thirty years his junior. Eight years later, her mother moved to California with an osteopath, whereupon Georgie's father resumed his amiable orbit between lunch at the pub at the end of their road in Hampstead, afternoon trysts at the flats of lady friends and the Garrick club in the evening. Georgie learned to fry fishfingers for two and make Buck's Fizz for Sunday breakfast. She became the real love of his life.

The year she left school, her father slipped on the stairs at the Garrick, under the portrait of Edmund Kean as Louis XI. Predictably, he broke his hip, then followed up with a stroke on the operating table while the bone was being pinned. Or so the surgeon had said.

Sometimes Georgie wondered if the issue of trust was so big between her and Felix because of that surgeon. Her father now had only one leg, and the use of one arm. His mind was delightfully unimpaired.

While the Sir Rudolph Trippitt Retirement Home for Actors ate up their capital, Georgie had switched from Art History to an MBA, determined to be able to meet the fees when the money ran out. In that she had exceeded her goal.

'Matron tidied up the chits for you,' he said, indicating a folder of papers.

Georgie opened the folder and began checking the bills. The shower of carnations, she noticed, came at £85 a roll. 'Daddy, I'm getting married,' she said, keeping her eyes on the figures.

'I knew you hadn't come home just for me,' he said sadly.

'He's a doctor. He's called Felix.'

'What sort of doctor?'

'Research.'

'No money then.'

'No.'

'But he makes you happy?'

'Every morning.'

There was a pause and a sigh. 'You know, I don't wish to know that,' said her father.

'I was in Chicago, not Kansas,' she quipped. There was a silence.

Georgie looked up and saw that his eyes

69

were shut and a tear had appeared on one of his finely wrinkled cheeks.

'You old crocodile,' she said.

He laughed and opened his eyes again. 'Still works! I can still do it and it still works!'

*　　*　　*

Donna called Flora at six, just as she had started to think about what to wear to the party she intended to go to later. The new trousers were essential, the top was the big decision. The choice was the net thing embroidered with beads or the crinkle silk shirt.

'I think Georgie's going to be a problem,' Donna warned.

'Hasn't she changed? She's got so dreary. We have to save her.' The net thing was sexier but the vest that went underneath it needed washing.

'She's not a laugh any more, is she? D'you think it's him?'

'That man? Probably. I hate to say this, but it seemed to me that she changed her mind about him when Dillon proposed to me.' Flora decided to try the shirt to see if she liked it better when she was wearing it.

'Funny what's happening with you two. When I first knew you, she was the alpha beast. Now it's like you're the dominant one and she's going out of focus.'

70

'It was the Scumbag. And Chicago.'

'Now she's hooked up with another one. What's happening to my beautiful, brave Georgie?'

'You're right. It's just dysfunctional. We've got to stop her. When she understands, she'll be grateful.' In the mirror, Flora frowned. The shirt was bloody tasteful, it was the kind of thing married women wore to drinks evenings in the suburbs thinking they were being daringly funky. Never, never, never.

'I could not *believe* that open relationship thing she said they had going.' Donna delivered this statement in the way she had of tying to the end of the sentence a hook which somehow snared the solution she wanted.

'I know. Sick.' Holding the phone to her ear with her shoulder, Flora rifled through the washing pile behind her bedroom door with both hands. No vest. 'But she really believes it's making the relationship stronger.'

'She does, doesn't she?'

Flora located the vest under the bed. She shook it violently to get rid of the dust balls. 'Before you came into the bar I was trying to make her see how weird this Felix guy must be but she wasn't having any of it.'

'For a sweet person, Georgie can be really arrogant sometimes.'

Really, the vest didn't smell too bad. There was some old guacamole on the front but under the net nobody would notice. Flora sat on the end of the bed with a non-specific sense of relief. 'I've got it,' she told Donna. 'I know just how to play it with Georgie. Leave it to me.'

'Smart as Prada, you are,' Donna's voice in her ear approved her. 'I knew you'd come up with the answer. We're going to do it, aren't we? We're going to save our Georgie. But listen, how about *you*? And your Dillon. Flora, don't let me get you into anything you aren't comfortable with here.'

'I'm cool, don't worry about me. You know Dillon. He's besotted. He'll be fine. Georgie and me, we never did appeal to the same kind of men.'

'I don't think women ever get to be really good friends if they're always trying to pull the same kind of guy. Not that men discriminate much, do they?'

Flora giggled in the act of pushing the silk shirt to the back of the wardrobe with the rest of the things she had ready to give away to friends likely to be impressed by her generosity and admiring of her superior taste. 'They're not really bothered, are they?'

'I heard another one yesterday,' said Donna. 'You want to hear it?'

'Go on.'

'What's the difference between a clitoris and a bar?'

'I don't know, what *is* the difference between a clitoris and a bar?'

72

'Nine out of ten men can usually find a bar.'

Flora giggled some more. Des called out from downstairs, 'Darling, if you don't know the difference between a clitoris and a bar by now you need to renew your commitment to drinking.'

When she'd finished talking to Donna, Flora let Dillon's call get through.

'What time are you picking me up?' she asked him.

'What time did we say I was picking you up?' he bluffed, assuming with terror that he must have forgotten a date they had made.

'Ten, maybe. Ten-thirty. Unless you want to eat before the party.'

Party! That was it. He must have forgotten about the party. Ten! Ten-thirty! Impossible. He couldn't live without seeing her for another four hours. 'Let's eat first,' he suggested. 'If I pick you up at eight . . .'

'Nine.'

He hadn't booked, he was a fool! And everywhere would be crammed by half past nine. Plus, bottom line, sex was the main event of the evening, and a late kick off plus a party would mean getting to bed late and knackered and perhaps unfit to deliver a class-A shag.

He pleaded. 'Eight-thirty?'

'If you like. See you, sweets.'

Flora rang off and thought about getting Des to start her bath.

CHAPTER FIVE

APRIL 15–16

On Saturday night, Felix and Georgie went to the cinema in Islington to see a Hungarian film that had won the critics' prize at Cannes. After ten minutes, Georgie fell asleep. They proceeded to the Wagamama noodle bar, where Georgie fell asleep again, standing up in the queue. This annoyed Felix; she was heavy and he felt unmanly when she slumped against his chest and knocked him off balance. He let her sit on the steps and sleep leaning against the wall until there were free spaces on the benches for them.

She managed to stay awake during the meal, although her nose nodded scarily close to the soup a couple of times. Thoughtfully, Felix told her about the film in so much detail she knew as much about it as if she had been able to keep her eyes open and see it herself. Going home, he let her sleep in the taxi until it was time to pay.

When they had finished having sex it was long after midnight. Georgie buried her face in one of Felix's scratchy linen pillow cases and consigned herself to self-indulgent unconsciousness for twelve hours.

On Saturday night, Des made a serious

mistake and went out in new boots. They took him to the Met bar without any trouble, where he met Donna. They consumed three strawberry Martinis each and agreed that Flora and Georgie were throwing their lives away.

'Chucking themselves into the Romantic Crap Swamp,' mourned Des. 'Drowning in the Bog of Icky Love Mush. Disgusting.'

'I never expected it of Georgie,' Donna grieved.

'I did,' declared Des. 'She was always the dilettante. Anybody's for a bad poem and an empty gesture. I'm surprised you never saw that.'

'I never did,' allowed Donna. 'But Flora, now—she started out useless but she was really coming round until this Dillon thing.'

'You don't have to live with it. But never mind,' Des assured her. 'We'll get them back on track. In six months they'll be just drooling with gratitude to us for rescuing them.'

'It needs a name, this project,' Donna proposed. 'You know plenty of military types. What's the right name for a mission to rescue two fine women from the Romantic Crap Swamp?'

'Project Heartswap?' he suggested.

'Project's too tentative. We must not fail. Operation Heartswap.'

'Genius,' breathed Des.

They drank to it. After that, his evening

became deranged.

From the Met in Park Lane he stupidly walked to the far side of Soho, queued an hour and a half for The Tube Club, threw down vodka-cranberries on top of the Martinis, danced madly then agreed to go down to Equinox for the Ginger Spice Tribute Night.

At Equinox he switched to vodka and Red Bull, threw a few of his famous karate kicks in Wannabee and pulled the venue's Top Shag. Top Shag was a Danish model, twenty-two years old, school of Johnny Depp. Top Shag demanded drugs. Des acquired drugs.

Together they went on to some place in Brixton. Des retained the impression of arm-waving, snogging and bad beer. Top Shag disappeared with the drugs. Des forgave him. He forgave everybody. He loved everybody. He wanted to huggle everybody.

Soon, Des huggled a body over whom another body wanted to maintain the illusion of ownership. The other body was very large and hit him in the face. Des forgave him. He captured the attention of another body that tried to have sex with him using a floppy penis in the alley outside. Des forgave them all. They went to some flat. Des wanted to take a piss but his trousers were uncooperative. The body tried to have sex with him in the kitchen but the penis failed at the last minute.

Des tried to throw up but the kitchen sink moved. He noticed that his boots were getting messy and sat down to take them off. That was when he discovered the blisters. His feet had become a mass of sacs of white skin. He told the body that they looked like a pair of thalidomide squids. The body said its mother had talked about thalidomide.

A few hours into Sunday, just as the body finally presented him with a standing penis, Des passed out in a pool of mingled bodily fluids on a kitchen floor in Herne Hill.

*   *   *

In a cab, it took Donna three-quarters of an hour to ride the glittering torrents of traffic from Hyde Park Corner to Tower Bridge. While the driver cursed fifty-two coaches of tourists, inched along the top of Trafalgar Square and waited out the roadworks on the Embankment, Donna retouched her mascara, repainted her lipstick, resurfaced her cheeks and meditated pleasantly on Operation Heartswap. Up to this point, she judged her evening a success.

At last she arrived at the Pont De La Tour and joined a colleague from Direct Warranty to entertain two global board directors over from Denver with their wives. The wives were malevolently polite to her. They ate small pieces of food stacked in miniature pagodas on vast white plates and discussed the state of the world reinsurance market, the economic prognosis for the former Soviet Union and the latest Washington sex scandal.

Donna's mood crashed. Boredom loomed. She was afraid of boredom, she felt her heart race when it attacked. Boredom always prowled the fringes of her mind, a savage, multi-headed monster with old entrails caked on its filthy jaws.

Over the de-caffs, she launched a politically incorrect dissertation on the attributes of lesbians. Once the company showed itself willing to be titillated by this iconoclasm, she indicated that she would be receptive to their views on African Americans. Eventually, the visitors felt uninhibited enough to speak judgementally of Jews. They left the restaurant with sparkling eyes, four more New Worlders exhilarated by the old forbidden thrills of Europe.

'How do you do that?' her colleague asked with admiration while they waited for their cabs.

'They were dreary,' she explained. 'I had to do something. I think they enjoyed it.'

'You bet they enjoyed it. I just hope they never tell.'

'They won't dare,' she promised him as he opened her taxi door.

The journey home was a short ride over Tower Bridge. In her flat, Donna sat at her desk looking out over the river. From nowhere, a vision of Dillon came into her

78

mind. He scurried, his shoulders were bent, his face was white and tense.

Operation Heartswap required men with blood in their veins and time on their hands. Dillon had the first, but not, at that point, the second. She needed him idle. Donna fired up her computer and planned a major rationalisation of the new business department of Direct Warranty.

*   *   *

Flora was not feeling hungry that evening, but Dillon pressurised her until she identified a need for sushi. He drove her across town to the nearest Yah! Sushi! and perched unsteadily beside her on a tall stool at the counter, choosing from a conveyor belt of dainty plates. While Dillon made a pig of himself with fish things, loaded up with ginger, mustard and God-knows-what, Flora dissected some disappointing rice rolls and extracted the chips of avocado.

Predictably, Dillon moved for cutting the party and going back to 17A for sex, making it necessary for Flora to explain that the party was an important networking opportunity and the host was an important client with a new office in Hampstead, who'd invested thousands in her special skills and now wanted to show off the results. The effort of this explanation annoyed Flora.

Dillon claimed to have heard of her client and said his reputation was dubious. To save energy and make sure Dillon never trivialised her work again, Flora expressed all her feelings, telling him that anybody who cared anything about her would have realised that her work was far more important than any bodily appetite, especially sex, and that he was an insensitive bastard.

These events took place as they drove north to Hampstead and waited out the traffic jam on Heath Street. To encourage Dillon to use his brain the next time he took her out, Flora also shared her option that he should have had the sense to leave his car and take a cab, whose driver would have known the backroads and not wasted so much time. Dillon began to feel hot and sweaty.

At the party, the client towered over them and made Dillon look embarrassingly young. The client was a massive man with steely hair, who used his hands like table-tennis bats, dispersing his guests about the premises to his liking. Paffff . . . he spun Dillon away into an airless little room occupied by the host's personal trainer and his reflexologist. Piffff . . . he chipped Flora into the big room by his side and introduced her to people.

Dillon needed air. He wanted Flora. Leaving his oubliette to find these two essentials, he noticed that the so-called office ended in a large room containing a bed, a wall of mirror and two pots of suggestive red orchids. He could not remember Flora mentioning this detail. Anxiety energised him, but before he could complete his crossing of the corridor, he started gasping for breath. He felt his face pulsing with heat. His neck was as stiff as a tree trunk. His chest was burning, his eyes were popping, he couldn't speak, he was on the floor. 'Who is that? I think somebody should take him to hospital,' said an irritated voice.

The paramedic was a fatherly man who was easy with the term 'anaphylactic shock'. 'Tuna does it, undercooked tuna, that's the usual suspect.'

'It was supposed to be raw,' Dillon said.

'Mad, you are. You gotta be mad,' the paramedic diagnosed as Dillon was rolled in a blanket and strapped to a stretcher.

After this embarrassment, Flora had a good evening. The energy was churning like a washing machine. Her host told his guests that the success of his party was largely down to her Environmental Aroma Balancer and the Euphoric Blend (neroli, ylang-ylang, black pepper). He claimed a 300 per cent increase in business since her visit and she passed around her cards. She promised that fishtanks were unnecessary and noted universal relief, which she expertly converted into an ecstasy of anticipation.

After the guests left, promising to call, Flora

mentioned a new club. The client called a taxi and took her there. Cash immediately resolved the question of membership. They were sucked into the depths of a squashy red velvet sofa. Flora reminded the client to book a follow-up consultation to cleanse the energy of his personal space after the party. Flora's client suggested that she ditch the loser, meaning Dillon. Flora invited her client to ditch his wife. As she expected, this question was not resolved.

When Flora realised that the synthetic smell of the sofa was making her nauseous, her client was properly shamed and whisked her home to 17A. Since he was richer, older and smarter than Dillon, it seemed only fair to allow him a goodnight snog.

Flora slept blissfully until midday on Sunday, when Dillon had the nerve to call from a hospital far away to ask her to pick him up. She gave him some indication of the scale of her disappointment and went back to sleep.

A couple of hours later, Dillon came round to 17A with a very large bunch of pink tulips. From behind her curtains, Flora saw him knocking at the door. He was about to give up, leave the flowers and go when a minicab pulled over and out of it crawled Des, who let Dillon into the house. For some reason, Des was walking barefoot and carrying his boots.

Feeling a little trapped now, Flora allowed Dillon to take her to Spitalfields market for peppermint tea and a bagel. In return for listening to Dillon telling her that he had nearly died, she accepted as a present a pyramid of labradorite, sold by the man who had crystals from Katmandu. It was obviously a highly charged mineral and well worth sixty pounds. In the evening, after she'd sent Dillon home to work, she meant to meditate for an hour, but as soon as she began, the next move with Georgie manifested itself in her mind so she made a call. Georgie's phone was on recall.

Despite this disappointment, Flora felt contentment. She inspected the whole canvas of her life and liked the picture. Ten years ago she had been her brothers' punchbag and her mother's therapist. Seven years ago, she had been so angry! She got her MBA at the University of Aberdeen, chosen because it was definitively too far from home for her to be able to get back more than twice a year. But all that guilt turned out into such terrible, unbalanced rage. It was only when she left uni that she really started to read: *The Celestine Prophecy*, *You Can Heal Your Life*, *What Colour is Your Parachute?*, *The Seven Spiritual Laws of Success*.

Those books had changed her life. She had worked on herself and now she had accepted her choices and changed her paradigms. She had her own space, a house in the East End; she had people in her life who supported her,

83

like Des and Georgie. She had a role model and a mentor, she had Donna. She had got out of the corporate madness, she had her own business and all these clients she could turn on to a true understanding of the universe. How cool was that?

CHAPTER SIX

APRIL 17–20

Dillon got ready to kill small-pet madness. He opened up his laptop and took control of the meeting. 'Small-pet policies,' he announced, giving his voice a dying fall as he put his charts on the screen. 'If we went into this area, the challenge would be that small pets don't live very long. A hamster lives three years, Russian hamster perhaps more, a gerbil will live five years, rabbits three to four according to the breed, small rodents less than two years.' The graphics got a laugh. He'd shaped each pie chart according to the animal and animated them so the hamsters washed their whiskers and the gerbil jumped. This was going to be all over in thirty seconds—max.

'That means that if we were to sell policies, they wouldn't run very long, the administration costs would be relatively high. In the large-pet market we get most sales in the vet's surgery. The owner's standing there looking at a massive bill for Fido's oncology and he sees the wisdom of his choice. That means commission payments to the vet. On a two-year policy, the commission we would be able to offer wouldn't be enough to be attractive. And small animals aren't like cats and dogs,

85

they don't go on for years with heart disease, diabetes, kidney failure, cancer . . .'

'Excellent,' Donna interrupted him. 'You're saying they just die and that's it?'

'Ah, yeah—more or less.'

'That's great, isn't it?' She canvassed the rest of the circle who nodded slavish approval. 'That gives us a minimal risk of high claims. Great work, Dillon.'

'Not quite. Before they die, they get lost.' So confident was he that he ignored the thunderclouds in Donna's eyes. 'They get lost with serious underwriting implications. They get down the back of sofas, inside pianos. A family in Macclesfield had their entire patio dug up because a hamster had got underneath the tiles.' Another laugh. The team were with him.

'Wow. People really love their small pets.' Donna nodded, round-eyed, the way people do when they believe they are hearing a great mystery of life expounded.

'Children,' he protested. 'Children love them, not the adults. Not the premium payers.'

'So, we market to the children. You're telling me there's no way we can get our premiums out of children's love?'

'Donna, what I'm saying here is the numbers don't stack up. My feeling is not to go any further with this product.' He'd lost them. The team was not with him any more, they were bouncing with Donna's enthusiasm and the cuteness of his bloody graphics.

'You're such a clever boy,' she returned caressingly. 'You'll fix the numbers. I'm really excited about this. The small-pet market is wide open! Direct will be the first in there! I'm making this your project, Dillon. Give it everything you've got! Pick your team, get out there, do some focus groups . . .'

Dillon had a flash picture of standing beside Flora at a party admitting that he was researching public attitudes to hamster health. On a woman lacking Flora's totally kissable lips, her expression would have appeared nasty.

'Development costs . . .' he remonstrated.

'Give me a budget. Great work, Dillon!' And she turned to her next victim.

*   *   *

On Monday Flora went about her business. She went out to see people, carrying her divining pendulum, her Ba Kwa chart and the Environmental Aroma Harmoniser in a yellow silk roll which she had designed to conserve their energies. She explained compellingly that she could make wealth, love and happiness flow through a workplace like a great river of blessings.

Back home at 17A, she hand-sketched maps of her prospects' offices and coloured the energy flow with red pencil. She left Georgie another message. She decanted her oils and cleansed some new crystals. She went to her shiatsu class. She sent Georgie an e-mail. She had a Thai massage and some reflexology. She waited.

*　　*　　*

Georgie downloaded her Monday morning prices at 6 a.m. and saw flashing red markers against a column of currency bonds. The red flashers she had programmed in to detonate when the bonds hit the level at which she considered they were overpriced and her clients might care to take their profits. She made a brisk round of calls.

By 10.00, the red markers had spread like a light-up plague across warrants and futures and forwards. Her screen was a firework display. Clients saw for themselves the wisdom of making the move. Calls came back like a dawn chorus of electronic songbirds. She spent most of the day standing with phones in both hands, screaming across the desk.

It was blissfully relaxing to get home. Felix took responsibility for their shopping, and did it on-line with an organic produce supplier, so there by their door to greet her was a box of freshly dug vegetables. She took them to the kitchen, put on an apron and started washing the mud off the leeks. She meant to turn her phone on before bedtime but it didn't happen.

88

She's avoiding me, Flora deduced. She's avoiding the whole issue. She'd actually let our friendship sink because she's so into avoidance. Donna will be so disappointed. I should support Donna, she has been my mentor and now it's my role to lighten her life. Flora made another call, to a useful friend from the Ardent Holdings days who now sold art from his own gallery off Hoxton Square.

'Georgie's back,' she announced.

'Who's Georgie?' he demanded.

'The one you had the hots for.'

'I never have the hots for your friends. Not so's you'd know, anyway.'

'You're pathetic. I always know.'

'Are we talking the one with the ripe hips?'

'What did I tell you?'

'She was the only one. She was special. Didn't she go to Cincinnati or somewhere?'

'Chicago. But she's back now.'

'Didn't work out, then?'

'Ask her yourself. Ask her to your private view.'

'What private view?'

'You have private views. You have openings. You have one on Thursday. You don't need to make up an excuse why you don't invite me. Just invite us both this time and we'll leave it there.'

89

'Give me her number.'

'She never gets back on calls. So driven, don't you remember? Hopeless. She needs slowing down. Send her a proper invitation. Do you want this woman or not?'

'This is one of your set-ups,' he sighed, 'but I'll do it because I'm a fool for love. Give me the address. Does she buy things? She must be rich by now, isn't she?'

'You mean is she going to buy one of your weird sculptures? What for? Scaring off muggers?'

'I am in business here, you know. I don't just do this for the good of your social life.'

'No, you do it for the good of yours. I thought the art world was totally chick-infested. Why are you always after my friends?'

'They're rich. I never meet a woman who can afford me. I suppose she's got a boyfriend. Whatsername. The one with the hips.'

'Of course she's got a boyfriend. For the moment, anyway.'

'Watch this space, huh? What's he like?'

There was real hope in his voice. Flora tried not to sound pitying. 'Never met him,' she said briskly. 'But I've got a kind of intuition about it.'

'Your intuition isn't going to pay my rent, sweetie.'

'Believe me. Anyway, I'm bringing my boss. She's seriously rich. And she buys stuff.'

90

'I'm a total studmuffin, you know. Have you told her that?'

'How would I know?' Flora teased him. 'I can't verify that.'

'Not my fault,' he claimed amiably, because he found Flora wispy, brittle and not at all attractive, even if she could be fun when she stirred things up.

Flora smiled her inward smile all day after this conversation and was pleased that men were slaves to their hormones.

*   *   *

'Messenger Gallery.' Georgie had time to read the franked logo on the envelope when she got home. She remembered the man who used to flirt with her at Ardent, smiley and beefy, not in the Great Lats league but . . . She felt a pinprick of self-pity because somehow her flirtability seemed to have evaporated. Felix was so sophisticated, so highly evolved; he understood how demeaning frivolous sexual attention could be for a woman. She stuffed the envelope in her bag and went to the kitchen to see how the leeks had marinated.

On the tube train at five the next morning, she was jolted awake at St Paul's station, half-dreaming about Flat Eric. She fumbled in her bag for her ticket, found the invitation and read, 'Merita Halili. My Homeland. Works on Aluminium and Glass, inspired by the artist's

flight from Albania. Private View, 6pm–9pm.'
Guilt attacked her on the score of her yearning
for flirting, of wanting to drive Flat Eric to the
office instead of caring for the planet and
taking the train, of failing to facilitate Felix's
fascination with the Balkan situation by
offering him the opportunity to share the
invitation to the gallery opening, of failing to
disclose the soft spot she had for Smiley-and-
Beefy.

There was still time. She vowed to call Felix
during the day. She called at ten, but he was
out of the office. She left a message. At twelve
he was in a meeting so she left another
message and virtuously refused to go for
coffee with the gang because Great Lats asked
her. At two she called for the third time but
did not leave a message because Felix was
saving doomed children and a third message
would have made him feel hounded. What was
a party beside saving the world from
Lightoller's Syndrome? By five, with a
hopeless mass of paperwork still to do,
Georgie submitted a final message with the
gallery address and went to refurbish her
makeup.

'It's you!' squealed Flora, dumping her glass
to give Georgie a hug.

'It is she!' boomed Smiley-and-Beefy, now
bearded and a ringer for Henry VIII. 'Darling,
I'll be with you in a minute,' and he turned
back to a woman in green satin, taller and

92

thinner than anyone else in the gallery with waist-length silver-blond hair and purple fingernails.

'She has to be the artist,' Georgie whispered.

'She so has to be,' Flora whispered back. An instant conspiracy. Excellent. Hold that energy.

Merita Halili, as the programme said, acknowledged her debt to Alexander Calder. She made mobiles. Blue glass discs on silver wires. A long horsetail of aluminium threads. A tinkling cascade of glass drops behind some large plates of metal which rotated slowly to display diagonal slashes in their smoothness. The pieces were turned by ingenious tiny motors. Occasionally, small natural forms were incorporated, fern leaves or snail shells. The works were oddly poignant. Flora saw Georgie get the kicked-cat look, which meant she was empathising again. 'You don't have to be sad,' she assured her. 'It wasn't our war.'

'Yes it was,' Georgie pointed out.

'It was the boys' war. All wars are boys' wars.'

'Madeleine Albright . . .'

'Advised by whom? Men are the experts on war. Women don't fight.'

'Then we colluded. We didn't . . .'

'God, what has happened to you? You're so earnest, Georgie. Is earnest how they are in Chicago? You used to be a laugh.'

Georgie was about to assert her light-heartedness when Merita Halili screamed and swooped like an enraged Valkyrie on a man who had just entered the gallery. A slap cracked through the party noise. The victim fell against one of the works, a sheet of aluminium which crashed like stage thunder. Fabric was ripped, glasses were broken, Merita howled, her victim bellowed. Merita waved a fork at his eyes. The surrounding British fell back in fear. Cowering in a corner, Smiley-and-Beefy got out his phone, rolling his eyes like a worried cow.

Flora, delighted with these helpful energies, drew Georgie away up the stairs and out to the roof terrace. There Donna was enthroned on a bench between two topiary box pillars, talking to a tiny blond woman who perched alertly on the edge of the seat. They were framed by the sordid pyrotechnics of the East London night sky, traffic signals and street lights, coloured bulbs left on cranes since Christmas and towers of empty offices with blazing windows.

'Fantastic surprise!' Donna greeted them. Flora preened.

'Well, I'll be circulating,' the tiny woman said in a surprisingly deep voice. 'Let me give you my card.'

'Yeah, thanks,' said Donna with an absent look in her close dark eyes.

As they sat, Georgie said, 'I can't be long, I haven't spoken to Felix.'

'You were always so sorted,' observed Donna and allowed a shadow of melancholy to gather under her brows before she launched the business of the night. Flora leaned back a little, putting Georgie in the front line. 'So, tell me, gorgeous. I've been meaning to ask you. Where is coming back to London in your life plan?'

'When I thought about it, it wasn't necessary for me to be in Chicago. At my level, you can be anywhere. Felix had this grant . . .'

'I don't quite see,' Donna persisted. 'Talk me through it one more time.'

'It doesn't matter where I am, I can earn the same money, relative to the local cost of living. But Felix had to be in London. So here I am again.'

Why did it sound lame, all of a sudden? Georgie felt awkward but Donna seemed to have taken her answer on board and was moving on. 'And now, my great girlies, tell me what you've been planning. What's the strategy?'

'Strategy?' Georgie's mind clung to Felix and the plan for her life, which she had to admit had been subsumed by the plan for Felix's life.

'Operation Heartswap. The strategy. The deal. Flora's plan for Felix. Your plan for Dillon.'

'For Dillon?'

'Our scam,' Flora prompted her. 'The boys'

fidelity test. You remember.'

'You're not serious,' said Georgie, but she saw that they were. 'Don't be daft,' she commanded them.

'Georgie! You're not wimping out?' This was Flora's opening move but Donna frowned, knowing it was a loser.

'Oh, for heaven's sake.'

'But I thought you were back up there. With your self-esteem.'

'Flora, give me a break.'

'OK, OK! I just can't . . .' The vibes from Donna were really evil. Flora started to panic.

'How can you think I'd do a thing like that? I love Felix, I respect him. You must love Dillon, don't you?'

'Darling, of course I love him. And he loves me, I know he does. Don't get me wrong, Georgie, I know you've always been a man-magnet, but the boy's in love and he doesn't know there's another woman on the planet except for me. And I love Dillon and I trust him, so where's the harm? It's just fun, isn't it?'

Just for a nano-second, Georgie wavered. 'Just a bit of fun,' purred Donna. 'Of course the guys adore you, both of you. You're gorgeous, they're in love and you're friends, it's just a game.'

'No,' said Georgie. 'It wouldn't be a game to me. This is my life you want to play with. My life, my future, the man I love. No way.'

96

A phone rang, a short, sour warble. Georgie reached into her bag and moved away to a corner of the terrace for privacy.

'Are you all right?' Felix hissed in her ear.

'Yes, yes—didn't you get my messages?' The blue lights of a police car pulsed over the street below. Georgie looked down while she talked.

'What messages?'

'I left . . .' She dared not say three. 'I called to see if you wanted to come to this gallery opening.'

He sounded weary, either from disappointment or tiredness, she wasn't sure. 'I suppose it's too late now?'

Down on the pavement three police officers appeared, struggling to propel Merita Halili towards their car. 'I think the artist is leaving,' murmured Georgie. She felt herself smile. No, she was not earnest. Life had joys, definitely it did.

'OK, sweetheart.' Felix went into enlightened magnanimity mode. She felt calmer. 'Enjoy the rest of the evening, take your time, have fun, I'll be here when you get back. There was something I wanted to see on the TV anyway. Take care, huh?'

As they said goodbye, Georgie caught a snatch of the side conversation Donna and Flora had started to fill the time. '. . . really has changed,' sighed Flora. 'I hate to see her losing it. I wonder if she'll ever get her confidence back.'

Losing it? No confidence? Was this about her? Georgie was indignant. She was alarmed. Damn it, she was scared. Without her confidence, what would she be? Useless, worthless—powerless! One of those weaklings straggling away from the herd just begging for the jackals to pull her down. No, never. Confidence was never her problem. Bullshit! She was invincible—but, as she switched off her phone, Georgie heard Donna whisper thoughtfully, 'I've seen that. I've seen people lose it. It happens.'

So philosophical! So accepting! Was it so easy for them to believe she was in some dying orbit spiralling to destruction? Georgie searched their faces. Yes—there it was! Pity. Pity for her. Well, that was unnecessary. Pity was premature. She opened her mouth, but before she could speak Donna issued a forgiving smile and said, 'Such a shame about the game, Georgie. But of course, we do respect your feelings. If you don't want to play, that's fine. Don't even think about it. But I was going to tell you . . . no, no point now.'

'What?' snapped Georgie, wondering what other damnations had been lodged against her name.

'No, really. Waste of time.'

'No, tell me. I want to know.'

'There's no point, darling. You don't want to do this and we're OK with that. Really we are. We'll just forget the whole thing.'

'So—what were you going to say? Come on,' Georgie remembered to smile. She even managed a careless giggle. 'What is this that you're hiding from me?'

'Donna was going to make it interesting.' Flora suddenly appeared to be bored to catatonia. 'I mean, really interesting.'

'You were what?'

'It's too trivial, Georgie. You're right. I just thought . . .'

'Come on, spill—for heaven's sake.'

Flora looked at the glaring night sky as if she expected a resolution was to be dropped by helicopter.

Donna confided very carefully, 'I was thinking of taking a bet on it, that's all.'

'What kind of bet?'

'Well, you know at Ardent we always said one day we'd have a real holiday, go somewhere divine, somewhere they make TV commercials, the Seychelles or the Maldives or somewhere, and spend two weeks on a white sand beach just doing fuck-all?'

'Yes, so?'

'And you and your Felix, and Flora and Dillon, you'll be planning honeymoons now?'

'We haven't really thought that far.' Georgie could hear Felix saying that neither of them could afford two weeks away. But already she was smelling the scent of Hawaiian Tropic.

Flora yawned. 'The groom does the

honeymoon. Dillon's going to surprise me. He's sweet like that.'

'So,' said Donna, spreading her fingers on her knees as she laid out her plan. 'I was thinking it could go like this. We set a deadline, say—what? Two weeks? You pretend you're going away somewhere, you hide out at my place and you go after each other's fellas. If you're right—and, ladies, I hope you are, believe me. I'd never lose a bet as happily as this, that's the truth. If you're right, and the guys turn you down, it'll be dream honeymoons for all four of you at my expense. And if you're wrong—we'll find that beach. Just us three. Win-win, huh?'

Rapidly, Georgie turned the deal upside down and inside out. Watertight. No holes anywhere. 'Win-win,' she agreed.

Donna stifled another sigh. Flora kept gazing at the sky. An angel passed. Then Georgie said, 'OK. It's too beautiful, Donna. I can't pass this one by. I'm in. Let's do it.'

'No, no. Georgie, you've said your piece. You really don't want to . . .' Donna began again, but Georgie was hooked and ten minutes later they had reeled her in and landed her.

CHAPTER SEVEN

APRIL 21–24

'Dillon, darling,' Flora began, winding both her arms around one of his while he made her lemon and ginger tea the next morning. 'I'm going to this conference on space cleaning. In Cornwall.'

'Good,' he murmured. Small rodents were pattering through his mind, a lemming-like torrent overrunning all other considerations.

'It's two weeks.'

'Great,' he muttered, wishing some Pied Piper would lead the horrible vision away to hell.

'You don't care!' She punched him in the back, causing him to slop boiling water over his thumb.

'Damn!' He lurched to the sink and ran cold water over the scald. 'Damn! Flora, I don't get it. What don't I care about?'

'That I'm going away for two whole weeks. We won't see each other for two whole weeks.'

'God.' He was thunderstruck. 'You're going away? You didn't say you were going away.'

'Yes I did, you weren't listening.'

'I was, but . . .'

'What were you thinking about? Don't tell me, I know. Work, work, work. You never think about anything else. Well, now you'll have two whole weeks without me to distract you.' And she darted out of the kitchen to the bathroom and slammed the door.

'Darling! Flora! Don't be cross, I didn't mean not to listen.'

He heard hissing shower water. She couldn't hear him. She was not going to ask him to join her in the shower. Flora had never asked him to join her in the shower. How could he even notice that about her, the beautiful spiritual creature who had agreed to marry him? Dillon went back to the kitchen and refilled the kettle so fresh water would be hot for the tea when Flora came out of the bathroom. Two weeks without her! It would seem like forever.

*   *   *

Georgie waited for the time when Felix was always good-humoured, immediately after they had sex in the morning. 'I have to be away next week,' she began as soon as she was dressed.

'Mnmn.' Felix's face was in the pillow. She went over to the bed and risked turning him over to make sure he stayed awake.

'Darling, they're sending me to the European Managers' Conference in Brussels.'

'Great city, Brussels. Beautiful architecture. Of course, it's neglected because everybody talks about Bruges, but really I think parts of Brussels are superior.'

'It'll be two weeks.'

'That long, huh?' He seemed very little moved. Georgie was annoyed.

'And I'd like to go in Flat Eric.'

'Who?'

'The car. I need the car,' she said. That got his attention.

'Is everyone at your level going?' he asked in bewilderment.

'Uh—no.' Yikes! Suppose they went to one of those with-partners evenings, like at Christmas, and Felix starting talking about Brussels and everyone went blank? 'Actually, the invitation was confidential,' she improvised swiftly.

'Great. That means they're fast-tracking you already. Superb.' He sat up and kissed her with great satisfaction.

'You'll be OK?'

'Of course. I'll rent a car for a couple of weeks. And I'll be able to work later, get things really moving. Don't worry about me. Go and get the best from it.'

'Thank you,' she said, and hurried off to work, pretended to be running late in case he saw that she looked guilty.

The air seemed unusually fresh. The leaves on the great plane trees shading Holland Park Road rustled with optimism. The buses grinding towards Notting Hill Gate looked magnificently red. Georgie felt elated, but was too busy to notice that.

They started out like four crazy teens at a sleepover. When Sunday came, Flora and Georgie packed their bags and arrived at Donna's place, Flora towing Des behind her as a porter. In case there were any fainthearts, Donna had the champagne chilled. She had also chilled the flutes for it, which Flora reckoned to be the apogee of style.

'Dillon,' Flora instructed Georgie, 'really loves ditzy, wacky, crazy, kooky women. Bubble-heads. Puff-balls. The intellectually challenged.'

'Don't we all?' commented Des, pouring the champagne.

'He watches old Goldie Hawn movies. You know the stuff I mean. Late for everything, putting the credit cards through the wash, forgetting your own phone number. Anything to make him feel all macho and protective.' She chuckled, thinking of Dillon's exasperation if she even misplaced her keys. 'And really obvious dressing, bright colours. Holey clothes, split seams, runs in your tights. Slutty stuff really turns him on.' She remembered seeing him wince when he noticed that smear of old guacamole under the net thing. 'And the old Gothic makeup. Black eyeliner. You *know*.'

'Yes, I know,' Georgie agreed. 'It's not me,

104

is it?'

'You'll manage. And Felix?' Donna prompted her. 'What does he go for?'

'Well,' Georgie winced with misgiving, thinking how thunderously Felix would disapprove of this adventure. 'He and Flora really have a lot in common, actually. He's a vegan, of course, no animal products at all, no smoking, no drinking, no alcohol. Cruelty-free cosmetics. He's amazing, he can tell.' She frowned, thinking of the things that made Felix frown. 'But what's really important to Felix are the emotional things. Being aware and caring and really, really honest. He can't respect people who don't share his values, think about the environment, social issues, peace. All that.'

'I know,' said Flora. 'I know absolutely.'

Donna smiled at them and said, 'Amazing. You've really studied these blokes, haven't you? Oh, this *is* going to be fun.'

'What about my hair?' asked Flora, letting a limpid strand run through her fingers.

'He'll love your hair,' Georgie promised her. 'Everyone loves your hair.'

'What about *your* hair?' Donna suggested, dragging a curl or two out of Georgie's obedient power pleat.

'It's boring, it needs some drama,' Des declared.

'We should have thought of this before.' Georgie clutched her hair to protect it but the majority were already voting for its reeducation with critical eyes.

'I can do something with it,' Des volunteered. They regrouped in the bathroom where he teased Georgie's hair into a haystack then slashed into it with Donna's manicure scissors. When he considered his work finished, he giggled, 'Well, that's sort of what I was thinking of,' and clipped up the ragged forelock in a pom-pom of the style which works only with two-year-olds and Yorkshire terriers.

'Great,' nodded Donna.

'Hot,' pronounced Flora.

'Really hot,' affirmed Des, standing back to admire the effect.

'It certainly is wacky,' sighed Georgie, covertly delighted that she now looked like a giant lap-dog, so this Dillon person would never fancy her so the whole mad scheme would fall apart. She noted that at the bottom of her heart she did not believe that Felix would fall for Flora, either. 'Can I go to bed now? I've got an early start.'

'Not yet—tell us the game plan!' Donna demanded, suspicious of Georgie as the weaker vessel in this conspiracy.

'She's got her ID picture and she's going to pounce on Dillon at the gym,' Flora assured them.

Georgie showed an overexposed picture-booth photograph of Dillon with red eyes kissing a cadaverously pale Flora. 'Tomorrow lunchtime. He gets there at twelve-thirty, I get there at twelve-forty-five. He will be wearing grey Calvin Klein shorts and a dark red rugby shirt. I take it from there. It's between asking him how the chin-up machine works or dropping a barbell on his foot. You did say he liked the obvious approach.' My God, Georgie exclaimed to herself, I sound so clinical here.

Des sniggered. 'I'd go for the barbell. Stop him running away.'

'So would I,' Flora confirmed. 'Who says he knows how the chin-up machine works anyway? He's there to sculpt his butt for me.'

'OK, barbells at dawn then. Can I please go to bed now?'

*   *   *

They sat up while Georgie tossed in her guilty sleep. 'And our Flora,' said Des. 'What's your plan for this pitiful creep?'

'You don't know he's a pitiful creep,' Donna reasoned.

'All that tree-hugging hippy crap. Of course he's pitiful.'

'If it's true,' Flora pointed out in a thoughtful voice. 'I never reckoned Georgie with a tree-hugging type.'

'Uh-huh.' Donna shook her head.

'What d'you mean, if it's true? Wickedness, what's on your mind?'

'She's not really up for this, is she? She'd

really like for it not to work. That's why I told you to cut her hair, you see. To commit her. She's buggered now, she's got to go through with it. But what if she told me exactly what this Felix creep doesn't go for, just to make sure I never get any action out of him?'

'Of course,' said Des at once. 'You're absolutely right. That's exactly what she's done.'

'She was always devious,' Donna commented. 'Never comes out with stuff. I think you're right.'

'I know I'm right. I think we can forget all that whalesaving anorak bullshit. I'm going for material girl. Big time.'

'You!' Des protested. 'You'll die, darling. You haven't a clue.'

'It's only a game,' Flora promised them, her smile more inward and mysterious than before. 'Donna, I need a car. A real car. You've got a Mercedes, haven't you? I can borrow it.'

There was a sudden hiatus. 'Uh—of course,' the Prima donna agreed.

*   *   *

'Dilbert!' As soon as Dillon dragged himself into the cardio theatre on Monday, his trainer bounded over and clamped him in a hefty Tasmanian handshake.

'Actually, it's Dillon,' Dillon told him. The

lunch-hour rush was starting, treadmills were roaring, music was pounding.

'Huh?'

'My name's Dillon,' he ventured to shout.

'Dillon! Dillon! Right! Sorry about that. Listen up my man! Congratulations! You're a star. You got third in your class in the Himalaya Trek! You get a T-shirt!'

'I can't have,' he said automatically. He had never won anything for sport in his life.

'No lies! Your name's on the board! Here it is, put it on! Increase your motivation!'

The Tasmanian was holding out a purple T-shirt with a jagged green line across it. Wonderingly, Dillon took hold and unfolded it. The green line was intended to represent the mighty skyline of Nepal. He had dim memories of a long time on a treadmill that lurched up and down of its own accord, of the Tasmanian holding out a form on a clipboard for him to sign.

'I won this?' He had to ask. Flora might be proud of him, if it was true.

'No worries! Your name's on the list! Runner up, beginners' section. Put it on, it's yours! You deserve it!'

'Cheers,' Dillon murmured. He put down his programme card, sucked in his stomach, pulled off his old red rugby shirt and struggled into his new trophy.

'Great colour. Matches your eyes.' The Tasmanian slapped him on the shoulder.

Dillon climbed aboard a treadmill and started to run. Soon his head was full of hamsters running wheels and rats running mazes. Focus group voices babbled of gerbils. He saw bright black eyes and twitchy whiskers and scampering paws. Marketing, it was all down to marketing. He needed a name. Bright Eyes? Mawkish, maudlin, forget it. Whiskers? Archibald Whiskers? Never. Marmeduke Whiskers? Could be! Cute plus wise! Cute plus traditional! Trad plus funky! Irresistible to the small-pet owner. Excellent!

From her perch on a Stairmaster at the back of the room, Georgie looked anxiously for a chunky form in a red rugby shirt. A dozen men were striding out in front of her, all of them tasty, especially the one in purple on the end, but none of them seemed to be in red, therefore none of them was Dillon. Georgie was hot, she was tired, she was sweaty and the trouble with cruelty-free mascara was that it was not waterproof.

Dillon moved to a rowing machine. He borrowed the Tasmanian's biro and noted 'Marmeduke Whiskers' on his record card in case his inspiration slipped away.

In another half-hour, Georgie was exhausted. Cramp was searing her thighs and the Gothic makeup was streaming down her cheeks. She couldn't work out how to reprogramme the machine and she couldn't move to an easier piece of equipment without losing her view of the room. This scheme was going to fail. Her heart felt lighter for this prediction.

In a few more minutes the cardio theatre was full. Purple T-shirt was rowing. He really had splendid thighs. Georgie was a thigh woman. She had often discussed this with Flora. It was another of their dynamic differences, for Flora liked buttocks. She was a self-confessed bum fascist. More than once she had vowed that she would rather be found dead in a ditch in shoulder pads and leg-warmers than be seen out with a man with a fat backside.

Georgina spied what seemed to be an old red garment lying on the floor beside the towel and the workout record card belonging to Purple T-shirt. Suddenly hopeful, she stepped down and checked the card under cover of visiting the water fountain. But the name on the card was Marmeduke Whiskers.

Damn! There he was! A man in a magenta jersey with a white collar had appeared in the cardio area and was making towards the weights room. On jelly legs, Georgie followed him, checking with Flora's ID picture, which was rolled in her towel. Yes, this must be Dillon. Her mood lurched back towards adventure.

She was barely aware of Purple T-shirt following her, and the Tasmanian following him. Dillon paused to survey the weights

111

room; his trainer took his programme card and added it to his clipboard. 'Let's take a look here. Time to move your weights up, isn't it?'

Dillon prepared to wait with resignation. 'You're not in a tearing hurry, are you?' The Tasmanian clearly had no respect for people who could not give their workouts prime time.

'Not really,' Dillon told him. 'I've someone to see at home at half-two, that's all.'

'You've got plenty of time then,' the trainer conceded.

For a moment Dillon allowed himself to watch the woman who had entered the room ahead of him making her way towards the pec-deck. The oscillation of her hips was rather beautiful. Amazing the way women's legs joined on their bodies, so different, so female. But he was engaged now, there was no other woman in the world but Flora.

On the other side of the room, the tide of fate seemed to have turned decisively in Georgie's favour. The man in the magenta jersey made straight for the chin-up machine, an awesome stack of steel stretching almost to the ceiling. Georgie passed time on the pec-deck while he drew on snazzy black leather weight-lifting gloves and began to perform. After thirty chin-ups, he released the machine with a crash of weights and stepped away.

Georgie jumped up to intercept him, then had to leap for the abdominal cruncher when she saw him go back for another set. The

112

second time he let go she moved more warily, gliding to the pull-down apparatus while he walked around in a circle, swinging his arms. Finally, he seemed to be finished.

'Excuse me.' Was she sounding ditzy enough? She tried a mad grin and fiddled with her hair. 'I was wondering—can you show me how this thing works?'

Breathing hard, his face as red as his shirt, the man pointed to the illustrated step-by-step guide screwed to the wall, gave her a thumbs-up and moved away to the floor mats at the far side of the room.

There was nothing to do but climb aboard the fearsome machine and attempt to master it. It was a steep learning curve, impossible to follow and keep your dignity. Georgie felt lucky to escape without dislocating her shoulders. At least her windmilling limbs fitted with the ditzy-wacky-kooky thing.

Luck was still with her, in its way. When she was able to look around she saw the man in the magenta shirt doing impressive things with a barbell in the free weights area. It was comparatively simple to skip over there, seize a pair of hand weights and let one fall on his foot. A very large foot.

'Silly me!' she squeaked.

Unmoved, her victim put down his barbell, picked up her weight and handed it back to her, then ripped open the Velcro fastenings on his gloves. He was, Georgie noticed, impressively large all round. Maybe it was the exertion, but there seemed to be a huge volume of first-class protein throbbing away under the red jersey. He did not give the impression of a man with buns of custard.

'You should be more careful,' he told her solemnly in a heavy German accent. 'Vy don't you take my gloves? Gloves are good when you get sveaty hands. You can grip good wit gloves.' The gloves reminded her of the Porsche mittens to which Felix had treated himself when she brought home Flat Eric. With a motherly gesture, the man in black picked up first one of her hands and then the other and strapped on the gloves. She had time to look over his record card in this process. The name on it was Dieter Apfeldorf. Damn.

'Now you azzume a good position, like zis, you vork from your ztomach . . .' The ditzy stuff had worked, at any rate. Dieter was now looming over her with an earnest concern that was unmistakable. His courtship ritual was a weightlifting lesson.

With arms aching in sympathy with her legs, she escaped after another half-hour, whirled into the changing rooms to shower and sprinted down to the underground car park. Now the mission to contact Dillon seemed the silliest waste of time imaginable. And horrifically embarrassing. Shameful, in fact. And crazy. If not totally insane. Her

114

relationship was the most important thing in her life. She loved Felix. She loved Flora. How could she have talked herself into risking the happiness of the two people she cared for most in the world? And screwing up her own life on the way?

When she dropped her car keys, Georgie realised that she was actually trembling with exhaustion. When she picked them up she found that she was also blurry eyed. Too bad. She had to get away, get back to reality. Fast. The car smelt of Felix's aftershave.

Flat Eric was feisty with the gas. In the gloom of the car park, she did not notice the dark Saab sneaking out of the bay directly behind her. So when she ran the back of Flat Eric smack into the Saab's rear, it was a double shock. She heard metal crunch and plastic shatter. Her seatbelt cut savagely into her neck just before the airbag burst into action and blotted out the world.

'I am so terribly sorry,' said a man's voice outside the white belly of the airbag. 'I didn't realise you were coming out so fast. Are you OK?'

Georgie heard another voice, Felix's voice, intoning inside her head, 'Never admit liability.' She groped for the switch that deflated the airbag but her arms were not behaving. Everything was white. The bag seemed to be wet. Her neck really hurt. She wanted to tell this poor man that she was fine, but the words were behaving even worse than her arms, she was yelping like a crazed poodle. She heard the voice repeat, 'I am so sorry,' and another man say, 'She's pretty shaken up, sir. Why don't you take care of her, and I'll take care of the cars?'

Thus Dillon, with the help of the security guard, extracted the hysterical woman from her Audi coupé. She was crying too much to speak. Dillon felt personally responsible when a woman shed tears. Thinking of the duty first-aid officer, he escorted her back to the gym, where it turned out that she was not hurt but shaken up and in need of a soothing hot, sweet drink. He installed her on the most comfortable sofa in the café and bought her fluffy cappuccino with two sugars.

'Don't try to talk,' he said, noticing that she was still trembling all over. 'I know it was all my fault. I'll call my insurance company and tell them. Look, here's my card.'

'Gff,' Georgie mumbled through teeth that wanted to tap dance. At least she seemed to have stopped crying. She concentrated on gripping her coffee in her shaky hands, then gave up and tried to focus on the card the man put in front of her on the table. It bore the logo of Direct Warranty and the name: Dillon MacGuire. It took ten seconds for her scrambled brain to compute that she had indeed contacted her target, rather more violently than planned. Panic exploded

116

somewhere in her traumatised mental equipment. She tried to take deep breaths.

Dillon saw the woman's eyes flash and her bosom palpitate dramatically. Probably a terrific bosom if seen in normal circumstances. An odd instinct suggested that the woman in front of him had nothing to do with normal circumstances of any kind. There was a definite air of drama about her. He wanted to take her in his arms and smooth her shaggy hair and say, 'There, there, it's all right.' The scent of her hair was almost real already. Extraordinary. He reminded himself he was engaged to Flora and other women did not exist. Foolish to crash into another woman, bloody silly, in fact. Flora was not going to be pleased. Nor would that estate agent friend of hers be thrilled to be kept waiting.

'Look, don't worry now,' he babbled on. 'I trust you. I'll sort everything out. We can leave the cars here. Let me get you home and you just call me when you're better and . . .'

Automatically, Georgie reached for the bag which had been rescued with her and opened it, intending to produce her own card. It was not her usual bag, big enough to carry work for her to do on the train. It was her little evening bag, last used at the art gallery party where this madness had all begun. There was nothing in it but the invitation, a pen and some peppermints. Her fingers, as if working on their own agenda, swooped upon the old art

117

gallery invitation and held it out to Dillon.

'This is you?' He turned the card around and read it. 'Merita Halili? That's you? You're actually Albanian?'

'Yes.' The word said itself quite easily. Georgie felt it needed a little ethnic shading. She dropped her voice half an octave and tried to feel Balkan. 'I am Merita,' she purred. 'I give you my telephone.' She took back the card and wrote her mobile number on it with a pen. Her hands were still shaking, so the figures came out a little jagged. 'I love my car,' she added, because it was true.

'It really isn't damaged badly. Just one of the lights. Easy to fix, I could do it myself.'

The advantages of this offer were several and obvious. 'Yes? You can fix it yourself?' She tried widening her eyes appealingly. 'That would be good. No insurance, no losing whatever you call it . . .'

'No claims bonus.' Perhaps Flora need never find out about this accident? Dillon felt less of a fool. 'My damage won't be expensive, not as much as the bonus, I shouldn't think. Would you really . . . ?'

'Why not? We never have insurance in Albania. Your car is bashed, you fix it. Simple. I don't understand insurance.' She tried an emotional gesture with one arm, and knocked over the flowers on the next table.

'Insurance is simple, really. You just find a way of making people pay as much as possible

118

for a policy, then find a way of never paying out if they make a claim. I should know, it's my business.' He picked up the vase and put back the flowers.

'You like this business?' Georgie heard herself growl.

'No. It stinks. But it's the only thing I can do,' Dillon heard himself confess. It seemed like the sort of thing an artist would like to hear. Flora would have been outraged, of course. Feeling disloyal again, he resolved to get himself out of trouble immediately. 'Look, shall I ask them to call us a taxi? I'll look into it, I'll buy you a new light and give you a call and then we can come back, I'll fix your car and probably apologise again and then that'll be the end of it.'

'Perfect.' Georgie felt extremely tired, but also obscurely pleased with herself. This was just a game, after all. A bit of make-believe, some harmless fun. She would tell her father about it, he would be amused.

*   *   *

Des was waiting, posed like James Dean, leaning against the outer door of the building with his hands in the pockets of his black leather jacket, staring darkly into the middle distance. No, he was staring at himself, Dillon noticed as he approached and saw them both reflected in the window of the kebab shop opposite.

'I see you are convenient for all the local amenities.' Des nodded at the sinister pink bulk of a fresh doner roast rotating beside the shop's encrusted grill. Smoke belched from the doorway.

'You could say that.' Dillon shook his hand.

'I will say that. And I will say "quiet cul-de-sac".' As Des pulled a palm-sized dictation machine from his jacket pocket, he turned his back on the sooty brick wall of a colossal railway bridge which blocked the end of the street, and watched Dillon struggle with the locks. 'And probably "state of the art security" as well.'

Once inside, they climbed ten flights of stairs walled with ox-blood tiles. 'Immaculate new conversion, original features retained,' Des muttered into the recorder.

'Spacious hall,' he suggested, taking care to squeeze past Dillon with a reassuring minimum of physical contact. 'Stunning living room, views over the river.'

'Only if you stand on the table and lean out of the window,' Dillon corrected him.

'Trust me,' Des advised him. 'Nice table, though.' It was a posh inlaid wood affair, serious quality, miles above the rest of the stuff in the room which Des guessed had been donated by the guy's mother because it was good but old and in need of polish and TLC. 'What else have we got? Two double

120

bedrooms?'

'The little one is sort of L-shaped. You can't actually get a bed in it.'

'That's not the legal definition. Two double bedrooms. Designer bathroom.' Moving on, he picked up a half-empty bottle of Allure Pour Monsieur shower gel.

'Flora gave me that.' Dillon felt himself grow an inch in height as he said it. I am not a boy, a kid, a youth, a student or a young person any longer, he told himself. I am a man now, I have a real fiancée, and she gives me shower gel. Here I am getting rid of my flat and buying a real home for us. Pretty soon there will be a bigger home, and a bigger mortgage and a big car for our children. My life has obviously started. I must try to get used to it.

Des watched him casually while he continued to inspect the property. His previous contact with Dillon had been limited to a few sleepy and embarrassed encounters at 17A. Extraordinary, the way the guy smiled. Slightly to one side, tough but shy, just like Superman. Flora never mentioned that. By the time she'd finished with the fat bum and the funny hair, you'd think Flora was planning to marry Pavarotti. This guy could be quite attractive if he took some trouble and got his clothes sorted. Women were strange.

'The kitchen lets it down,' Dillon apologised, leading Des up some steps to a

121

space under the bare roof tiles. Where a tile was missing, a plastic bag had been stuffed into the hole—some time ago, judging from the cobwebs. A tap dripped into an old sink and toast crumbs on an upturned packing-case seemed to have enticed some mice to hold ceilidhs day and night for weeks.

' "Period fittings. Exposed beams. Scope for the owner to customise the property." Very personal, kitchens. New owner always wants to rip out the kitchen. You'd have wasted your money spiffing it up. Any more? Roof terrace?'

'Afraid not.'

'What's that then?' He pointed to a lop-sided window at the far end of the space.

'Nothing. Fire-escape.'

Des took hold of the latch and forced it open, rattled the window frame with a dominant hand and forced it open. Outside he saw a rusting metal walkway leading to the edge of the roof. A small, ugly tree had seeded itself in the blocked gutter.

' "Balcony. River views." Right. Now the dimensions.' He turned off his recorder and exchanged it for the electronic measuring device that could always find another twelve inches which the old tape-measure would not register.

'You're doing the smart thing. It's a seller's market,' he told Dillon over a beer in the stunning living room. 'I could get you five

122

offers in a week for this. Question is, what do you want? What can we find you? There's not a lot for sale. But since you're, like, family, you'll get first refusal on anything that comes in through me.'

'Great.'

'So what's it to be?'

'Well, for Flora and me, of course. Something she'd like. By the river, maybe. No offence, but I mean, like, really by the river. Near the water, you know. She likes the water.'

'Really?' Des's enthusiasm moderated. He considered Flora very hard to please. Buying things was some kind of power trip with her. Even if she was only buying lettuce, she never seemed to know what she wanted, only what she didn't want. It was not difficult to imagine her turning down everything that came on the market for the next eighteen months. He asked, 'What are we talking about for a price?'

Dillon named what Des considered a reasonable figure and he considered a small fortune. 'Going on a mortgage up to three times my salary,' he added.

'They're giving five times now, some of them. I know a few guys, if you want to go higher.' No, the customer was looking seasick. Not ready to drown himself in debt just yet. He would get more ambitious when he saw what he could buy for the figure he first thought of—they always did. And Flora had this way of making a man reach into his pockets. Another reason to be glad to be gay.

'If you're making that much, why are you still living here?' Des enquired, in the boyishly cheeky tone he used to protect himself when asking personal questions. 'It looks like it was your first flat or something.'

'It was,' Dillon admitted. 'Three of us moved in. The others moved out. One got a girlfriend, the other got a diving instructor's job in Thailand. I could afford it, so I stayed. I never really thought about moving until I met Flora.'

Des finished his beer and put the bottle on the floor because the table looked too good to use. 'This is like Beidermeier. Where d'you get this?' he asked, running a finger along the strip of ebony inlaid an inch from the edge.

'I made it,' admitted Dillon. 'Design project. At school.'

'It's great.' Des allowed his admiration to show. 'How old were you?'

'Fourteen. Fifteen? I can't remember.'

'You were good, then.'

'Yes, I was. But I had to give it up. People don't pay you to make chairs, do they?'

'Well they do,' Des pointed out, 'but not as well as they pay you to make insurance policies, I should imagine.'

'True.' For the first time for three hours, Dillon thought about small pets.

CHAPTER EIGHT

APRIL 24

Felix was performing for an audience of one. 'The tragedy of Lightoller's Syndrome is that it's preventable. I believe that it is one hundred per cent preventable. A biochemical imbalance that is genetically transmitted to the mother affects the DNA in her genetic material, leading to a faulty gene here . . .'

His office was in a Portakabin in a corner of the car park. The hospital, a mountain range of red brick and rusting fire escapes, blocked the daylight on one side. The only decoration • in the room was a blown-up DNA analysis strip. It was six feet high and looked like a stack of giant barcodes. Felix had had it laminated and pinned to the wall behind his desk. He stood up, picked up a red marker and circled a section of the molecule where one gene, instead of being a straight black bar like the rest, was crumpled like a cigarette butt. Flora, in the role of a pharmaceutical research executive, seized the excuse to lean forward and let her Wonderbra do its work.

'On the X chromosome. So Lightoller's Syndrome afflicts only boys, because in females the X chromosome contributed by the father is still normal.' A touch of ruefulness

125

shaded his smile, admitting the superiority of women. 'But in male children, who of course inherit the much shorter Y chromosome, that defective gene is not compensated for and the result is an abnormality in the structure of the adrenal cortex, which in turn produces the anomalies like ADD, hyperactivity and so on, which result in educational underachievement and antisocial behaviour. In short, wasted lives. Do you know that one third of men under the age of forty have criminal records? Excluding vehicle offences.'

'I didn't know that. That's very serious.' Flora thought it was time to cut to the chase. 'And your research is funded by . . . ?'

'A grant from the University of Middlesex. Which is fine, as far as it goes. I believe that I can do enough to substantiate the biochemical basis for a cure. My research will show that a simple nutritional supplement is all that is needed to rectify the brain chemistry and allow boys with Lightoller's Syndrome to lead normal, law-abiding and productive lives.'

He was not what Flora had expected. He was blond, for a start, a pale Scandinavian blond, the hair mowed as short as grass. She was never quite sure if she found blond men attractive. At least his eyes were dark. He was well dressed. Very well dressed. That was a silk polo, and a bespoke jacket, and a Tag Hauer watch. Flora was impressed.

'I've read your paper in the *Journal of*
126

Biochemistry. When you talk about a simple nutritional supplement . . .' She adopted a tone of stern analysis. 'What exactly are you saying?'

'The chemistry is simple. The difficulty is that the compound is rare. Methyl ethylapotomaze. Normally synthesised in the body and essential to the brain metabolism. My research will show that children with this disorder are unable to make their own methyl ethylapotomaze, but the amino acids into which it breaks down in solution, administered intravenously, will be taken up by the brain and will correct its functioning.'

'You mean the kids will have to take this stuff for life or turn back into psychopaths?' Flora allowed her eyes to sparkle with greed. Her hasty research had made it clear that from a drug company's perspective, a condition requiring lifetime medication was a goldmine.

' "Psychopath" is not the appropriate term.'

'Of course not, forgive me. But you expect that this will be a lifetime maintenance programme?'

'That's the finding I anticipate, yes.'

'Have you done any work on synthesis?'

'Not so far. Methyl ethylapotomaze is a blessing of biodiversity. It is also found in the spores of a small fern that grows in the rainforests of central South America. The next phase of my research will involve harvesting that plant.'

'Ethically, a problem.' Flora tested the water.

'Well, quite.' Felix did not seem deeply moved until he added, 'And the expense of extracting and purifying it on a commercial scale would be prohibitive.'

'So we'd be talking cultivation or synthesis.' She tapped some notes into her Psion. Flora had attired herself as much like an air hostess as she could bear. From Donna she had borrowed a blue suit, and the silk blouse had been retrieved from the back of the wardrobe. Blue eyeshadow and pearlised lipstick, the whole nine yards. This kit did not lend itself to seduction, but she did her best, tweaking the skirt higher under cover of recrossing her legs. 'And who else is working on this?'

'Nobody, as far as I know.' Felix was not really looking at her. He was leaning back comfortably in his chair, his gaze hovering around a spot on the wall behind her. With a trace of bitterness in his voice, he added, 'Little boys with behavioural problems don't hit people in the wallet the way mastectomy patients do. There is a culture of blame, I think. We don't get supermodels begging to wear ribbons for us.'

'We like to think long term at Pforza. Perhaps the only thing predictable about public opinion is that it will change.'

'That's very true.'

'Enlightenment pays. It's almost our

company motto.'

' "Enlightenment pays"?' And he sighed, allowing his eyes to roam around the box that was his office, resting momentarily on the dented metal cupboards and sagging second-hand furniture.

'It seems to me that the social benefit of this work, the potential saving to society in terms of reduced criminal activity, more stable family structures, whatever . . . I'd like to make a recommendation to the funding committee on those lines.'

'What exactly are you saying?' Now Felix was thoughtfully running a fingertip along the edge of his desk.

'I'm saying I think this is the kind of work Pforza should be funding.'

'That's excellent.' A smile, at least. But it didn't last long.

'And we like to do things properly. A five-year trial, at least. High grade personnel, top salaries. The funding board meets every month and I'll draft a proposal for them straight away.'

'Great, excellent.' A little excitement, just a little. He was really making her work.

'Look,' she suggested, 'you must be incredibly busy right now setting up this project.' Did his face fall? Was there a shadow of disappointment there? Flora couldn't tell. 'But it's crazy for me to duplicate work you've already done. If you could maybe spare the time to talk me through the basics . . .'

Felix reached out for his keyboard and put his schedule up on the screen. 'Thursday next week?' he offered.

'I was thinking about lunch tomorrow. I'd like to get moving right away. The board meeting is at the end of next week.'

'Lunch is difficult for me, I'm seeing new patients all day.'

Flora took a deep breath and tried opening her fifth chakra to release its sensual energy. 'Then dinner, perhaps?'

Hesitation, still. Maybe even reluctance. Finally, Felix ran his cursor down the screen and tapped in some words. 'We finish at eight tomorrow. I could manage dinner.'

'Good,' said Flora, briskly getting up to leave. 'I'll book somewhere.'

'I should tell you, I have some reservations about this,' he said, holding open the door for her.

'We can talk about that too,' she promised him with her most luscious smile. He shook her hand.

Outside the Portakabin the first patients were assembled, a small group of women standing with their backs to the wind and their hands deep in their coat pockets, exchanging tentative confidences. They were ignoring their sons, a bunch of boys who were kicking about a can at the end of the car park. They did this as if ignoring the boys was the shameful solution to their problems which they had been forced to adopt a long time ago.

Flora climbed into Donna's Mercedes. Damn this Felix. What was the matter with the man? Five years on a top salary, and dinner with her thrown in, and he had 'reservations'. How did Georgie tolerate this creature? She pondered the question as she crossed the potholed car park and drove down the shabby road connecting to the route back to the city centre. Recognising that her mood was low and the exhilaration of the night before had gone, she shook a few drops of neroli oil into the prototype In-Car Aroma Harmoniser and breathed deeply.

After a mini-meditation at the first red light, the answer came to her. Simple, really. He was playing hard to get.

*   *   *

A staring eye appeared in the centre of the dummy Marmeduke Whiskers Web Page. The computer made a noise like a police siren. A message appeared below the eye. 'Caution! You have activated the Desktop Surveillance Programme. Review your screen NOW! Delete inappropriate material.'

'What the hell's that?' Dillon demanded.

'We must have been naughty boys,' explained the anorak with his hand on the mouse.

'I wish! We're designing an insurance proposal form, for God's sake.'

'The thought police put this beauty in the system last week. It's monitoring your key-stroke rate, checking up how much work we're all getting through. It modifies the spell-check to suggest appropriate language. And if you put in one of its trigger words, the evil eye comes down and nukes you.'

'What trigger words?'

'The thing's designed to stamp out inappropriate behaviour. Stop people downloading child pornography or whatever.'

'That's ridiculous. We're asking clients to give us the insured details. What's the big deal with that?'

'Sex,' sighed the anorak. 'It picked up on sex.'

At the top of the form gambolled an animated parade of coloured rabbits, their ears flopping and their whiskers quivering. Below that was a box with the instruction, 'Enter your pet's name.' Next came, 'Enter your pet's age.' Then followed, 'Enter your pet's breed.' Finally, the offending line read, 'Enter your pet's sex.' A flashing red bar was highlighting the word 'sex'.

'OK.' Dillon took a deep breath. It was late in the evening. He was tired. The anorak was irritating. He missed Flora. The dummy site had to be ready for Donna's meeting in the morning. 'Why don't we put in, "Is your pet a boy or a girl?"'

'I don't think so,' said the anorak, looking as if he was chewing a lemon.

'This is for kids, we need to make it fun. The idea is that kids finding out about their pets on the Net will get to the portal site and then—'

'No way. You don't get it, do you?' The anorak turned around to eyeball him, a sign of extreme emotion. '"Boy" or "girl" could also be trigger words. If my terminal keeps getting hits from the evil eye, I'll find myself on an integrity report. You want to try those words, do it on your terminal. Then come and tell me.'

'Look,' said Dillon wearily, 'it's not a big deal. It's only a dummy. Let's put in "gender". Enter your pet's gender.'

'Thank you,' the anorak mumbled.

'What's an integrity report, anyway?'

'You don't know what an integrity report is?'

'Well, no. That's why I'm asking you.'

'OK. Each of us working here has an integrity file, right?'

'If you say so.'

'On that file go discipline ratings, timekeeping, target achievement, all this surveillance data, and the confidential reports.'

'Confidential reports?'

'From other employees. If an employee

133

feels that you have behaved inappropriately to her or to him, she or he can go to Human Resources and ask to put a confidential integrity report on your file. Then it's three strikes and you're out. They fire you. It's in your contract.'

'My God. I never saw that.'

'In the small print on the back.'

'So—what kind of thing are we talking about?'

'Sexual harassment, racial abuse, judgemental language . . . whatever would be against a good atmosphere in the workplace.'

'And you never know who filed the report?'

'No. Their ID is totally protected.'

'My God,' said Dillon again, trying to review his conversations since joining the company. In fact, when he thought of it, there had been very few. He seldom had time to waste in talking. But had he called anyone 'love'? A dreadful habit he had acquired from his mother. Or used the word 'good' carelessly? Or at all?

'What do you think,' he asked the anorak suddenly, 'of the animal rights implications of this product? Is this really compatible with the dignity of the small pet? Is it in their best interests?'

'It's gotta be, hasn't it?' the anorak reasoned. 'If we're paying for top notch medical treatment for an animal, that's gotta be in their interest.'

'I suppose so.' Paranoia had Dillon in its crushing grasp. 'People use rats for research, don't they? Maybe we should build in an ethical dimension. A donation to the Blue Cross with every policy?'

'I can put in a link to the World Wildlife site,' the anorak offered.

'Good call,' said Dillon, finding the patience to wait while it was done.

Back at his own desk, he contemplated his terminal. The grasp of paranoia slackened. Disbelief asserted itself. He called up the in-house help menu and asked for Human Resources, then typed in 'Integrity File'. The screen asked him for a name and he put in his own. Then it asked for a password. He entered his employee number and got a flashing 'Access Denied' sign with a box explaining, 'Integrity Files may be viewed only by authorised personnel.'

So they existed, it was true. Fascinated and fearful, he cleared the screen. He typed in 'girl'. The computer made a throat-clearing noise and an animated figure resembling a Disney princess appeared with a message: 'Do you mean a female under the age of 12? If not, click here and change to WOMAN.'

He deleted the word, and typed in 'boy'. The evil eye flashed up.

Dillon cleared the screen again and typed THIS IS JUST ORWELLIAN, I HATE THIS STUFF, I HATE THIS STUFF, I HATE

135

THIS STUFF. The evil eye appeared once more.

'It must be "hate",' said the anorak, watching over his shoulder. 'Try putting in, "Donna is a shagging cow."'

'All right,' said Dillon recklessly and entered the words. The machine did not respond.

'American programme,' the anorak suggested. 'Can't recognise shagging.'

'I've been there,' Dillon muttered, intending to think of his life before Flora. He had spent most of it in the clutches of a woman who had picked him out at the Freshers' Ball and had devoted the next five years to trying to make him grateful. Plus fifteen months of bleak, sordid, work-obsessed loneliness once he had found the courage to break up with her. He didn't want to go there again.

From nowhere, the thought of the girl who had run her car into his came into his head. His ragged mind had an impression of messy hair, mobile shoulders, dark eyes with tears standing in them. Some new emotion was trying to form in the swamp of sensations at the bottom of his mind. It seemed like a pleasant feeling but he couldn't quite identify it. For no reason, paranoia's strength failed and it let him go.

'I can get you a boss alert programme,' the anorak was saying. 'Cunning device that tells you when she leaves her terminal, then saves your game or whatever's on your screen and puts up a nice spreadsheet or something. I can get you a bootleg copy for twenty quid. Good one.'

'That's OK,' Dillon told him, shutting down his terminal. 'I don't do games, there's never time.'

'Wow. You really give it all that?' The anorak shook his head in pity.

'Good work on the Whiskers page. She'll like it. Let's go for a drink.'

'Cheers.' The anorak smiled sarcastically. 'You sure you've got the time?'

CHAPTER NINE

APRIL 24–25

'Nobody goes out on Monday, we can't possibly go out on Monday,' Flora dictated. 'We'll look like total prats. People only go to the gym. Or have dinner with their parents or something. We can stay home and order in.'

Accordingly, Operation Heartswap's first review was conducted around the glass table in Donna's dining area. 'I'll be mother,' she said, pouring vodka-cranberry from a crystal pitcher into tall glasses. 'So how did it go?'

'I felt like an idiot,' Georgie said flatly. 'This is so stupid. The adult thing for us to do would be to forget it.'

'So you're saying you got no action, then?' Des picked over the olives for the one with his name on it.

'No,' Georgie affected martyred patience. 'I'm saying I felt like an idiot.'

'So you got some action? Dillon's dead meat already? We're on our way to Mauritius?'

'*No*. Will you give me a break?'

Donna smiled and said nothing. Georgie was flustered. Flora preened, put down her glass and admitted, 'Felix is having dinner with me tomorrow.'

Georgie felt a stab of anxiety and rushed

into asserting her own success. 'And I'm seeing Dillon after work. He's going to fix my car.'

'I call that a result. Way to go, girls!' Donna raised her glass to toast them.

'Well I don't.' Des shrugged petulantly. 'Who needs dinner, for God's sake? You hate food. What's this dinner thing about?'

'And why does your car need fixing?' Flora demanded of Georgie, flaring a contemptuous nostril.

'I ran into him. Busted my lights on one side.'

'That desperate, huh?' Des yawned. 'Flora's wasting time eating a dinner she doesn't want and you've wrecked your car? Why don't you just go up to these guys and tell 'em you want to shag 'em?'

'It doesn't work with straight men,' Flora argued. 'Unless they're too pissed to shag in the first place.'

'It always works for me,' Des told her.

'Are we saying it matters how pissed they are?' enquired Donna of the company in general. 'We just want to score the guys, don't we?'

'I think it matters.' Flora was alarmed. Half a bottle of wine and Dillon was ridiculously suggestible. No way was Georgie going to take unfair advantage of him in that condition. That was her prerogative. 'We're saying all men are the same, they're programmed to shag, they're basically anybody's. Alcohol isn't

139

part of the theory.'

'It's supposed to be a disinhibiter,' Georgie proposed, trying to remember Felix chilling out after a few drinks. There was nothing in the file. Felix could consume astounding amounts of alcohol and never lose control. 'But there's nothing disinhibits my man.'

'I say getting them drunk is not fair,' Flora insisted. 'We want to find out if they really care enough about us to turn down sex on a plate. It has to be a conscious decision.'

To her surprise, Donna agreed. 'OK. Rule Three. If they're drunk it doesn't count,' she announced.

The doorbell rang. It was the porter bearing a sushi box from Nobu. Donna distributed her chopsticks, her rice bowls and her bamboo mats. Des raised the lid and looked inside. 'Urgh,' he exclaimed, pushing the box away, 'how can you eat that stuff?'

Flora switched her attention to Georgie. 'What about his car? You were supposed to be in the gym. You didn't damage his car, did you? I can't have Dillon spending all our money getting his bloody car fixed.'

'It was an accident. Eric came off worst. His hardly got a scratch.'

'Horrible thing. Like running into a tank, I should think. I wish he'd get rid of it. He must qualify for a new car, doesn't he? Can't you do something, Donna?'

'I'll have a word with our fleet manager,'

Donna promised. Her chopsticks fussed about like a beak, selecting morsels from the box. 'I never thought you'd be so dedicated to this, Georgie. Flat Eric's the love of your life.'

'I didn't mean to do it. I didn't see him backing out at the same time as I was. I thought I'd blown it, actually. I missed him at the gym.'

'You can't miss Dillon in the gym,' Flora giggled. 'He's the only one who wobbles when he walks. He's like a man-sized crème caramel. I'm thinking I'll have to put the wedding off until he's fit to be seen with.'

Georgie said nothing and speared a nori roll. She did not recall that Dillon wobbled. She saw no resemblance to a crème caramel, apart from the appetising contrast between the dark brown hair and the light olive skin. She did remember him asking if she was hurt when she hit his car. Nobody around the table had considered that question.

The doorbell sounded again. This time the porter presented Des with his pizza. 'Urgh,' Flora wrinkled her nose as he opened the box. 'Get that glycaemic index. How can you?'

'It's no trouble,' Des assured her, sinking his teeth into the first slice.

She watched in fascination as he caught up the trailing strings of hot mozzarella with a sweep of his tongue. 'They say that's your ideal man, don't they? He has sex all night then turns into a pizza?'

'That sounds like love. Make it a Quattro Formaggio and he'll do me,' Des mumbled as he munched, pulling out a second slice that trailed more cheese across the table top.

'I want to hear more,' said Donna. 'Juicy details, come on. What's the vibe you're getting off these guys?'

'Not promising,' Flora admitted. 'He's a bit of an ice-man, isn't he?'

Georgie remembered her first meeting with Felix. He'd persuaded her to leave a dinner party because there were people smoking at the table. Three in the morning had found them walking along the lakeside. Some kids were throwing chunks of ice across the frozen surface to hear the whistling noise they made. A group of drunks were swaying in a circle around an oil-drum fire. Tiny snowflakes blew in the wind and clustered in their eyelashes. Felix's nose went white with cold. She had to take him home in case he had frostbite. He looked like the hero of an ancient Norse saga. 'He's passionate when he cares about something,' she offered Flora in consolation.

'He's got to care about me,' she insisted.

'Well, I have no idea about your Dillon. I was so freaked by crashing Flat Eric that I can hardly remember anything. He was kind, though.'

'I suppose he is kind.' Flora did not see the point of kindness. 'When he has the time.'

'He looked kind of pink when he came back

to the office,' Donna confirmed, winking at Georgie to encourage her.

'Pink?' said Flora crossly. 'What do you mean, pink?'

'Pink. Disturbed or moved or . . .'

'Clapped out?' Flora suggested. 'He always claims he's working so hard. And let's face it, I'm not marrying a natural athlete.' She laughed. Donna and Des laughed with her. This is what Donna wants, Georgie observed. Laughs. Fun. Bitching about the fellas. I've got to get out of this. It can be done. Just let me think about it.

'Des,' she murmured, somewhat later, when the pizza was nothing but a belch, a memory and a grease stain in the box. 'What exactly do you say when you go up to some bloke and say you want to shag him?'

'Well, I say just that,' he replied, rolling his round black eyes while he thought about it. 'Like, "I'd like to shag you." Or, "Fancy a shag?"'

'Subtle!' gurgled Flora.

'Or, "Gissa shag," if it's someone I've shagged already and I know they're up for it. Or ask to see his piercings, if I want to be subtle. Or if he's a bit of a toff, I might say, "I say, I'm feeling rather randy—I was wondering if you'd care to have sex tonight?" Or you can just look at them kind of moodily and go for the nuts.'

'And they say romance is dead,' Donna

143

poured them another round. 'Hey, listen up. Have you heard about the new sensitive condoms?'

'No,' said Flora and Des together.

'They stay awake and talk to the woman afterwards.'

'Mellow,' Des observed. 'You really are mellow tonight, Donna.'

* * *

Georgie's plan was simple. She would take Flora's advice. Flora knew a lot more about seducing men than she did, because while she had been wasting her life with the Scumbag, Flora had been having a ball. If Flora said the straight pass never worked, she would make a straight pass. Which would never work. Dillon would turn her down. Then honour would have been satisfied, the whole horrible thing would be settled and they could go back to normal life. She put on some high-heeled sandals, freaked out her hair again and set off for the car park.

Dillon was there before her. She saw him from a distance, walking respectfully around Flat Eric.

'It's very stylish,' he said with admiration when she arrived.

'Good car,' she agreed in the husky monosyllables she had rehearsed for Merita Halili.

144

'Very good car,' he agreed. 'The man I got the light from said there was a waiting list for them.'

'I never wait,' she announced.

'OK. Well, if you just open up for me, this won't take a minute.

Georgie had developed reasonable screwdriver skills. They were the surprise bonus of her life so far. Felix never touched a screwdriver because he needed to keep his hands nice for his patients. Her father believed that screwdrivers were imps of Satan and would stab you through the palm if you messed with them. The Scumbag had seen screwdrivers as something you paid the underclass to master. Dillon, swiftly releasing her broken tail-light, appeared to be a natural with the tool. She found it relaxing to watch him work. The obvious moves came easily.

'I like a man who is good with his hands,' she purred, leaning provocatively against a handy pillar.

He dropped something and had to look under the car for it. 'I used to like making furniture,' he told her when he emerged. 'But I never get the time now.'

'People will always need chairs,' she said vaguely, wondering why Flora hadn't mentioned this.

'That's what my mother used to say. Then she said, "But you can't possibly make a living out of that."' The new light took to its position

145

happily. In a few more minutes he was tightening the last screw. 'There!' He stood up and felt pleased with himself for a job well done. 'As good as new.'

'You like a drive?' Georgie invited him rapidly, opening the driver's door.

'Uhhhhhh . . .' He who hesitated was lost. 'Could I really? Would you trust me? Well, why not? Just around the block, maybe.'

'No, not around the block,' she insisted. 'You got to drive fast to enjoy this car.' And she incited him to sprint down the underpass to Westminster and then over a bridge and around Battersea Park, which was as much driving excitement as the city can offer. The weather cooperated with a fast-moving Constable sky.

'I love these evenings in London,' she informed him, sticking her head out of the window to let the wind blow her hair. 'Everything is so beautiful! You can feel free here!'

'I suppose you can,' he agreed, anxious to be tactful with a refugee from poverty and oppression.

As they approached Battersea Bridge, she spotted the tea stall and demanded that they stop.

'English tea!' she improvised. 'I love it. I drink it all the time.'

'How long have you lived here?' he asked while they leaned against the balustrade and waited for the scalding beverages to cool.

'What does it matter?' she demanded, panicking because she had not invented a cover story for Merita. 'I am here now, that is the only thing that is important.'

'What about your country? Your family? Are they still . . .'

'My art is everything,' she declaimed with an inclusive arm sweep which splashed tea into the river. 'My life is nothing. I can't talk about my country. It makes me sad. When I am sad, I make my art!'

'I must go and see it.' Dillon found that he was feeling good, meaning younger, fresher and less tired than usual. In addition, it was somewhat exciting to be with this woman. The handful of people standing around the tea stall were looking at them benignly. Life seemed to contain possibilities. He could not remember discussing happiness or sadness with anyone before. He realised that he had not thought of a gerbil for almost an hour. He felt he could do with a second cup of tea. And perhaps a fried egg sandwich by way of dinner.

Georgie reached towards him, shut her eyes and grabbed. She opened her eyes and found that she was clutching a chunk of Dillon's jacket and the wrist of the hand that held the styrofoam cup. 'I think you are very sexy,' she announced. 'Will you go to bed with me?'

'Huh?'

'Go to bed with me!' she repeated wildly.

147

An extremely foolish laugh broke out somewhere behind Dillon's tie. 'Let me put my tea down,' he suggested, playing for time. Was she serious? She seemed extremely serious, she looked suddenly deadly earnest. Would she be more insulted if he said no or if he pretended he thought she was kidding? If she was insulted, would she hit him? Or scream? Or claim he was attacking her so he'd be locked up and interrogated on suspicion of being a serial rapist?

'Look,' he said, instinct telling him to try the reasonable approach. 'I should have mentioned it before. We hadn't talked for long, it didn't come up really. But I'm getting married. I am engaged.'

'You are . . . engaged?' Oddly, she seemed to like this idea.

'Well, yes. Very much so, as a matter of fact.'

'Very good!' Definitely, she was pleased. She was even smiling, a sort of all-purpose, life-affirming smile.

Dillon felt violent relief. He was not going to be charged with sexual harassment after all. 'Yes, I'm getting married. I'm sorry . . .'

'Why sorry?' Georgie felt violent relief. It was over. He'd passed the test, he was OK, whatever voodoo Flora had performed on him had worked, this man was no longer a victim of his hormones. 'It is I who should be sorry. I make mistake.'

'Please—look, we can forget it. Shall we do that?'

'Yes. We forget. You go home, I go home, we forget.' She rolled her Rs outrageously. Merita was a lot of fun, she was going to miss her.

They set off back to the car with one will. 'But I will go and see your paintings,' Dillon promised in consolation.

'Not paintings!' Georgie exclaimed. 'Art! Works on metal and glass. Very noisy when you fall in them.'

'Are people supposed to fall in them?' Dillon enquired, wondering if she would still let him drive the car back. She seemed to find the question hilarious. He had to drive because she was laughing so much. She had, he noticed, a very deep laugh. For no reason at all he thought of hot dark chocolate.

*   *   *

Flora visualised Felix, his silk polo shirt and his flashy watch, the home in Notting Hill and the office in a Portakabin in the hospital car park. Into her meditative mind came an idea. She booked a table at the most expensive restaurant within a quarter of a mile of the flat where Felix lived with Georgie.

'I do hope you will stay in touch with us,' she told him. 'However our funding proposal is received. At Pforza we believe in bringing

149

together the best minds in medicine on a regular basis. Being a new company, we know we need to make friends. Part of my remit is to organise a conference every few months or so. Nice places. Five-star hotels. People think much better when they know their physical needs will be taken care of.'

'Oh, yes,' Felix commented.

'Our last conference was at Monte Carlo. We gave the delegates a thousand pounds each to go gambling in the evenings. Instead of just eating and drinking. One of them was a pretty mean player. He went home quite rich, I think. Entertainment is tremendously important, it stimulates creative interaction.'

'Absolutely,' said Felix.

'It would mean so much to me if you could join us. We were thinking of going to Capri next. Or maybe Istanbul. Which would you prefer?'

'I'd go for Capri,' he said, dragging his eyes away from the menu. 'As a man, I'm never really comfortable in a Muslim country. Even though Istanbul is a cosmopolitan city. The assumptions people make about you, the things you know are going on, the beliefs you know people hold . . . I suppose the bottom line is I just can't feel happy somewhere where women still wear the *chador*.'

'So sensitive,' she murmured. 'Do you have a lot of sisters?'

'Oh no,' he confessed, 'I'm an only child.'

'But you seem to have extraordinary understanding of women.'

'Perhaps because of my mother. We've always been very close. Things were tough for her, she was widowed when I was still quite small. I identified so much with her, struggling to make a home for us. Until I was able to start discovering the female in myself, my mother was my *anima*. So she was closer, really, than a sister could ever be. My mother made me a feminist.'

Flora considered saying, 'If I give her the wool, will she make me one too,' but she felt that Felix did not admire flippancy. 'How fascinating,' she breathed. 'I sensed it, you know. When we first met. You have this rapport with the female, don't you?'

'That's hardly for me to say.' At last, Felix had the decency to blush. Or perhaps he was merely hot. Flora's flattery had inflated him like an amorous frog and his jacket seemed tight around his shoulders.

She disdained to open her menu and caught the eye of the waiter, thinking that this whole affair was turning into a long luxurious picnic. 'Do you have *escalope de toro*?' she demanded.

'Oui, madame.' His accent was a veneer of Geneva over several generations of Capetown.

'It's the bullfight steak,' she told Felix, waiting for a reaction. He blinked, but that was all. 'They have it flown in from Andalucia. Utterly delicious. The tenderest possible meat,

151

because the death was instantaneous and the muscle fibres are completely relaxed. And not hung too long, so the taste is out of this world. I'd like mine rare,' she informed the waiter. 'And the oysters to start.'

Felix was gazing at her with large eyes. 'The same for me,' he said obediently. Flora felt she could certainly help him with some of his integrity issues.

Flora commanded the most expensive Burgundy on the list. Then she poised her chakras in perfect alignment, summoned the kundalini serpent coiled in her solar plexus, moved to invade the border of Felix's personal space and asked him, 'What was it, Felix, that led you to explore your feminine side?'

Ninety minutes later they were elbow to elbow and the last spoonful of his chocolate sorbet was sliding between her freshly reddened lips. She looked at him moodily and, under the camouflage of the tablecloth, went for the nuts.

'Please,' he said. At least, the quick hiss that escaped his lips sounded like that word. The matter in Flora's hand tightened eagerly. She smiled and applied delicate fingertip pressure.

'Please don't.' His voice cracked a little. She felt increased eagerness and awarded it a feathery caress. She leaned towards him and blew gently on his ear. Felix opened his mouth but had difficulty finding words.

'Why don't you take me home?' she

152

whispered, cradling possessively. 'Just for coffee. I promise to behave.'

'No.' It was nearly a moan. 'No. I can't. It wouldn't be right.'

'I've never felt anything so right in my life,' she suggested.

'Right for me,' he explained, settling the knot of his tie with an uncertain hand. With downcast eyes, he coughed. Flora felt the movement and responded to it, smiling some more as she felt the substance in her grasp increase.

'Just right for me,' she repeated softly.

'I've worked so hard to transcend my conditioning.' Felix paused for a battle-weary sigh before continuing. 'I believe the emotional quality of a relationship is everything. It's much too precious to compromise at the beginning by falling into stereotypical roles. Don't you agree?'

Flora translated this as 'we don't know each other well enough', high on the list of her own top ten favourite strategies for playing hard to get. The correct response was obvious. Lightly but instantaneously, she removed her hand. 'You must forgive me,' she said with gracious regret. 'Suddenly, I just wanted you so much. You are an extraordinary man.' The pliancy drained from her body, she sat stiffly upright and gestured at the waiter for the bill.

Outside the restaurant she gave him a cheek kiss as quick as a kingfisher's dive and said,

'It's been a wonderful evening, Felix. I'll call you tomorrow.' Then she slipped into the Mercedes and was gone without a backward glance, leaving Felix on the pavement with an uncomfortable degree of turmoil in several different regions of his being.

CHAPTER TEN

APRIL 26

'Flora, you were right.' Georgie kicked off her shoes, dropped her briefcase on the floor and dived into the aromatic depths of Donna's suede sofa. 'That man is all yours. I made the most outrageous pass at him and he nearly died of terror.'

A warm giggle came from Flora in the kitchen area. 'That doesn't sound like my baby boy at all.' She appeared in the doorway, swinging a crystal on a silver chain. 'Blow by blow, come on. What the hell did you do?'

'Grabbed hold of him and told him he was sheer sex on legs and how about it?'

'You didn't!' Flora shrieked. 'Way to go!'

'Des inspired me. He was right, I was just pussyfooting. Men don't faff around, do they?'

'And where was this?'

'The tea stall on Battersea Bridge. I was letting him drive my car.'

'You let him drive Flat Eric! Are you crazy? You love that thing. Dillon's useless with cars. He didn't hit anything this time, I hope?'

'I think he enjoyed it,' Georgie said artlessly, not noticing the green flash through Flora's eyes at the word 'enjoy'.

'You're a star,' Flora assured her. 'More

155

balls than me, anyway.'

'I wouldn't say that.'

'Well, I'm getting nowhere fast with your Felix. It's like smooching a glacier.'

'Funny, I never saw that side of him.' Georgie stretched her legs and wiggled her toes complacently.

'I keep vamping him and he just sticks to business.'

Georgie sighed happily. 'That sounds like *my* baby, all right. Unless you're talking to him about Lightoller's Syndrome, he doesn't hear a word you say.'

'So,' Flora proposed. 'Twelve days to go and no progress on either front.'

'That's right,' agreed Georgie with satisfaction. Too much satisfaction, Flora considered. Just as she had failed to declare her game plan, or mention that the affair of Felix had progressed precisely as she had hoped, so she reasoned that Georgie had to be holding back.

'Where shall we go for these honeymoons Donna's going to be paying for?'

'Felix will never take time off. He's a short break man, it'll be a weekend in Venice if I'm lucky.'

Flora twirled her pendant, making rainbows over the glass tabletop. 'You can do better than that. Motivate yourself, woman! I was thinking about one of those houseboats in Kerala. Drifting through the giant waterlilies to the temple of a thousand gods. Dillon will get bitten to hell by the mosquitoes, I expect. But I'll enjoy it.'

'What's the crystal for?' Georgie enquired, hoping to get Flora off her case.

'Shopping,' said Flora. 'Des wants to cook us dinner. I thought I'd swing by Planet Organic and buy some vegetables. You use the crystal to dowse them. The freshest ones have the most energy.'

'Oh, right.' Georgie sat up, suddenly in the mood for play. 'This I have to see. I'll come with you.'

As they waited for the glass-walled lift in the marble-floored hall, Flora said casually, 'So what's your next move with Dillon, then?'

Georgie had no intention of making another move. As far as she was concerned, she had played her part, honour was satisfied and the game was over. Nor did she wish to incite Flora to move any more towards Felix. Flora was a great mate but she could take things too seriously sometimes. 'I'm going for the strategic withdrawal,' Georgie said. 'I think I scared him off. The thing to do now is give him back the initiative.'

'Good. I don't want you sending my poor boy into cardiac arrest before I can be a grieving widow. That's where I'm at, too. Time to back off. Give him space.'

The lift arrived and the doors opened, sighing along with Georgie as she observed,

157

'They do like their space, men, don't they?'

*   *   *

Through the half-open door of her office, Donna watched Dillon moving around his desk. Three days without Flora and the man looked different. Thinner, perhaps. More confident, maybe. Dominant, even. She could see a lean, mean, boss Dillon emerging from the bright but undirected young man she had hired. He was morphing into one clever bastard. She had handed him a poisoned chalice and he had come back with a Holy Grail, rot him.

In the presentation suite that afternoon, Dillon had unveiled his concept for the small-pet policy. The all-animated Marmeduke Whiskers Home Page, projected on the wall of multiple screens that Marketing used for their TV commercials, had wowed everyone. The minute Dillon had finished, people had jumped up all over the room with ideas for sales, for publicity, for merchandising, for franchising, for export, for God-knows-what. They'd made so much noise, the managing director had looked in and sealed Dillon's success.

For the first time in her life, Donna had found herself powerless. She had visualised the event as a damp squib, an embarrassing exercise that would have left everyone muttering apologetic monosyllables and remembering urgent appointments. Instead, Dillon had triumphed. There had been nothing to do but sit there and let the man bask in his victory. Now she was stuck with the Marmeduke Whiskers policy, which had argued itself into her development strategy on its graphics, in defiance of business logic. Her own calculations insisted that the product couldn't possibly be viable financially, but there was no way she could tell that to the MD when his brain was full of jumping gerbils and hippity-hoppity bunny-rabbits.

Donna wanted a cigarette and she didn't even smoke. She walked around her corner office looking for things to put in their places, but everything was already in its place. She had long ago mastered the nitty-gritty habits of success. There was no paper on her desk because she read every item of print and actioned it immediately. Archives, research, resources—they were for underlings. She gloried in minimalism. Her desk was naked. Her floor was bare. She had spent prime time on buying furniture that effaced itself and choosing a paint colour that seemed to dissolve the walls. Ideally, Donna would have liked to exist in a vacuum. Things just slowed you down. People were worse.

The floor-to-ceiling window was lined with a blind which allowed her to see out but prevented outsiders from looking in. Over at the product design desk, Donna saw her wunderkind preparing to go home. He scooped papers into his wastebin, tossed pencils back in their pot and closed down his terminal. He was preparing to leave her sphere and take up a life beyond her control. Even before he moved to take away Flora, there had always been something wayward about Dillon, something subversive, inaccessible. A bubble of rage exploded in her mind. As he stood up and prepared to leave, Donna pulled open her office door and raised her voice to coo, 'Golden boy! I want to talk to you.'

'I'm here,' he said, with that irritating Superhero smile she thought she'd buried with a stake through its heart. Lean, dominant and somehow more mature. All at once Donna could see Dillon as an MD. A popular one, at that. More popular than she would be. Such men were dangerous. She made her way through the desks towards him.

'Brilliant presentation. Absolutely brilliant,' she said.

'Thanks,' he answered.

'Have you got a moment?'

'Sure. I'm meant to be playing squash, but not for an hour.'

'I didn't know you played squash.' An idea was forming in Donna's mind. She made conversation while the details became clear.

'I don't really,' he was admitting. 'But with Flora away, I thought I'd better keep myself off the streets.'

'Can you put that Web page up again?' she asked him. 'I'm doing a brief for the reinsurance actuary, I need to make sure I've got the details.'

'No problem,' he said cheerily, sitting down again and switching on his terminal.

She watched his keyboard as he tapped in his password. His fingers moved too fast for her to follow. The page appeared in all its nauseating charm. 'Show me the links,' she asked, grabbing a memo pad on which to squiggle notes. 'And can I access this from my terminal?'

'I haven't posted it in the system yet. But if you use my password . . .'

'What's your password?'

At least he had the grace to blush when he told her. 'Flora. And three xs.'

Pathetic. Predictable. To be sure, she said, 'That's so sweet. Space before the xs?'

'Yes. Flora space xxx. That's it.' He blushed again. 'Flora suggested it. She said hackers always started with obvious stuff like your birthday.'

'Good point,' Donna commented. 'Thanks for that. I'll shut down here. You get off to your game, eh?'

So Dillon left, swinging his sports bag with the enthusiasm of a man who has had such a good day that he has temporarily forgotten that for him to pick up a racquet is to invite

161

total humiliation. Once he was out of sight Donna shook her head sadly and returned to his screen.

She closed the Marmeduke Whiskers page and opened up the Web connection.

She searched on the word 'sex'.

The search engine found 4,988,210 Web pages for her. She sat in Dillon's chair and browsed the first twenty of them, looking for plausible options—nasty enough to be offensive, but not so exotic as to be unbelievable. She registered Dillon with something called Klara's TeenSex Chat Club, clicking on the special interest menu for Wet Chicks, Hot Haystacks and Three in a Bed. In his full name, she posted a few comments on the torrid topics in debate. From her own files, she then extracted a standard notification programme, pasted in the signature picture of a site called Barely Legal Bare-Assed Babes, and installed it in Dillon's desktop. Then she signed off and closed his terminal down before being tempted to any more creativity.

When Donna left the office, she too stepped out with the ebullience of someone who has had a good day.

*　　　*　　　*

'And has your son been excluded from school?'

'Yes, Doctor. The boy's home more often than he's there. I say home, but he doesn't stay

162

in. He goes out getting into trouble. We've been having the police round since he was seven. Taking cars. Getting into people's houses. Throwing things on railway lines. Going into shops. Annoying the neighbours. His sister would help me, but she left home because of him. Couldn't stand it no more. He's too young to go to prison, you see. Otherwise there wouldn't be a problem.'

'A problem for you,' Felix corrected the mother. She was a large, vigorous woman with tightly curled hair. The crumpled green fabric of her cheap suit flapped around bare legs speckled with broken veins. 'There is a problem for Wayne in any case, isn't there? But no criminal record as such, then?'

'No, he's too young, I told you,' she repeated defensively. 'Does that mean we can't come to this clinic?'

'Not at all,' Felix assured her. He turned over another page of the file to find the referral letter, which was from a doctor in a former mining town two hundred miles away. 'You've been sent to us by your GP?'

'That's right. He said Wayne needed a specialist. He said he'd been on the Prozac too long already and he didn't want to prescribe any more.'

'And he's better on the Prozac?'

'No, not really. The boy smiles more, that's all. He gets into the same amount of trouble but don't get so depressed about it.'

163

She spoke furtively because her son sat at the far end of the humid little room, completing psychometric tests under the supervision of the intern. He was a scrawny grey-faced boy, whose age was given as eleven although most people would have estimated him about four years younger. As he toiled through the paper he kicked the table-leg with thin feet, which were loose in his overlarge trainers.

'Good shoes,' Felix smiled at her. It was about the only positive thing he could find to say about the child.

'Yeah, well,' the mother said. 'I don't know nothing about them. You don't ask, do you?'

'How did you get here today?' he asked her. The parameters of patient compliance with the programme were becoming depressingly clear.

'His sister brought us in her car.' She seemed unwilling to admit any relationship with either of her children.

'We'll be running this trial for two years and during that period I'd need to see you every month. Would that be a problem?'

'What, you mean I'd have the fares to pay? Every month?'

'The treatment your son received here would be free, of course. The prescriptions, the assessment, any tests we did. The fares would have to be paid. You'd have to get here somehow. Tell me, is there a social worker involved with your son?'

'I suppose so.' She was defensive again. 'He's seen social workers sometimes. Not one in particular that I remember.'

'If you can get me some names, I'll have a word and see what we can do. Sometimes we can find a budget for travel expenses. Now, if I could ask you and Wayne to step over to our nurse, she'll finish the assessment.'

The nurse was housed in the next-door Portakabin. As Felix shut the door the thin wall shuddered. The atmosphere in these temporary rooms was sticky. It was a warm day, and already the windows were half-misted with condensation. Since most of the glazed panels in the wall were not capable of being opened, it seemed grandiose to classify them as windows at all. The ones that did open slid jerkily apart like windows on a toy car; the room was so small that the breeze they let in blew all his papers about. So they stayed shut, Felix perspired in his shirtsleeves, the beauty of his intern was blemished by the sweatmarks under her arms and the acrid smell of his patients lingered long after the admission clinic closed for the day.

He retired to his chair and finished opening the morning's mail. 'I am enclosing a copy of a paper to be published in our next issue,' the editor of the *Neurological Digest* had written. 'Given your interest in Lightoller's Syndrome, you may wish to respond to the points made by Professor Knudson and Professor Kjell.'

Knudson and Kjell, in Felix's opinion, were charlatans. Kjell wasn't even medically qualified; he was just a teacher. From their research centre in Gothenburg, they broadcast the heresy that Lightoller's Syndrome did not exist. They advocated crude behavioural modification to 'treat' hyperactivity and ADD. They gave children praise, biscuits and play sessions when they behaved 'well'. They showed the kids old Western films so Alan Ladd and Randolph Scott could supply the template of socialised manliness which their fathers had not provided. They copped out by citing the inherent sexism of Western educational methods. They were reporting from a state-funded trial, which used two thousand children. Felix had estimated that his budget would allow him to treat about fifty. He hated Knudson and Kjell.

Felix saw a medical conference, a big one, perhaps in a hotel in Las Vegas. He saw himself giving his paper on Lightoller's Syndrome. He saw five thousand delegates listening intently to his penetrating arguments. He saw his graphs, he saw his statistics. He saw the applause, the approval, the handshaking, the backslapping and the headhunting. He saw himself condescending to address a studio audience of worried mothers on daytime television.

There at his old hospital he would have his parking space right there in the senior

166

consultants' car park by the entrance, with his name on the tarmac in fresh white paint. Each morning—when he was not lecturing around the country—his new BMW would glide home in that beautiful receptive space and he would cross the entrance hall as a living god, followed by the worshipping eyes of his colleagues. Perhaps even some of the patients would recognise him. His clinic, his famous clinic, would be on the ninth floor. He could feel the thick carpet, the refreshing air conditioning, and the swish of the potted palms as his trim assistant swayed by them on her elegant high heels. Waiting humbly would be a couple of middle-class madonnas, classy blond mothers with gold earrings and modest clean-limbed boys. They would shake his hand and thank him for saving their lives.

A disrespectful wind gusted through the car park and rocked the Portakabin on its shaky foundations. Felix's reverie hit the buffers. He breathed the stale air, brushed a dead spider from the scratched desktop. The distance from reality to dream was long but it could be covered. The journey of a thousand miles began with a single step. He had taken that step. It was time to take more, to stride out for his goal. On the desktop his hand formed itself into a resolute fist and thumped the surface. That woman from Pforza Pharmaceuticals. Damn her, why didn't she call?

In certain circulatory backwaters, Felix's

blood started tingling. He thumped the desktop again, a little harder, then picked up his pen and started drafting the rebuttal of Knudson and Kjell.

CHAPTER ELEVEN

APRIL 26–27

Flora had a word for it. She had the derivation wrong, she thought it was something to do with destiny or the universe or whatever she believed in, she didn't understand that it came from the old name for Sri Lanka, but even she understood the principle: an amazing coincidence. Such a wonderful amazing coincidence that even Dillon was tempted to believe that God or somebody had organised it. He got the feeling that it was all meant to be. Normally he left sensations like that to Flora; perhaps she was right when she claimed she was educating him. Serendipity, no question.

Stretching his sore calves, he stood outside The Messenger Gallery entranced by the works of Merita Halili. They shone. They shimmered. They floated in front of his eyes. On their arcs of silver wire, the blue glass discs swayed like lazy fish in a slow river. The horsetail of aluminium threads swished. Solemnly, the aluminium doors rotated before their cascade of glass drops.

So clever! Such ingenious motors, such magically miniaturised gears and such marvellously deft levers! Discovered by

169

accident, just because cramp had seized his legs after that fiasco of a squash game and he had considered it wise to pull his car over and walk about for a while. And there, enticing him like will-o'-the-wisps, were the works of Merita Halili.

The pain in his calves transferred to his neck. Dillon realised that he had put his head on one side to watch the way the silvery wires joined to their elegant little crank-shaft. He was, in fact, standing in the street in the light radiating from the gallery window contorted like Quasimodo. The man in the gallery was watching him, a massive figure with a beard standing hands-on-hips in the pose adopted by Henry VIII for his Holbein portrait. As Dillon restored himself to normality, the man in the gallery beckoned him with a wave of his huge hand.

'Aren't you shut?' Dillon asked him, checking the time. There was music playing quietly throughout the gallery, something reedy with a voice singing in a language he assumed to be Albanian.

'Technically we're closed, yes. But I'm going to be here doing my blasted VAT for another hour at least. So look around, if you'd like to. They're great, aren't they?'

'Yes,' Dillon agreed humbly and stepped forward into the world of art, a world he considered the real world, the only world, but a place that he, in his profit-oriented dullness

170

and his leaden lack of talent, would never be fit to do more than visit. He wasn't sure he even knew the proper way to say he liked something like a sculpture. And this was Merita Halili's world. In his memory she acquired a golden halo of creative glamour. 'My Homeland,' he read on the catalogue cover. 'Inspired by the artist's flight from Albania.'

'Take your time,' Smiley-and-Beefy advised him. 'There're some beers back in the kitchen if you'd like one.'

Dillon found this suggestion welcome. Floundering around the stupid squash court had left him hideously thirsty and he had been too ashamed to join his partner in the pub afterwards. A bottle of something Belgian and highly agreeable went down easily. Smiley-and-Beefy encouraged him to have a second.

Upstairs, a discreet pile of price lists allowed him to discover that the smallest works in the show cost about as much as the bonus he expected for the Marmeduke Whiskers account. Another coincidence with the intoxicating smell of destiny about it.

Dillon was drawn back to the blue glass number. It was, clearly, the masterpiece of the whole show. Flora always said that shade of violet blue was very spritual. In fact, the whole thing made him think of Flora. It was delicate, scintillating, mysterious and fundamentally out of his reach. In fact, since a red spot had been applied to its label, indicating that it had been sold, it seemed out of his reach entirely.

Smiley-and-Beefy watched him with half an eye. 'That has been very much admired.' Dillon felt flattered that his taste was shared. 'The buyer is actually an American collector. He was delighted to get it before all these pieces go off to New York next month for her debut show over there.' Dillon felt positively proud of himself. 'The artist won't reproduce it, of course.' Dillon shook his head. 'But if you were interested in something like that, I could find out if she would be interested in a commission.

'Could you?'

'Of course. She is very busy at the moment . . .'

Dillon's mind jumped into the future and found only Flora. 'I was thinking of giving it to my fiancée as a wedding present,' he heard himself say. 'It's the sort of thing she'd love.'

'And when are you getting married?'

The man was taking notes, this was serious. 'We thought in about six months. A winter wedding.'

'How original. It would make a memorable gift.'

'Yes, it would.' Dillon suddenly felt himself being schmoozed. Did he not know this artist, now found to be on the threshold of global fame? Hadn't she described him as very sexy? A pack of indignations beset him. He saw no reason for this amiable giant to be doing any contacting on his behalf. Besides, he would save the gallery commission on a direct sale. Flora liked him to save money. She would be twice as happy if he presented her with a gift which celebrated her unique femininity, symbolised his love for her and also represented a bargain. 'Let me mull it over for a couple of days,' he suggested, making for the door. 'Thanks for the beer.'

'No trouble.' Smiley-and-Beefy put a brave face on defeat. 'Come again.'

In his car, Dillon extracted the gallery card from his wallet and dialled Merita Halili's number.

*   *   *

There was so much noise in the J Bar that Georgie hardly heard the phone when it first trilled for attention. The TV at the end of the room was relaying the early evening news. The lead story was the Fraud Squad raid on the offices of the National Bank of New Caledonia. A large, animated crowd had gathered around the screen.

When she heard her phone, Georgie decided to let it ring until the message service was activated. 'It'll be Felix,' she explained around the table. 'He thinks I'm in Brussels. I can't let him hear this, it's hardly chocolate-throwing or Eurorolling or whatever the

173

Belgians do for fun, is it?' To make her point, the group by the TV broke up in cacophonous discussion as the news bulletin moved on to the less interesting topic of war crimes in Serbia.

'What?' Flora shouted at her.

Des dispensed what his grandmother called an old-fashioned look and seized the telephone on its final note.

'Da?' he enquired menacingly. 'Ochin priatnik. Vskorie nagdia doshdi.' He put his head on one side and listened to the answer. 'Myuzit bylt. Myuzit.' He listened again. Georgie tried to look sporting. Felix hated playing a part in any kind of joke. 'Da,' Des announced once more, then, affecting a heavy accent he asked, 'Vooman?'

The caller responded. 'Da,' Des nodded at them. 'Byootiful vooman? Da!'

Georgie lost patience and tried to grab her phone, but Flora pulled her back.

'Let me get it,' Georgie hissed, suddenly anxious. 'It's not Felix.'

'Dot ferry ferry byootful vooman? Name Mereeeta?' Des was rolling his eyes. 'Nyet. Nyet Mereeta. Pozhalista . . .'

'Will you give it to me!' demanded Georgie. She pushed Flora back into her own seat and felt her sweater snag on Flora's bracelet. It was her favourite sweater, a silk one, laundered out to an extremely flattering old-rose pink. Georgie was unworthily annoyed.

A sense of the caller's identity suddenly snapped Donna out of her apathy. She felt a rush. A hit of pure power made her pulse race and her blood sing. Yes! It was working. She was going to win. Her superior powers made her the master of everyone around her. Flora and Georgie, those two ridiculous men, they were all just creatures of their limbic systems, trying to hack it in the modern world with the mental equipment of lower mammals. They were her puppets, chess pieces on her personal board, snips of her own creation who could be altered and moved as she liked. This was how it must feel to be God. 'Let her take the call, Des,' she ruled.

He grimaced disappointment and gave Georgie the phone. Saying, 'One minute please,' she scrambled to her feet and took the apparatus outside the bar.

'Sorry,' she said. 'A lot of people.'

'Is that Merita Halili?'

'Yes.' What was she doing? Why had she said that, just when she'd put an end to this idiotic pretence?

'I thought I'd got the wrong number.' The sound of his voice induced in Georgie a frisson of what she assumed was embarrassment. 'Listen, is this a bad time?'

'No, no. Good time. Who is this?' Without an effort, she had slipped back into character. She found herself purring into the microphone, leaning provocatively against the

175

wall and running her fingers through her hair to make it messy again.

'It's Dillon MacGuire. The man who ran his car into yours.'

'Oh yes. Hello, Dillon.'

'I've just been to your gallery.'

'Gallery. Very good.'

'To see your exhibition. It was great. Really great.' Beginning to feel stupid, Dillon switched back to the facts. 'The owner says you are going to New York soon?'

'What? Oh—New York?' Damn, she wasn't ready for this. Georgie sprang away from the wall and began to walk round in an agitated circle. An unusual chill down her side led her to discover a hole in her sweater. A large hole. 'New York,' she repeated, hoping for a sign.

'So good they named it twice. Yes.'

'What?' She hit a few buttons to fake the sounds of connection breaking up. The line held clear and unbroken. The hole in her sweater, she saw with dismay, was growing with every movement of her arm.

'Sorry, you don't understand. Listen, we can't talk like this. Could we meet sometime? Sometime soon? Before you go? I need to ask you something.'

'Ah . . .' Georgie pressed the cancel button. Nothing happened. She pressed it again. Dillon's voice was still talking. Her sweater was running into ladders like a silk stocking.

'Coffee, if you like. There's a coffee shop

176

near my office, we could meet there any time you liked, really. I could just slip out for ten minutes. That's all it would take, just ten minutes.'

'OK.' It seemed easiest to give in. Besides, Georgie felt ready to annoy Flora. Just a little. A sweater's worth, in fact. 'Tomorrow. Twelve o'clock. What is this place for coffee?'

He told her and rang off. Georgie pulled her jacket around her ruined knitwear and strolled back into the bar.

'Cat's got the cream,' Des announced, looking at her face. 'All I said was yes, hello, nice to meet you, maybe it's going to rain. In Russian. I don't know any Phlegm or Wally or Sprout or whatever language they speak in Belgium. So, was Felix OK?'

Georgie was considering a white lie when Flora said, 'It wasn't Felix, it was Dillon, wasn't it? I know it was, I heard his voice.

'Good going, Georgie. That's a great result.' Donna said this in precisely the same tone as she used to congratulate people for meeting their sales targets.

'So, you sexbeast—what did he want? As if we don't know, eh?' Des tickled Georgie under her chin. 'He wanted to see you, didn't he? So when's it to be?'

'You were chilling,' Flora accused her.

'Didn't he wonder why someone was yelling at him in Russian?'

'I think he expected something like that. He

thinks I'm that Albanian sculptor.'

'He what?' Donna demanded dramatically. 'Georgie, what have you done?'

'I don't know. It just happened that way. I was shaken up, I needed a name and that invitation was still in my bag.' The three of them were looking at her in bewilderment. Georgie realised she had made no sense. It would have been nice at that moment to be Merita Halili and be released from the obligation to make sense.

'I never saw you doing something daft like that.' Des sounded as if he thought she had acted out of character to annoy him.

'Why not? We agreed we'd use fake IDs. Flora's being a witch from the pharmaceutical industry. I can be a sculptor. When the bet's over, we'll all four of us have dinner together and have a good laugh about it.'

'If he can actually laugh. Your Felix,' said Flora drily. She had recoiled into a defensive tangle of limbs. Her face was pinched with anxiety.

'Of course he can laugh.'

'So, when are you seeing him?' Donna sensed them straying.

'Tomorrow. Just for coffee.' The ruin of Georgie's sweater was rankling. I will not fall out with Flora over a sweater, she lectured herself, editing the self-satisfaction out of her body language. A sweater or anything else. This is a game, it is not a competition. Flora is

178

hurt. I will not let it look as if I must be a more desirable female because her man is making moves on me. I will make this right. I must make this right.

Georgie sat with her friends, trying to think of something she could do to heal the wound she had inflicted on Flora's feminine pride. Feminine pride, she felt, was easily hurt but not at all easily repaired. No useful ideas came. Most of her mind wanted to wallow in anticipation of the moment when she would leave her desk, head for the ladies' room with her black eyeliner and a can of hairspray and transform herself into Merita Halili.

In her handbag, her telephone rang again. She rapidly answered it, fearful of another prank from Des.

'Sweetheart, is that you?' It was Felix.

'I'll call you back. I'll go outside,' she shouted into the phone, hoping to drown any identifiable London background noise. On the pavement outside the bar once more, she told him, 'We're out in some bar. It was really full.'

'How can you network when there's so much noise?' Felix sounded tired and peevish.

'I'm not exactly networking,' she told him. 'We're just having a drink. It's been a long day. Seminars and stuff.'

'I tried you earlier, you were on recall.'

'We were calling a taxi,' she improvised. 'Did you leave a message?'

'No, I did not leave a message. I didn't want

179

to leave a message. I wanted to speak to you.'

'I'm sorry. I was thinking you wouldn't be calling until later.'

'You're an hour ahead, don't forget.'

He talked on for a couple of minutes, until it became clear that there was nothing much to say. To fill the sudden silence, Georgie invented some facts about emerging markets.

'Well, sweetheart,' he said suddenly. 'Take care. I'll talk to you tomorrow.

'You take c—' Georgie realised that he had cut the connection. But Felix was not a phone man, he did not chat even when the line was good.

*   *   *

'It was this one. "River Number Four." The blue glass mobile. The one at the front of the gallery, by the window on the left.' Was he making an idiot of himself? Had he got it wrong? Was she going to be tempestuously insulted because in his philistine stupidity he had been unable to identify the marvellous sculpture which he claimed he wanted to commission? No, he was right, there was a picture. To hide his nerves, Dillon put the gallery catalogue on the counter and took a swig of his large skinny latte.

'River Number Four. I know it. It is blue.' Thank God, there was a picture of the thing. Shit and thrice shit and I say again, shit.

180

Georgie blew on her double espresso and set her mind to finding a way out of the elephant trap she had apparently dug with her own hands. 'You like it?'

'Very much. It's . . . ah . . . it makes me think of . . . well, I think my fiancée will like it.' Had he said that? Had he really said that? Banal, or what? He had shown himself a cretin and unfit to own art. Let alone an exquisite work like "River Number Four". She was going to refuse. Her eyes were definitely dark, she was smouldering. Very expressive, those eyes. Real windows to the soul. And what a soul.

'You want to make a present to your fiancée?' You are not disappointed, Georgie informed herself immediately. You are pleased for Flora. You are pleased for yourself, because you didn't want to seduce him and you obviously haven't so that's absolutely fine. You are pleased for yourself and for Flora, because this was getting out of control. What a nice man. 'You are a nice man,' she told him.

'No,' he said, meaning that she should not start with personal stuff.

'Yes!' she insisted, because it was fun to make him blush.

'Look, um . . .'

'I am sorry again. I embarrass you. We start again. You like my art.'

'Yes, and I like this one, River Number Four.'

'And you want to give it to your fiancée.'

181

'Yes. As my present to her when she gets married.'

'That is very sweet.'

'Ah . . .' Maybe, being an artist, she was above all the dreary stuff about sales and money. Her head was probably full of wonderful creative impulses. 'But you've sold this one. The one in the exhibition.'

'I have sold it?' Yes, she was looking quite amazed.

'So the man who owns the gallery said. But he said you might accept a commission?'

'Commission?'

'Commission to make another one. For me.'

Georgie immediately saw her escape. 'Please,' she asked him, laying on a flourish of hot-blooded supplication. 'You ask gallery. Better for me. Gallery handles commissions. It is my contract.'

'Oh,' he said, feeling disproportionately disappointed. 'You want me to go back to the gallery.'

'Please.' She nodded encouragement at him.

'But their commission . . .' How to open this subject without looking mean? Mean in the question of a wedding gift to his bride. Tricky.

'Don't worry. I make you a special price. Special for wedding.'

'Would you? That's so kind . . .'

'I like to be kind,' said Georgie. 'I like to make people happy.' Was that over the top? No, he seemed to buy it without any trouble.

182

How pleasant to be Merita Halili, Albanian sculptor, and say exactly what she felt. And as soon as she got back to her office, she would call Smiley-and-Beefy and sort out the price thing. The least she could do for Flora, after all.

'Thank you,' said Dillon.

They sat and smiled at each other over the empty coffee cups, allowing an angel to pass. Then another. It seemed necessary to find a reason to leave. Eventually, Georgie said, 'I have to go.'

Dillon watched her walk to the door. The way she moved really was very beautiful.

CHAPTER TWELVE

APRIL 27

Twenty-two floors above the struggling street, a deep peace existed in Donna's living space. The triple window glass muted the distant drone of a jet, the thick city air muffled the noise of human activity. Flora could hear the hands ticking round on the clock in the kitchen area. The tiny sounds fell into the stillness like drops of water, ricocheted between the steel work-tops and the shiny walls, and disappeared before they hit the dark wood floor. Gently, she shut the door. Quietness was such a luxury.

Flora enjoyed all luxuries, especially those that belonged to Donna. Being in this great apartment was the best thing about this silly Heartswap business. Being in the place by herself was a pure pleasure. It was also a pleasure which she was not going to be able to enjoy much longer. This Flora had decided.

Seventeen-A did not have the luxury of quietness. Nothing protected her little leaning house from the night-and-day snarl of London—the shapeless sound of people, vehicles, machinery, movement, striving, business and hate. Above that grey noise you could hear the traffic on the road and the planes on the flightpath over the river, and the neighbours on one side who screamed at each other and the neighbours on the other side who played Turkish flutes.

The house talked to itself. It was old, its beams cracked and its fabric rustled. When Flora was there alone with her work she thought sometimes that ghostly footsteps came up the stairs, weighting each tread in turn. Flora did not like to share ownership of anything; the spirits of long-dead occupants of 17A nagged at her. It was an annoyance to know that other people had lived between her walls. When she felt particularly harassed, she went about the rooms ringing bells and throwing flower petals into the corners to chivvy away their invading presences.

The beauty of Donna's apartment was that there was no trace of life in it. The walls were perfect, no pin had ever pierced them and no pictures spoiled their emptiness. The chairs were not crushed by the people who sat in them, the hard surfaces were never marked. There was never any impedimenta of eating or drinking in the kitchen. There was no colour and no scent except the faint animal smell of the sofa. Donna collected stuff and her objects stood self-consciously on shelves, contemporary art glass and monochromatic Chinese pottery. Apart from Flora and the sofa, the only organic things were the lilies in a black ceramic vase, and they were dying with elegance. The silence was so deep that when pollen fell from their stamens Flora heard it sprinkling the glass table top. She put her shopping beside the fallen grains, a plastic bag from a charity shop, a grimy, discordant thing evocative of scarcity.

Walking slowly across the room, she swung her arms, imagining the air stirring like water in a pool, ripples spreading to the walls and returning to her. Flora became aware that she was not satisfied. She wanted. What she wanted was not clear. It would become clear. It always did. She let herself fall face-first into the sofa.

Heartswap was finished. She had decided that as soon as she heard Dillon's voice from Georgie's phone. What had she been thinking? Gambling on a man's fidelity made as much sense as taking bets on the weather. Men were always ready for sex like it always rained in London. Game over. No rematch. The others could bitch all they liked, she was reclaiming the boy immediately.

To that end, Flora rolled off on to the floor and lunged for the telephone. Dillon's phone was on recall. Presumably because he was still at work. 'You'd better be still at work,' she told the electronic emptiness. 'This conference is crap. I'm coming home. Call me when you get in.'

The bliss of being alone! She lay on her back on the rug and put her feet on the stool, a clever little stool which matched Donna's sculptural chair, the two fabulous blobs of upholstery being placed just perfectly in front of the fourteenth-century carving of a Buddhist monk with his begging bowl, their greyish horizontalness enhancing the carving's pinkish verticality. Was it possible to be too relaxed to meditate?

Flora was not angry with Dillon. His lapse was natural. In fact, it made him more of a man. There were times when Flora could wish Dillon had more manliness in him. He was consistently eager, always bloody bright-eyed; there were no challenges in him. Look at the way she had asked him to marry her. Flora always said, 'Let's get married, darling,' when she got out of a new bed. It smoothed over the weirdness of being naked with a stranger.

Most men knew to laugh. In fact, all the men she'd said that to had laughed away the M-word immediately. Dillon had said, 'Wow,' in a rather idiotic way, then gone for a massive snog. When she came up for air she found she was supposed to be a fiancée. Everyone was cool with that. Dillon was storming ahead, buying them a place to live. Flora felt the thing was out of control.

She was happy thinking about herself. She discovered that she felt good in Donna's place. Being alone here had a quality that being alone in her own house lacked. It was almost a meditation in itself, just being here with

187

Donna's things. If Dillon were with her, he would be all over her like a rash, wanting reactions, expecting her to know what she wanted to do. Flora had little difficulty knowing what she wanted to do, but it was a bore to be asked, even by the implication of being with someone else. Most of the time, she wanted to do nothing.

From somewhere, Flora had acquired the idea that Dillon was the kind of man she ought to marry. Their marriage would be like some American comedy series from the fifties; she would be tripping around her big dope of a husband being sassy and getting applause. His dopiness would be the kind that all men had. He would never understand what she talked to her girlfriends about or why it was necessary to redecorate the bedroom. Her role was to use her superior understanding to manoeuvre the dumb beast into doing what she wanted without him realising what was happening. The only problem was that Flora found it irritating to be communicating all the time with someone who really might as well be a Martian. She did not want to be irritated. She wanted calm. That was why she liked being alone in Donna's home.

Satisfied that she had worked out what she needed, Flora got up and reclaimed her shopping. She drifted into her bedroom to put Plan B into operation.

*   *   *

An hour later Georgie dragged out her keys and unlocked the apartment door. Tonight, she felt exceptionally tired. Guilt, of course. Guilt about Felix. Guilt about Flora. Georgie knew she was hopelessly honest, which was why deception made her guilty and guilt ate away at her strength like some moral tuberculosis. That was why she loved Felix. And Flora. They believed in honesty just as she did. So no wonder the Heartswap thing hadn't worked.

When she thought about that madness, Georgie shuddered. Well, that was all over now. Without great enthusiasm, she opened the door.

The flat was exquisite but it made her feel sad. Sharing Donna's life was depressing. Nothing about her had changed in the time Georgie had been away. Flora had been a winsome, scatty girl but was now a poised and focused woman; Georgie had left London as an angry victim and come back healed. They were both moving on, moving up, getting married. Nothing had changed for Donna; the same meetings in the corner office, the same evenings in the same bars, the same laughter and the same jokes. Georgie found that this bothered her. She saw Donna's life unchanging until she was sixty. Or seventy. Or until she gave up work. But Donna loves her work, Georgie argued with herself. It's her whole life. And being single is a valid choice. She's perfectly happy. You want more, but she doesn't. Live and let live. Even if you wouldn't really call it living.

The silence was creepy. Georgie went straight to the stereo and put on some music. Goodness, she hadn't played music for herself for months. Choice! So exciting. Donna had no Chopin. She seemed to have mostly compilations, racked alphabetically: Abba, The Beatles, Boyzone, The Best Disco Album in the World Ever. Felix would have had to go and lie down if he'd been asked to choose from such a selection.

'If there's one thing I can't stand, it's people being judgemental.' Georgie said it aloud to herself and giggled. Felix couldn't understand why she found things like that funny. Felix did not like paradoxes at all. He always tried to argue them away. Georgie giggled again. The prospect of music was lifting her mood. She found a Tchaikovsky Pas de Deux compilation and wondered if she could make do with that. Why not? There was no one else to hear.

Just as she was loading the disc, she heard something. A little animal-like noise, a snuffle or a sniff. She looked around. The door to Flora's room was open a crack.

'Flora? Are you in?' The snuffle again. Georgie forgot her music and went to investigate.

The blinds were down and the room was dim. Flora was curled up on her bed in a foetal ball, her hair spread out on the pillow. Her face was pressed against her teddy bear, an ancient toy plaything with fur that was matted and colourless from so many years of giving comfort.

'Flora? Are you OK?'

The noise that answered her was more than a snuffle. If Flora's face hadn't been buried in the teddy bear, it would have been a sob.

'Flora?' Georgie sat on the bed and stroked the amazing hair. Some of it was damp. 'Flora? You're not crying?'

A sharper noise, still in the sob area. 'You are crying. Flora, what's the matter? What is it, sweetheart?'

Flora heaved herself up, grabbed a tissue, then flopped back on the pillow and sobbed again, several times.

'Is it us? Me and Dillon? This stupid game?'

Back to the snuffle. Georgie passed her the box of tissues. 'Don't cry. Please don't cry. It wasn't what we thought. He really loves you, Flora. He thought I was that artist and he wanted to commission something from me for a wedding present for you. That's all, I swear. There's nothing for you to worry about, nothing at all. He adores you. He said this mobile thing reminded him of you. Because it was beautiful.' Steady, she told herself. No more lies, remember?

Flora sat up and crossed her legs, patting her flushed cheeks with a tissue and continuing to sniff.

Again, Georgie explained Dillon's reason for seeing her. 'So you see, it was all for your sake,' she told her friend, hugging her lightly around the upper arms. 'Nothing to do with me. He doesn't know that any other woman exists, I promise you.' Flora whimpered and blew her noise delicately. 'I feel terrible you've been crying,' said Georgie helplessly.

The poise of the Degas dancer had gone. Flora's shoulders slumped with misery and she let her head flop from side to side. 'Look, we've got to stop this,' Georgie urged her. 'I'm not happy, either. We should never have let Donna talk us into it. It's really unfair on the guys. It's not right, it's deception, it's betrayal, it's dangerous. We must have been crazy to think it would be only a game.'

'But . . .' Flora gulped pathetically, folding over her tissue as if she was hoping to find a dry area in it.

'Donna will be angry, but that's her problem. If she makes a fuss about money, I'll sort it out; I've got plenty. What's it for, after all, if it can't get what you need? We need to get out of this. Forget it ever happened.'

In a shaking voice, Flora whispered, 'Really? You really want to stop?'

'I didn't want to start, remember?'

Flora did not wish to be reminded and took

192

refuge in another snuffle. 'You're sure?'

'Of course I'm sure. Let's just stop it. For heaven's sake, it was just something between friends. Not like a contract or anything. We can stop whenever we want.'

'Well, if you're really sure . . .'

'I really am sure. It was a terrible mistake. We must stop and put things right. Things between us, as well as with Dillon and Felix.'

'You're a wonderful friend,' Flora told her, hugging her in turn. 'You always know what to do. Donna's going to be so diappointed.'

'I can handle Donna,' asserted Georgie.

*   *   *

'So—too tough for you, is it? You want to quit?' Donna laughed at Georgie, a gloating, buccaneering kind of laugh, and she put her feet on her smudgeless glass table and wiggled her toes in her pink kitten-heeled slingbacks. Donna had always been a sucker for silly shoes. That killer elegance stopped at her ankles.

Georgie refused to be challenged. 'You know I wasn't comfortable with the idea.'

'You were comfortable with it when Dillon was taking the bait,' Des reproved her. He prepared to loll over the back of the sofa, but Donna frowned at him, so he sank on to the arm, which made her hiss. 'Oh, all *right*.' He subsided to the floor and sat with his back

193

against the seat and his legs in a half-lotus.

'That thing cost what you'd make on a penthouse and it's meant for sitting on.' Donna attempted to stab his backside with one of her sharp pink heels. 'So what's your problem with fucking sitting on it?'

'Boring,' he claimed. The heel struck home. 'Ow. Bitch. Leave me alone. I like the floor.'

'I never thought you'd crack up so fast,' Donna returned to Georgie. 'I thought you'd do the week before you came up with some pathetic excuse to back out.'

'At least you didn't put money on me,' Georgie tried a submissive smile. It got her nowhere.

'Oh, yes she did,' Des informed her with satisfaction, holding out his hand, palm upwards, towards Donna. 'Pay up, madam.'

The pink kitten heels were motionless. Smiling non-specifically at them all, Donna stayed as still as marble. The don't-move move had won her many a dodgy meeting in the past. Georgie remembered them well. Such was the force of her will that all Donna had to do was indicate the outcome she wanted and sit still and smiling while the underlings found a way to make it happen. The first to crack would be the most emotionally involved. It was Flora.

'Don't you get it, Donna? That's what's so wrong about this. It's like it's sport, it's all about competing. Georgie and me, we're

194

having to fight each other. It just doesn't feel right.'

'It just doesn't feel right!' Des mimicked her, rolling his eyes. 'Poor touchy-feely-huggy-kissy Flora. Everything has to feel right for you.'

'When something feels right it's because I'm in touch with my intuition,' Flora informed him crisply. 'I believe in being guided by the wisdom of the spirit.'

'Oh really?' Tauntingly, Des arranged his fingers like flower petals, imitating the carved monk. 'That's the spirit which tells you that your relationship is over because Dillon's splurging all his cash on your secret wedding present? Great wisdom, Flora. Really.'

'Oh, shut up.'

'I'm just jealous. I want somebody to buy me a nice piece of art because I'm so deep into negative self-esteem that only a really expensive present will make me believe that he loves me.'

'It isn't about my self-esteem.'

'Everything's about your self-esteem.'

'Keep your pathetic left-brain delusions to yourself.'

'And leave you believing all that right-brain moonshine?'

'It's about spiritual energy. Don't try to understand, you'll go into integrity overload.'

'I suppose that means you want me to mix the Martinis again?' He stretched his legs.

'God, how's anyone supposed to meditate sitting like that? All I'd be able to think about would be the pain.'

'Testosterone, darling. Makes you stiff. Have the change, you know you want to.'

The suggestion threw Des onto his feet immediately. 'I do not. I'd rather shave than have periods, anyone would. Anyone with any taste. Compare the razor to the tampon—one a design miracle, the other just a wad. Which object of desire would you rather have in your home?'

'If you had the change, you wouldn't have to mess with either. No periods and no more shaving. Transsexuals get it all ways.' And Flora giggled, which displeased Donna. It was not part of her strategy for the conversation to drift away from her target.

She demanded, 'Are you making those drinks, or what?'

'I'm making, I'm making.' He retreated to the refrigerator, while Donna gave an automatic small sigh.

Flora giggled again. 'When God made man, she was only testing.'

'Only joking, you mean.' Donna did not bother to lower her voice. 'And frankly, I don't appreciate that sense of humour.'

The maenad spirit appeared in their circle and danced between the three of them, bringing sparkle to their eyes and tingle to their blood. Georgie discovered that she was

196

no longer tired. Flora found her own arguments absurd. Donna concealed herself in stillness again, but saw victory coming her way.

'I suppose I am being insecure about the dear boy,' Flora mused, rearranging her bracelets on her wrist while she arranged her thoughts. 'It is rather sweet, isn't it?'

'Yes,' Georgie said bluntly. 'I'm jealous as well. Felix only buys art for himself.'

'There isn't anything for me . . . for us to worry about, really. Is there? Men would do this, wouldn't they? Men wouldn't even think about it. It's just a laugh, isn't it?' She leaned across and patted Georgie's arm. 'I just had a little lapse there. I'm fine now. Let's go on with it, Georgie. We were just starting to enjoy ourselves.'

'You're sure?' Caring for another was so easy, so familiar, almost a habit. Georgie slipped back into it like an old horse accepting its bridle. 'I'd never do anything to hurt you, Flora. I couldn't.'

'We should do this, you know. I was thinking that. We should have our fun. While we can. We're getting married, we might even have children, we'll have to be sensible and grown-up and all that stuff. I feel like I've never really been a girl, you know? I never played enough, and now playtime's nearly over. Everything's been so heavy, the work and exams and career and stuff. Don't you feel that?'

Georgie said what Flora knew she would say. 'I suppose I do.'

'So,' said Donna, wiggling her toes again, 'does this mean . . .'

'I think so,' replied Flora, looking at Georgie, who said, 'It's only a week, isn't it? What can happen in a week?'

'We're on again. Heartswap is go.'

CHAPTER THIRTEEN

APRIL 27–28

'You have—NO—new messages,' announced the bright electronic voice of Felix's mailbox. His thumb crushed the action button on his phone, as if he squeezed the device hard enough a message would be extruded from the remote vastness of its memory. Damn no messages. Fuck no messages. Shit no messages. And the same to she who was not messaging him. Both of them.

Extreme states required extreme remedies. Felix recognised that his emotional condition could become extreme if not managed appropriately as a matter of urgency. He took his own pulse. Yes, it was elevated. Music had been proved to slow the pulse rate. He put on some unchallenging dinner jazz. Alcohol? Also sedative, in reasonable amounts. Perhaps a glass of the Merlot he had just bought. Not strictly ready for drinking just yet, but likely to be more appealing than anything he could buy at the late-night supermarket. He unpacked a bottle and drew its cork. A gratifyingly complex aroma flattered his nose. Felix felt he was gaining control.

Flawed femininity, that was the problem. Why was he always drawn to these Amazons who'd maimed their own womanliness in some kind of struggle? The Amazons of classical mythology had each cut off a breast to be able to draw a bowstring. How apt a metaphor that was! A warrior woman had to disfigure her own femininity to be effective in battle. Perhaps because he loved bright and brilliant women, he would always be attracted to partners who were struggling with their own gender issues.

Felix had clearly defined concepts. His concept of a real woman was a flexible and communicative creature which did not struggle at all, except perhaps a little token resistance to him in the beginning, just to sharpen the appetites. Georgina had struggled promisingly. She had flexibility, she could be quite good at moulding herself to the needs of their relationship. In fact, there were times when he thought she was a little too adaptive. It was necessary to give her the space to find her own balance sometimes.

Communication was where Georgina was lacking. He had felt it from the start. She kept things back from him, she held out, she failed to disclose. His impression was that she had been getting worse in this respect since their return to London. There was too much of Georgina that was reserved to herself. Felix did not like this. It was unreasonable. It was wrong. It was not truly and deeply female. Poor Georgina. It was not her fault that in the scramble to compete in the workplace she had compromised her essential self. When she came home, he would open a dialogue with her about it. She needed a man of his perception to contribute these insights to her life.

He decided to call his intern and talk over the file format she had proposed. He might share his analysis of his relationship with her as well; she was a bright girl, she would be interested. His intern was also not quite beautiful, but arousing, in her way. She was also in Paris for the weekend, according to her voicemail. From his briefcase, Felix extracted his Psion and made a note to review the intern's salary. After all, she was not much more than a trainee, at this stage in her career.

He poured himself some more wine. Perhaps the Merlot was not really too young at all. With the chance to breathe a little it developed a pleasing complexity. He resolved to start a cellar book in which to jot down these observations. While the Psion was running he opened a new file named CELLAR BOOK and wrote a note to himself: MERLOT ALREADY FINISHING WELL.

The case, the Psion and the wine had all been bought with the rewards of Georgina's scrambling but this connection was not clear to Felix. Since his first year at medical school, Felix had relied on seven brilliant, achieving, scrambling women, one after another, for financial support. He moved up, in material terms, each time, as it had become clearer what his real needs were as far as housing, décor, food, clothing and a car were concerned. This progression was also not clear to Felix. Nor had he told Georgie his complete relationship history. Disclosure did not sit with Felix's concept of a man. A man diminished his own masculinity by saying too much. Men had no imperative to talk, quite the reverse. So his silence on the subject of five of his former partners did not compromise his own ideals of personal honesty.

Pensively, he walked the floor. After a while, he chose to estimate the potential represented by Miss Pforza, as he thought of Flora. Staying in touch. Making friends. Capri or Istanbul, which would he prefer? Hah! A lack of sincerity, undeniably. She needed to understand the importance of keeping her word. As for the sexual aggression, it probably indicated promiscuity. Quite irresponsible. Cervical cancer, STDs including HIV although hepatitis was probably more dangerous now, or resistant gonorrhoea . . . Felix refilled his glass. He could make her aware of the risks she was running. He should also take responsibility for his own protection. As he always did.

Could he actually contemplate a relationship with a woman who worked in the pharmaceutical industry? Perhaps it would not necessarily be ethical suicide. The greatest good, after all, was the work. Funding from the industry would make all the difference. If his research was good enough, nobody would be concerned about who had paid for it. He swilled the wine around in his glass and allowed himself to imagine the conferences, the applause, and the clinic with the ankle-deep carpet and the rustling palms. An irrational thing, imagination. It leaped on to the swish of her silky skin as she crossed her thighs and then in a nano-second it recreated the feathery clutch of her fingertips. Insincere, irresponsible, obviously promiscuous; it could hardly be wrong to objectify a woman like that for a couple of minutes. He allowed his imagination to move upwards from the swishing thighs.

In a while, Felix returned to the kitchen and found one more glass remaining in the bottle. A shame to let a good wine turn sour. As he refilled his glass, the insinuating tones of his phone sounded from the next room.

'Felix?' It was Georgina and she was clearly in another bar. He could hardly hear her over the hubbub.

'Who else would it be?' he demanded.

The signal failed. Or was cut. In a minute, the phone rang again.

'Georgina?' No background noise now, she had gone outside. Unwise. Probably dangerous to use a mobile on the street in Brussels.

203

'Where are you?'

'In my room,' she told him.

'I couldn't hear you before.'

'I couldn't hear you.'

'So . . .' Resentfully, he softened his voice for her. 'How's it going?'

'I nearly gave up today,' she told him. 'I've been having problems with it.'

'Problems?' Anxiety prickled the back of Felix's neck. He never liked his partners to have problems. Since he counted on their support, a problem affecting their ability to support him would rock his world on its axis. It drained his energy to have to respond to an external stimulus like that. Moving up was effortless if he chose who and when. When the move was forced on him, things could get ugly.

'It's me, not the course,' she explained. 'Someone else was really quite upset. But they're over it now. So I've decided to press on,' she told him. He breathed deeply, thinking that she sounded quite positive about the decision.

'That's not like you. Picking up on someone else's problems and letting them slow you down.'

'I had a weak moment, I suppose. But it passed. Only another week, after all.'

'Missing you,' he said. It was not Felix's way to make a direct statement.

'I miss you too,' she said, feeling ashamed that it was her way to hear a direct statement

204

when none had been made.

There seemed to be little more to say. He brought her up to date with his progress at the clinic, then said, 'Take care of yourself, sweetheart,' and ended the call.

Georgina was losing it, definitely. Losing it was part of Felix's concept of a woman. Not to imply any inferiority by that. Nobody could make up thousands of years of conditioning in one generation. Historically, women were always able to leave the workplace for the home without any loss of status. Quite the opposite, until feminism degraded the position of motherhood. So it was understandable that their commitment might falter. That was another subject on which a man's insights could be valuable. Georgina, however, could be arrogant. She could ask his advice then ignore it. Part of whatever she had going on about communication, no doubt. When they got a dialogue going, he would point that out to her. When a woman lost it, she also lost Felix. The usual pattern was that he got out while the going was good.

Felix savoured his final half-glass of Merlot and weighed nurture against nature. He thought of studies of identical twins separated at birth. Nature was powerful. If it was Georgina's nature to be uncommunicative, if her gender deficiency was actually biological, then opening a dialogue would be a waste of energy. If it was a secondary response to an infant trauma, the prognosis was not much better. Trying to repair traumatic lesions on the psyche was pointless. Tough but true. In reality, he had only two choices: he could accept her as she was, or not.

He decided to defer the decision, then finished the wine and went to take a shower. Alone in a bed, he always slept badly. In wakeful periods during the night, the vision of a small white rectangle floated above him. It was Flora's card, inscribed 'Pforza Pharmaceuticals' with a double P logo in clean clinical blue. He knew exactly where it was, tucked into a pocket in his computer case. It would be quite justifiable to ask her when the grant application had been made.

*   *   *

'Shit!' Dillon fumbled frantically for his mouse. The cursor, as if infected with his own panic, swooped around his screen. He tried to stop his hand shaking. The cursor was jumping like a flea. Furtively, Dillon looked left and right. There was a God. His colleagues were at lunch. The nearest person was at the end of the row. But looking his way. Getting up. Coming towards him. Shit, shit, shit! Only a man, but he couldn't risk it. Dillon reached for the off switch and liquidated his morning's work.

'Bloody software,' his colleague observed,

holding out a rosy red apple. 'D'you want my apple?'

'Don't you want it?'

'I only like green ones.'

'Cheers. Thanks.' Dillon took the fruit and sank his teeth into it, praying that the man would go back to his own desk. Instead he parked his backside on a nearby chair and started a ramble around the Marmeduke Whiskers project. This was the price of success. Being the department's official golden boy meant that all Dillon's conversations had become extended. People had started to regard him with something like wonder. Quite often this made them so nervous that they chattered at him for precious minutes while he cranked up the courage to break off the encounter. Dillon found himself promoted to the level of departmental icon. It made him deeply uncomfortable.

'Look, would you mind very much if I gave IT a call?' he said at last. 'I've got to get this problem sorted.'

'Oh, sure. Sorry. Really sorry. I didn't realise. I . . . well, I'll get out of your way.' And his benefactor stumbled back to his own chair, making him feel worse.

'Thanks for the apple,' he offered, trying to mitigate his own perceived superiority.

He picked up the phone and put it down again. Before he made an ass of himself with the anorak, it might be wise to make sure that things really were as bad as he feared.

Dillon turned on his terminal once more. The screen filled and refilled with technical messages, then cleared and asked for his password. He typed in 'Flora xxx'.

The screen cleared, then his folders appeared. So far, so good. He opened the file he had been working on earlier. The autosave was programmed to work every five minutes. Some of the day's work should still be there.

The screen filled with text. Dillon folded his arms and watched. The time window in the corner told him it was 13.27 p.m.

At 13.30, the trouble began.

A pink spotted drop-down menu promised:

LICK FUCK TEEN PUSSY HOT BABES NAKED SUCK TONGUES KLARA'S TEENCHAT! TONITE WET'N'WILD 10pm EST

The menu then disappeared, to be replaced by pictures of three breasts, two mouths, a hand and a red lollipop shaped like a spaceship. Or a penis, if your mind worked that way. In fact, it probably was a penis. Dillon's mind was frozen with fright. The breast gave way to four buttocks, some legs ending in white ankle socks and a hairbrush. Terror splashed over his head like a drench of cold water. For an instant, he was convinced that he had pee'd his pants and he found himself staring at the crotch of his trousers. No stain. It was just an illusion. He killed the power again and reached for the phone.

'I've got a bit of a problem. Quite a serious problem, in fact,' he mumbled into the anorak's voicemail. 'I'd really appreciate it if you gave me a call as soon as you could.'

His luck was out. The anorak was getting vaccinations for his holiday and did not return to collect his messages until four in the afternoon. To fill in the intervening hours, Dillon called an unnecessary meeting of the focus group team; he told them that they needed to review the videotapes of the discussions they had held the day before. They sat in a claustrophobic little room, huddled over a blurry screen for two hours. The focus group team were all monthly contract workers, which meant that they were the only subordinates he could call away from their daily grind without the computer system detecting their absence. When the tape was finished, he moved them to a meeting room, squirming while he extemporised a second phase of research into small-pet ownership among the under-fives.

'Never fear, I am here,' the anorak told him.

'This is delicate,' Dillon began.

'You gotta virus from one of them porn sites.' The anorak smirked and assumed his seat. 'Fuckin' clever, they are. Let's hope it's not one of the new ones. They've figured out this tamper mechanism that makes 'em multiply through all your drives if anyone tries to get rid of 'em . . .'

Dillon looked around, violently apprehensive. The office was now full. In fact, it was crowded. Every seat was occupied, every screen was bright, every keyboard was clattering. He tried to stand in front of his own screen. For a paranoid second, he imagined that all his colleagues were already busy composing integrity reports on him.

The door to the corner office opened and Donna appeared with the bright-eyed look which usually meant she was about to pay her underlings a visit for no specific purpose apart from general intimidation. It was not hard to intuit her pleasure as she progressed through the room, watching people cringe with fear as she approached them.

'Can it wait a minute?' pleaded Dillon.

'D'you want this sorted or not?' demanded the anorak.

'I'm desperate to get it sorted but Donna's coming this way.'

'I'm outta here,' the anorak responded fearfully, hitting the power switch as he leaped out of Dillon's chair. 'Call me when it's all clear, yeah?'

'Everything all right?' Donna enquired as she surged past Dillon's work station. He imagined that she stared directly at his screen as she passed. Paranoia again.

In a few more minutes, one of his phones rang. 'Dillon, can you give me a moment?' enquired Donna's voice.

'Of course, right away,' he assured her, and set off for the corner office.

'All you have on your plate right now is the Whiskers project?' she said as he came through the door. He decided to leave it open. Strangely, he felt that he wanted the rest of the office to see whatever was about to happen.

'Yes,' he agreed. A new account, perhaps? His hopes budded in a small way.

'Are you up to the deadlines with that?' She was walking slowly up and down behind her desk. The paranoia convinced him that she was deliberately avoiding his gaze.

'Well, yes,' he assured her. 'We're still aiming for the beginning of next week, aren't we?'

'I'm asking because your work rate has been dropping. The on-line figures for the month just came in and it looks like you ran into the buffers a couple of days ago.'

'I've been brainstorming Phase Two with the focus groups,' he offered. Thank God he'd covered his back with this one.

'Do I know about Phase Two?'

'It was your suggestion. Marketing to the under-fives. It's looking good.'

'I'm glad to hear it. You've been brainstorming two days?'

'Not the whole time. I've been working on

211

the figures as well. There's been a . . . a technical problem.'

'Are IT helping you with that?'

'Oh yes. Actually, they sent someone down just now.'

'Good. Get it fixed, Dillon. Your time is our money, don't forget. And we've got a lot riding on the Whiskers thing. It's got to be up and running on schedule.'

'Absolutely,' he promised, sliding crabwise out of the door.

Donna watched him leave with some irritation. Brainstorming. Phase Two. Technical problems. Fool! Didn't he know he was already dead? His only real option was to lie down.

At his own terminal, the anorak wrestled with his conscience and let it slam him to the canvas. In situations like this, he liked to see himself as a cyber-outlaw, a Robin Hood riding to the defence of Direct Warranty's oppressed peasants. But Robin Hood had the Merry Men to watch his back, and the anorak was only on a three-month rolling contract. It was only reasonable to cover himself. With jittery fingers, he picked out an integrity report on Dillon and mailed it to Human Resources.

CHAPTER FOURTEEN

APRIL 28

Flora was reaching the end of the week in bad shape. The day began badly; she overslept and had to cut down her morning meditation time, so she left Donna's without getting a proper connection to the source at the beginning of the day. Two client visits were in the diary, both initial consultations, and it always drained her spirit to confront people's cynicism.

The first client had a sense of scarcity about money and the second client was locked into an ego thing about the colour of her carpet, all of which created a sensation of tightness around Flora's heart chakra. The stress of having to travel across town at midday in a period of high humidity and ionisation created a stuffed-up feeling in her sinuses which she hadn't noticed since she gave up eating dairy. Three of her fingernails broke, meaning that she wasn't getting enough chromium. Her intuition felt faint, her energy was blocked and she was sure that her aura was murky.

Relief was elusive. Her favourite masseur was already chilling on some mountain in Scotland for the weekend. Her reflexologist was booked solid. The acupressure practitioner was on holiday. The flotation tank had sprung a leak and was closed for maintenance. All she could do was make an appointment to see her nutritionist the following week and, against her better judgement, drove back across town to the home of a fellow shiatsu student to offer herself for a practice session. The clumsy cow decided to walk her spine and stumbled over the solar plexus, leaving Flora with a menacing twinge around her left ovary.

Shivering with negativity, she went back to 17A, put some rose and frankincense in her personal Environmental Aroma Harmoniser, plugged it in and blew the fuses. Or blew something electrical. A blue flash came out of the socket, there was a smell of scorching and all the machines in the house turned themselves off. At least the universe was giving her some signs. Probably the electro-magnetic field in the house was causing all the problems. Flora found a lotus incense stick, a tea-light and a match folder from the Bit Bar which had two matches remaining. She lit the incense with one and the tea-light with the other, then sat down to do a flame meditation.

Her telephone rang. It was in her bag by her desk.

Flora allowed her mind to notice the ringing. Her phone was set to announce a call with a little snatch of Bach. She encouraged the sounds to float away like blossom petals which had fallen into a stream.

The ringing stopped.

Flora welcomed the energy of the flame and directed it to the pain in her back. There still was a pain in her back. Also a twinge in one of her ankles. She decided to count her breaths.

At the fifteenth breath, her telephone rang again.

Flora allowed her mind to notice the ringing, which it was eager to do. Fifteen. Sixteen. The petal thing wasn't working so she decided to welcome the energy of the music. Seventeen. Bach was quite stimulating. Eighteen. Wasn't there something about classical music being the same tempo as alpha brain waves? Nineteen. Or was it beta brain waves? No, twenty. Twenty-one. Twenty-three. No, twenty-two. It was only Dillon calling. He really ought to get a grip on his neediness. Twenty-five. It was so disruptive to get calls from him all the time. Like now, for instance. Had she done thirty yet? Her whole meditation was spoiled. Typical. She might as well answer the phone.

As soon as Flora got her phone out of her bag the ringing stopped.

After that, she realised that her spiritual condition was quite serious. Emergency therapy was needed to cleanse her mind of its negative thoughts, replace them with a positive visualisation and do some affirmations to alter her focus before her whole being was overwhelmed by bad vibrations. Flora took the candle into the bedroom where she kept her affirmation book on the night table. The text for the day was, 'I am surrounded by love.' She found the love affirmations troubling, they always seemed to be invoking more problems rather than helping her with what she had already. She flicked forward to the next season and picked, 'I am a whole, perfect being. I have everything I need.'

'I am a whole, perfect being. I have everything I need,' she said aloud, sitting on the bed. 'I am a whole—'

Her telephone rang again.

'You have TWO new messages,' it informed her.

The first message said, 'HiFlorathis isGeorgieBitBarateightyeah? Onlycallme ifthere'saproblem. Loveya.'

The second message said, 'This is Felix. Any news on our funding application?'

The voice was almost angry. It was a tone Flora knew well and she enjoyed hearing it. It was the sound of a man in need who hated the way he was so much that he was acting offensively to kid himself that he didn't need anything, or anyone, not at all, not ever. Hah!

Flora's spirit soared like a skylark. The blood in her veins felt as gassy as Diet Coke. She was empowered. It was a beautiful evening. Thrilling events were about to cram themselves into the empty space of her

216

weekend. Donna was right, she was an uber-babe and brilliant with it. World domination might be a laugh. She swooped into the kitchen and made herself some hibiscus tea.

In the normal way, Flora would have allowed Felix to leave at least two more messages and then found herself able to answer his fourth call in person. With a bet to win, Georgie to beat, Donna to impress and fun to be had, the action parameters were unusual. And there would be a special bonus in calling back now. She knew that the peripheral traffic circulation of London was completely clogged every Friday afternoon, and that a man was never so suggestible as when trapped in tedium behind ten thousand fellow commuters on an ugly overpass at least an hour from any civilised amusement.

'I've been *meaning* to call you,' she assured Felix, her voice lush with insincerity. '*Very* positive response from the board. Just a few *tiny* details we need to clarify before the next meeting. I've been *so* busy, I've let you slip out of my schedule for a few days. We really *should* get this wrapped up by Monday. Where are you now?'

'Shepherd's Bush,' was the unhappy reply. Flora could not remember Shepherd's Bush but it sounded like a traffic nightmare.

Felix instantly understood that the most practical arrangement would be for her to call by his flat the next morning, though he was

217

correctly embarrassed to make the suggestion. The effort it cost him to keep the eagerness out of his voice was really rather sweet. Much more appealing than all the gibbering and fretting she would have got from Dillon.

*　　　*　　　*

'I assure you, Donna, no one out there will recognise me. When I go undercover in an organisation it is a completely professional exercise. If you decide that you need my services, I will make absolutely sure that no one in your organisation becomes aware that I am an investigator. The assignment I've just completed, at the London office of an offshore bank, took months of preparation for the office culture, as well as learning how to do the job that was my cover.'

Donna wished that everyone who worked for her would be so professionally eager to please. All the same, she was cautious with anyone who was trying to tell her what she wanted to hear. She sat back in her chair and frowned at the tiny woman poised on the edge of the largest chair in the room. 'What was that, exactly?'

'I was a risk assessor.' She gave a husky laugh. Her voice was surprisingly deep for such a pixie.

'Wasn't that difficult to sustain as a cover? I mean, what happened when you actually had to assess a lending risk?'

The sparrow-like blonde pursed her lips. From the depth of the wrinkles that appeared around her mouth, Donna judged her to be much older than she looked when her face was blank. 'Normally, my work is confidential, of course. But in this case I was retained by the United States Federal Fraud Agency. They picked up on the situation and worked with the Fraud Squad here. You may have heard about it, the case is going through the courts. The National Bank of New Caledonia. They never actually made any loans. Their clients were all fake. I found a whole room full of files on companies which did nothing registered to addresses that didn't exist. But not a lot of people were ready to get the street map of New Caledonia to check them out. The risk assessor's job was just to go through the motions. The challenge for me was to create a character with a CV which would put them in a position where they would be credible going along with that.'

Donna was momentarily crucified by indecision. Should she be happy that the CEO of New Caledonia, the fuckwit she had shagged in a moment of deep boredom, had finally got his just deserts? Or should it concern her that even at a moment of deep boredom her judgement had been so far off that she'd shagged such a fuckwit at all? Knowing that she'd got so close to a big-time loser made the hairs on the back of her neck prickle.

Swiftly, Donna elected to congratulate herself for creating the Heartswap thing to stop her sense of humour getting her into any more trouble. Ever since Heartswap, fancying mad, bad and totally inappropriate men had not been a problem. It was so much more amusing to screw around with other people's lives than to screw up your own.

'How did you do that?' she asked her guest, projecting flattering interest. 'Do you have any training?'

'Three years of Stanislavsky. Inner motive forces. The difference between seeming and believing. You know.'

'Uh-huh,' allowed Donna, who did not know at all.

'I was an actress,' her guest explained in a crisp tone.

'An interesting transition.'

'It wasn't a sudden thing. I got into role-play work and then I was headhunted. Believe me, if there's one thing I know, it's how to prepare a role.'

'Of course.' Donna agreed. 'But in this case there's not much time for preparation. This employee is showing badly in our monitoring system and there's been a bad integrity report on him this week. They both suggest we should be seriously concerned. I've got to move quickly. The company could already be in the

220

position where other staff could take action against us for retaining him while we were aware of his inappropriate behaviour.'

'You need to know fast,' the little blonde agreed. 'But this is an individual you want investigated. Just one person?'

'Just one.' Perhaps the job was going to be too small for such a highly trained operative. 'But a key player,' she added.

'What is it you're worried about? Theft?'

'Sex.'

The investigator rolled her eyes around the ceiling. 'Men! It is a man, I presume.'

'Of course it's a man. Will you have a problem with—er—the problem?'

'Not at all. The cases I hate are the ones where I've got to check up on people for subverting the franking machine or extending fag breaks to more than five per cent of office time. The pitiful stuff. Cases where people want to pay me thousands to save themselves twenty quid a year.'

'Thousands?' The slack in Donna's budget went to four figures but not five.

'In a long investigation, yes. You pay me for the work I do as cover as well as the inquiry. But sex things never take long. They can't help themselves usually.'

'And he's a really bright guy.' Donna sighed with fake regret. 'In terms of intellectual capital, the major asset of my entire department.'

'So you wouldn't want him pissed off if he's in the clear.'

'Ah . . . no. Of course not.' Being proud of the ingenuity with which she had incriminated Dillon, Donna had trouble remembering to seem uncertain about his guilt.

'That's the great advantage of an undercover investigation. If it turns out that there's nothing to worry about, nobody need ever know. I'll just be somebody who was hired and then didn't work out. I can disappear and they'll forget I was ever here.'

'That's what I need. What's your availability?'

'I'm on leave now while the court case is running. I don't expect to be called to give evidence until the end of the week. I could give you a couple of days at least. If we work out some kind of temping as a cover, I could come back again after that if you needed me. Which I'm sure you won't.'

'Perfect,' said Donna, feeling in control again. 'Can you start on Monday?'

'Surely.'

*   *   *

Georgie sipped her margarita and made a face. She discarded the straw; she despised straws in cocktails. She sipped again, then a third time, through the gap made by her lips in the salt rim, just to be sure. 'Hey!' She called

222

to the waiter before he could wander out of range. 'I asked for a margarita with Triple Sec.'

'So?' the waiter replied.

'So this is with Cointreau,' Georgie informed him pleasantly. 'I asked for Triple Sec.'

'The classic margarita is with Cointreau,' he pouted. The bar was heaving. It would have been hard to fit one more girl with an eating disorder between the tightly packed bodies. Flora had obtained their table by projecting maximum fuck-off vibes at the previous tenants from her third-eye chakra, ripping into their ankles with her heels and upsetting their drinks with a dextrous twitch of her handbag.

'The classic margarita is with Triple Sec,' Georgie returned briskly. 'And whether it's classic or not, that's what I asked for. And it's not what I've got. So you can bring me another one or we can go and get the barman to settle the argument.'

The barman was whirling like Roadrunner between glasses, shakers, blenders, optics, mixers, juicers and plates full of sliced fruit. The waiter pouted some more and scooped her glass back on to his tray before struggling away through the crush.

'Do you know the difference between men and toilets?' Flora asked Georgie as they watched him disappear.

'You mean you can never find one when you

really need one?'

'No, no, no. The clean ones are all taken and the rest are full of shit.'

'Felix is certainly clean,' Georgie sighed. 'The best thing about this week has been getting a shower to myself and not choking to death on his Gaultier Pour Homme every night.'

'Jean-Paul Pour Homme, eh?' Flora's eyes sparkled.

'Forty quid a throw and I don't even like the stuff.'

'I wish Dillon would spend forty quid a throw on smelling nice for me.'

'You could buy it for him. Eighty-five per cent of men's toiletries are bought by women. I buy the Jean-Paul.'

'You mean you buy him Jean-Paul and you don't even like the stuff?'

'Isn't that what I said?'

'Then don't buy it, for God's sake.'

'Felix likes it.'

Flora smiled. That was her mistake. Just that once, instead of her habitual inward lip-quivering smile, she gave a wide, curling, maximum-teeth smile, the sort of smile that a person does not stretch to unless they are experiencing genuine pleasure.

'You're smiling like Julia Roberts.'

'Have I got sesame seeds in my teeth?' Flora made a number out of diving into her bag for a mirror, then realised she might be making things worse. Georgie was in a high good temper in spite of the margarita affair and whatever Flora's smile had given away, she seemed not to have picked up on it. 'And what about you?' Flora went on rashly. 'Your energy's really good. Did you have a great ass-kicking week?'

'Yup,' Georgie said, marginally bewildered. Flora only ever commented on her energy status when she wanted to hand out one of her lifestyle lectures. Her usual position on ass-kicking weeks was that they caused a lot of stress, which deranged your bio-dynamic integrity.

'That's wonderful,' Flora encouraged her, hiding behind her mirror and picking an imaginary seed from between her small, flawless incisors.

'Yup.' Georgie considered explaining why the past week had been exceptionally ass-kicking. It was technical. She'd spotted something when it was a cloud the size of a man's hand in Jakarta and taken profits for everyone by the time the storm was gathering over the Bourse. Flora's eyes always glazed when she started talking about the markets. Now that she considered the subject, Georgie's mind was beginning to glaze as well. Was it possible she'd been watching them too long? Up and down, boom and bust, bull and bear— it was all so predictable. The markets were like a switchback she'd ridden on too many times.

Thinking of switchbacks, it was surprising how much she'd got done in the past week while she had been riding out the Heartswap affair. In fact, that day had been so ass-kicking she had forgotten she was supposed to be chasing Dillon. A dear man. Flora had really scored there. Even if he wouldn't spend forty quid a throw on asphyxiating French designer aftershave. Georgie found she respected his position on that.

'There's something about you tonight,' Flora continued rashly. 'You're really glowing.'

'So are you,' said Georgie automatically. Then enlightenment finally reached the high plain of mellow from which she had been enjoying the view. 'So,' she said casually, 'when did Felix call you?'

Flora startled. Georgie watched the light and shade in her eyes while she considered lying then decided to tell the truth, cause pain and enjoy the kudos of having scored again. 'Just after you, this afternoon,' she admitted. The smile came back, she couldn't help it. 'It was just business. I think he really needs more funding for his research.'

The view from the high plane of mellow was exceptionally clear. 'This is wrong,' said Georgie, taking one of Flora's hands in hers. 'You know it is. We're lying to each other, we're lying to Dillon and Felix, we're undermining all the relationships that are most important to us and we're in serious danger of

226

screwing up our lives. We should never have got into this. I really want to stop now.'

'You're right,' said Flora, grateful for the opportunity to appear gracious. How had Georgie managed to manipulate the conversation to her own advantage so quickly? 'I'm not comfortable with the way it's turning out,' she added generously.

'Why don't we call Donna right now and tell her it's over?' proposed Georgie at once. As if to reward her decision, the waiter appeared with her margarita.

'OK,' said Flora. 'I'll do it. She's probably still at the office. She said she had a late meeting tonight.' She reached into her bag for her phone.

As Flora dialled, Georgie noticed that Donna's number was the first one in the phone's memory. Even from the high plane of mellow, this appeared to be a significant fact.

Georgie said, 'I know you owe Donna a lot. She'll be disappointed, she was enjoying it all. But it's different for her. She's got another agenda. Relationships can be fun for her, her life isn't involved with anyone else the way our lives are.'

'Lucky bitch,' said Flora, using one finger to hold the tiny hands-free microphone in her ear while the call connected.

*   *   *

Donna caught Des just as he was leaving 17A. 'Where are you going?' she demanded. 'I've got to see you, Des.'

'What's happened?' he demanded, eager for incident and delighted to be needed. His weekend was looking terribly flat at that moment.

'They've wimped out. The girlies. Both of them. Flora just called me.'

'Flora called you? But she was winning.'

'I know. I can't believe she's really buying into that marriage crap.'

'Pathetic.'

'Pitiful.'

'They can't give up now. They're half-way there.'

'And I've bought our tickets.'

'Goody, goody, goody. Where are you going?'

'I thought Bali. I got a great deal on some place with five different pools and a scuba school.'

'Right. Well, we'll see about this. They can't get away with ruining your life for their own selfish motives.'

'No, they can't. This is an emergency. We've got to talk tactics, Des.'

CHAPTER FIFTEEN

APRIL 29

With a twinge of anticipation, Georgie opened her front door and entered her home as quietly as she could. Felix was usually in bed until at least ten on Saturday morning. She might tiptoe into the bedroom, slip off her clothes and slide into bed beside him. With any luck she would never have to explain anything. No, he'd call that childish. Unless he was really gagging for sex. Which he usually was. All the same, Georgie decided to forget the tiptoe plan. There was enough on her conscience already. Her jokes always irritated him. She chose not to admit that it had been pleasant not to have sex with Felix for the past five days.

'Coo-eee!' she called. There was a powerful aroma of Jean-Paul in the hallway.

As she passed the kitchen, Georgie noticed with relief that it was perfectly clean and tidy. A freshly washed espresso cup stood with its saucer beside the sink. He had treated himself to some Gourmet Roast Jamaican Blue Mountain, the absolute top of the coffee range at Planet Organic.

'Honey! I'm home!' called Georgie, walking into the living room where the windows were open and a fresh breeze stirred the bird-of-paradise flowers in the vase on the table. Felix called them strelitzas, knew that Colombian drug cartels made use of the hollow stems for smuggling cocaine, and thought that their orange and purple spikes were tremendously erotic.

Beside the vase the periodicals had been arranged in a fan so that the old issue of the *Neurological Digest,* carrying his last article on Lightoller's Syndrome, was casually nestled next to the new *Vanity Fair.* Florence Purim was cooing from the hi-fi.

On the sofa, the *New York Review of Books* was open at Susan Faludi's review of a treatise on fourteenth-century Japanese erotica. Georgie clearly remembered that when she had bought that publication Felix had called it The Sunday Masturbator.

'Felix?' In the bedroom, the bed had been stripped. In the bathroom, the sheets she had put on for them both on Sunday night were bundled up in the linen basket. Georgie was rapidly getting the picture. Felix was expecting a woman. A woman he wanted to impress. A woman he intended to seduce. Flora.

Georgie giggled to herself. She remembered her first visit to Felix's apartment in Chicago, which he had set-dressed with velvety red roses, the same old issue of the *Neurological Digest,* Ella Fitzgerald and an article by Susan Sontag in *Apollo* on some sickly etchings after

Fragonard. She remembered telling her father, who chortled, 'My God! All those sleepless nights when you were a baby were for that? If I'd known, I'd have let you scream.

Should she be miffed that Flora appeared to rate more exotically than she had? Difficult, when she couldn't stop giggling. Ella Fitzgerald and *after* Fragonard! Guilt, begone! When she heard Felix leaping up the stairs she straightened her face and went to recline on the sofa. This was going to be fun.

'Darling!' she greeted him as he dashed through the door.

Felix dropped the laundry. The packet burst on impact with the floor and an assortment of crisply folded linen tumbled out on to the white rug. 'Georgina!' he gasped.

'I'm back, darling!' she purred, folding up the *New York Review of Books* and tossing it aside with a beguiling flourish before holding out her arms.

'Yes you are,' he agreed, stepping awkwardly towards her over the fallen sheets. He tripped as he did so and lost his grip on the small brown paper bag that he had been clutching in his left hand. Six ripe figs fell from it. One of them split as it hit the rug. Another flattened itself in a red smear on a white pillowcase. The rest rolled saucily in different directions across the floorboards.

'Fuck!' said Felix as he stumbled.

'Oh well.' Georgie reached out and dragged

him towards her. 'If we must.'

With relief, Felix decided that action would definitely speak louder than words at that point. He had been thinking of Flora. He saw, smelt and touched Georgie. Nothing turned him on quite as violently as the idea of sex with two women, in any configuration. A red flash temporarily burned out his brain. There was a short, thrilling flurry of kisses, fingers, buttons, buckles, underwear and flying shoes.

As his intelligence circuits reconnected, Felix held Georgie and remembered Flora. He kissed the nearest one of Georgie's nipples, holding her breast with one hand, smoothing her hair with the other and sneaking a look at his watch at the same time. Miss Pforza was due in a quarter of an hour.

'Mmmm. Missed you,' Felix whispered near Georgie's ear.

'Mmmm,' she answered, turning her head slightly. Laughter was bubbling up from somewhere around her diaphragm and she didn't want him to see her face break up.

He licked her ear, his mind racing.

Two and a half years, thought Georgie, and he still can't remember that I can't stand having my ears licked. They had finished up on the floor. One of the runaway figs had halted under the coffee table. It looked succulent. She reached out for it.

'Damn,' Felix murmured, raising himself on his elbows. 'I've just remembered. I bought some lemons as well. I must have left them on the stall. I'll have to go back for them.'

'Lemons for ecstacy,' sighed Georgie, wrapping her free arm firmly around his waist and biting into the fig. He was planning to call Flora as soon as he was outside the building.

'It won't take a minute,' he insisted.

She held the fig to his lips so he was forced to sample it. 'Who needs lemons anyway?' she asked while he was swallowing.

'Lemon zest for an espresso,' he explained. 'I was going to treat myself. Sensual deprivation, you see. Without you.' He rolled over on to one side and kissed her forehead. There was a deep vertical wrinkle between his eyebrows. It was always the first sign that he was nervous.

'Let's both go,' Georgie suggested, sliding to her feet and smoothing down her skirt. 'I love browsing round the market on Saturday.'

'It was terribly crowded,' he tried. In vain. She went to get her knickers from the top of the TV, at the same time ascertaining that his jacket had fallen behind the sofa. The phone was usually in his jacket pocket. While Felix was readjusting his socks she leaned over the back of the sofa and let the phone slip from the pocket while she picked the jacket off the floor and shook imaginary dust from it.

'Thank you, darling,' he said, slipping arms into sleeves one by one. His movements tight with tension, he patted the jacket pockets and found no phone. She gave him a luminescent smile and fondly tucked in a fold of shirt. Rather than make her suspicious, he kissed her hand and decided to find a pay phone outside somewhere.

Hand in hand, they walked towards Portobello Road. Felix set off briskly. Georgie lagged and dawdled and looked in shop windows.

'Let's have a coffee,' he proposed jovially when they at last reached the Brazilian café.

'Let's have it when we get back,' she countered. 'With the lemon zest. Nobody does that better than you.'

It seemed likely that Felix would soon explode with anxiety. Thirty seconds later, while she was lingering by the door of a boutique, he bounded across the road like an antelope leaping for its life and plunged into the flower shop. Towing an agitated florist, he carried on into the workroom at the back of the sales area and disappeared from view.

Ten minutes later Felix reappeared, carrying a vast assembly of roses and foliage. Peachy pink roses, all overblown and unlikely to last until Monday, lashed with expensive wired ribbon to an outlandish frill of palm leaves. He forgot his credit card and the florist had to run after him and return it. She seemed to be irritated by the whole transaction. Felix's face was radiant with relief.

'Welcome home, darling,' he murmured,

crushing the bouquet into Georgie's arms.

* * *

Four people apparently wanted to view Dillon's flat on Saturday morning. He went out early to buy a loaf of bread. His mother had advised him to put a fresh loaf in a warm oven when buyers were expected, to give the flat a wholesome and appetising atmosphere. 'All the smoke from the kebab shop blows straight in your windows,' she warned him. When he first received that advice, Dillon resolved immediately to ignore it.

On Saturday morning, however, a stale smell of the previous night's kebabs seemed to permeate the whole building, so he reconsidered. Freshly baked bread that actually had a smell was thin on the ground around Madagascar Basin. The nearest bread was a shelf-full of sliced loaves wrapped in plastic at a petrol station. The next nearest bread was a stale and scentless old baguette at a corner shop that was waiting for its weekend delivery. The supermarket was too far away. Dillon went back to the petrol station and bought a cheese and bacon croissant, which smelt reasonably attractive if not precisely as wholesome as fresh bread.

Feeling martyred because he had had no breakfast, Dillon put the croissant in the oven and waited for his first viewing at 9.30.

By 10.50, when his bell rang, the smell of the croissant had made Dillon ravenously hungry but he had not dared to eat anything for fear of making the kitchen look more sordid than it was. Nobody had come to see the flat. Nobody had called.

'It's me,' announced Des's voice on his state-of-the art security device, which buzzed as ferociously as a wasp but refused to unlock the door to the street when Dillon pressed the button.

'Bit of a bummer.' Des began a hectic gabble as soon as Dillon opened the street door. 'The thing is, they've blown you out.'

'What, all of them?'

'Well, the first three. Taking a rain-check, decided to go away for the weekend, offered on another place down at Millennium View. Sorry, but what can you do? It's a buyer's market at the moment. Got number four here.' He jerked his head rapidly in the direction of his car, which contained an elderly Asian couple. 'But they're my fault. Bit of a mixed message coming over. They're looking for a shop and a flat together. Flat above. Should have seen the commercial department, not me. I'm doing what I can.' He let his hair flop cutely into his eyes and gave Dillon an appealing smile. 'Gotta run. It's madness in the office Saturdays. Give you a phone in the week.' He whirled back to his car and drove away.

Back upstairs, the powerful smell of browning cheese had obliterated the whiff of stale kebab. Dillon was on his way to the kitchen when the telephone rang. It was Des once more. 'Madam wants you to call her,' he said.

'Flora?'

'She's coming back tomorrow,' Des told him.

'I thought the conference was two weeks,' said Dillon, then realised he was talking to a dead line.

The phone sounded once more. Assuming that Des was courteously finishing their conversation after getting cut off, Dillon answered it by saying, 'What time is Flora coming back?'

'Flora?' said the voice of Smiley-and-Beefy. 'I didn't know she was away.'

'She was at some conference on space clearing in Cornwall.' Dillon assumed he was talking to a friend whose identity would become clear shortly. At least someone wanted to talk to him. Since getting engaged, he had neglected his friends.

'What, again? She went to that last year. Must be bored already with that sad suit she's decided to marry. No surprise there, anyway. She doesn't let the grass grow, does she? I didn't know you knew Flora.'

'I'm the sad suit,' said Dillon with annoyance. 'Who are you and what are you

237

calling me for?'

'Oh God. I'm terribly sorry.'

'OK.'

'I'm jealous, that's all.'

'Don't mention it.'

'Kind of you. It's the Messenger Gallery. So you were going to give Flora River Number Four when you got married?'

'We are getting married. What do you mean, I *was* going to give her River Number Four?'

'Ah.' For the first time, Smiley-and-Beefy seemed embarrassed. 'That was why I was calling. I contacted Merita Halili and I'm afraid she doesn't want to do it. The River series was her first big success, you see, but she did begin making them about five years ago now, and she says she's explored the idea as far as she can and doesn't want to go back to it. She's doing trees now. You're welcome to go round to her studio and—'

'But I know her. I've spoken to her already,' Dillon broke in. 'She was delighted. She said the best thing was to commission through you and she'd—ah—talk to you about it.'

'Oh. You've spoken to her,' said Smiley-and-Beefy, speaking slowly and with caution. 'She is pretty volatile, I suppose. She never said anything to me. When I got in touch with her, she didn't know anything about it.'

'Did you give her my name?'

'Possibly not. Artists don't often want to

know who's buying their work. It can upset them.'

'Well call her back and tell her it's for me,' Dillon instructed him.

No home. No present. Dillon felt that he was failing Flora on all fronts. He needed to do at least another six hours on the Marmeduke Whiskers report to get it ready for Monday morning. He called Flora and left a message with her voicemail. He called Merita Halili and left her a message too. Her English seemed to be getting better and better.

He was hungry enough to eat a chair. In the oven, the former cheese and bacon croissant had cooked down to an oily, dark brown crust. He threw it away and decided to go over the road for a kebab before he started work.

*   *   *

In her bed at 17A, Flora pulled the quilt around her chin and listened to the sound of Saturday. Weird that the London noise was just as loud even though nine-tenths of the people who worked in the City were at home and three-fifths of the East End was still a wasteland of building sites and new property waiting for tenants.

Next door, the people with the Turkish flutes seemed to be rehearsing a new song. On the other side, they were screaming at each other in Bengali. Someone out on the street

239

was trying to start a car whose engine would not fire. Further away some builders were hammering. Summer was just beginning and the holiday jets were circling above the Thames.

From the middle distance, she heard Des roll out of bed, wallow in the shower, crash downstairs to the kitchen, rattle the plates in the dishwasher, pick a fight with the ironing board then rush out of the door and slam it behind him. None of this was what she needed to hear.

Flora was tired. The kundalini serpent had gone down its burrow and was coiled up in a coma somewhere in front of her coccyx. The silver thread connecting her to the cosmic flow felt frayed. Her arms were heavy and her neck was stiff. The phone had been ringing all morning and she hadn't had enough energy to turn it off. Dillon, of course. He never stopped to think that she might not be in the right place to talk to him.

The idea of making Des bring her some tea was forming, but the effort required to decide what kind of tea she wanted was too much. Then she remembered that Des had gone out and the idea of tea dissolved.

She decided to focus on her tiredness and make it disappear. What shape was it? It seemed to be flat. And long. Narrow at the foot end. About the same shape as a coffin lid. It was hard and dense. It was heavier than wood, heavier than MDF, nearly as heavy as stone. Or metal or something. It did not seem at all organic.

What colour was it? It was brown. Red-brown. Very dark red-brown, darker than rust, almost black. Perhaps it had black speckles. Veins, black veins. Maybe it was some kind of marble. The kind people once used for gravestones. It was also cold. It crushed her to the bed, pressed on her chest and slowed down her breathing. Deadly tiredness, in fact.

In her imagination, Flora coated this marble slab with golden light. She created a picture of it bathed in radiance, losing its weight and its coldness. She visualised it floating upwards past her wind chimes in a golden cloud. She made it pass through the ceiling and disappear. She took several deep breaths and sat up. A desire for lime flower tea became identifiable. But Des was still out. For a gay man, he could be very selfish sometimes. Flora flopped back on her pillows.

The next time her telephone rang she forced herself to roll over, shake it out of her bag and answer it. 'I hear you've been away,' said the voice of Smiley-and-Beefy.

'You're having a slow morning then,' she deduced.

'How do you know?'

'You must be desperate if you're trying to talk to me.'

'I had to talk to him. Your man. He told me

you were back.'

'Des told you I was back?'

'No, no, no. Whatsisface. That sad suit you're marrying.'

'Oh, Dillon. When did you speak to him?'

'Just now. He knows my artist, so he says.'

'Dillon knows your artist?' Flora recalled Georgie's undercover identity for the Heartswap affair. She laughed, a little bitterly because that source of entertainment had come to an end. 'Oh, yes, that's right. Well, he thinks he does, anyway.'

'What do you mean, he thinks he knows her? I mean, he does think he knows her. She can't remember him. Did you bring him to the opening or something? I don't remember.'

'He thinks he knows her but he doesn't really,' she explained, making it as simple as she could.

'What's that about? He's not the sort of saddo that has an imaginary girlfriend, is he?'

'Oh yeah, like I'd definitely be hanging out with one of those. No. He's sad, but not that sad.' Flora felt mildly malicious. She felt a little more awake. She sat up and folded her legs in the lotus. 'I can't tell you any more. It's complicated. But believe me, he does think he knows her and really he hasn't any idea.'

A meaty sigh sounded in her ear. 'Speaks for most men nowadays, I suppose.'

'Give me a break.'

'How's your friend?'

'Which friend?' Flora knew perfectly well who he meant. She knew perfectly well that for all Smiley-and-Beefy had the hots for Georgie, he would not be able to remember her name.

'The one you used to work with. The one with the hips. Although I thought she was looking a bit skinny last time I saw her. You know the one. You said she was leaving her boyfriend.'

'They got back together.' Flora took pleasure in telling him.

'Blast,' he responded. 'What are you doing tonight? I suppose you're getting together with your fian-*say* and he's taking you out for champagne somewhere flash with all his disgusting money.'

'I've got one more night of freedom. He thinks I'm coming back tomorrow. I'm going to have dinner with Donna.' With the excitement suddenly drained from their lives, they had made a half-hearted date for the evening. 'We're going to check out this new place that's doing Cambodian cooking with Pacific Rim influences.'

'The Pol Pot, I suppose.'

Flora computed the man's entertainment value. He was a trier. He was new blood. He was tall. He was not known to be gay. He was not actually bankrupt yet. The word was he was something of a shagmeister. 'It's off London Fields. Why don't you join us?' she invited him.

'You and Scary Power Woman?'

'And Des.'

'You and Scary Power Woman and Flop the Fop at the Killing Fields?'

'I'll guarantee your safety,' Flora promised him. She yawned. She stretched her legs. The kundalini serpent raised its head and tasted the air. 'It's called Le Khmer Bleu. Get there about nine.'

CHAPTER SIXTEEN

MAY 2–6

London started to get silly. The winter had gone on for too long. Irrationally, a couple of sunny days gave people hope. For another year they dusted off the belief that living could still be a pleasant experience. Trees, where they could be observed, shook out their clean new leaves. Currents of fresh-smelling vapour swirled in the atmosphere; occasionally, it was possible to think that oxygen rather than hydrocarbon gases was the dominant note in the air.

Those who could cleaned their grimy windows. The tube trains rattled cheerfully through their tunnels. The buses were almost nimble as they lurched round Hyde Park Corner. Near Georgie's flat the Brazilian café put out new parasols and the boutiques redressed their windows with silly floral frocks, bright coloured sandals and mad straw hats.

The torpor of work lifted and people stepped lively in the streets. The surging crowds at crossings got daring and ran red lights for the hell of it. It seemed good to linger, to talk, to be together with other human beings. In the long light evenings people sat out on their steps, their balconies and their patios, wondering if it was going to rain. The clientele of the pubs spilled out on the pavements in heedless chatting mobs, clutching bottles of foreign beer by their necks, while restaurant reservations were forgotten and the theatres were yielded to the tourists. Men put on their shorts. Girls asked their friends if they could really wear vests. The lucky some took holidays. God willing, there would be a summer.

The mid point of the year appeared on the horizon of the diary. The new season caused folk to review their commitments. Have I spent six months with this woman already? Will I last five weeks in Thailand with this man? Can I be seen on the Tahiti Plage with him? Can I face another year with her? The sunshine let people see each other clearly, perhaps too clearly to keep them happy.

Flora saw Dillon and he annoyed her. He was a ball of tension until his goddamn presentation, after which he became a pool of ick. She turned off her phone and complained to Donna that he was all over her like a rash.

Donna saw both Flora and Georgie as inferiors. She always saw Flora that way, although Flora was amusing. Georgie could have worried her. The inferiority was a revelation but a comforting one. Donna felt good when she could feel superior.

Des saw Flora and she irritated him. When people found that her mobile was turned off, she got calls at the house: calls from Dillon, calls from Felix, calls from the man-mountain in the art gallery, even calls from her mother. She didn't want to talk to any of them so she made him do it and lie for her. There had been a lot of work involved in taking Dillon's flat off the market as soon as it had been offered. There was good commission there for him. Some of the punters had given him grief. His lovingly worded details were lying wasted in the file. He didn't care to be foxing around the office keeping up a smokescreen story about the seller changing his mind. Flora could be a real madam sometimes.

Georgie saw Great Lats and thought he was a nice kid but a bit boyish-looking. Particularly his legs. Specifically his thighs. A bit slender, a bit shapely, a bit Michaelangelo's David. Really nice thighs made you think of grabbing hold of them in a flash of passion, of how your hand wouldn't go round their mass very far, of how your fingers would only sink into the flesh a tiny way before getting hold of the solid muscle. And how solid that muscle would be. Yum.

Unfortunately Felix had been quite far back in the queue when God was handing out thighs. Frankly, with the white skin and everything, he sometimes made her think of the chickens at Planet Organic which had given their happy, active lives so that people could hold low-cholesterol dinner parties. But

247

of course, it was not appropriate to evaluate your partner on the same scale of day-to-day recreational lust that you might use to fill up the boring moments at work. There seemed to be a lot of boring moments at Eon plc.

Dillon saw himself and was disgusted. How could he have put so much juice into the idiotic Marmeduke Whiskers business when it amounted to swindling children out of their pocket money? How could he have felt proud when the Shagging Cow told him he'd done a great job? And now that was over, and with any luck he'd never have to go down that road again, his mind was running on that artist woman the whole time. He'd lost her. The phone number she had given him was taken out of service, he couldn't even leave a message. The art gallery man must be thinking that he was a complete prat.

Underneath all the bewilderment and frustration, setting aside the fact that he wanted to give Flora a present, he had been looking forward to seeing her. He liked her. She was fun. She was interesting. She had a great car. OK, she was sexy. Really sexy. And he was engaged. It was all wrong.

To make up for this infidelity of the heart, Dillon tried to be extra nice to Flora, but Flora went off in a frost. She seemed to have one of her instincts about the thing. Dillon was sitting at his desk feeling mildly wretched when the call came.

'We need to talk. Come into my office,' said Donna. No 'Golden Boy'. No 'Wunderkind'. He shivered and complied.

It was obviously as bad as he could have imagined. The whizz-kid from Human Resources was already there. Donna had closed down all the charm circuits and was looking like a total witch.

'Direct Warranty is a company with a commitment to ethical relations in the work place,' Donna began the instant that Dillon's backside made contact with the chair seat. 'Our policy is set out in your contract of employment. Unfortunately you have not been able to maintain the standards of conduct to which you committed yourself when we offered you this job.'

'Someone has made an integrity report about me, haven't they?'

Donna ignored him and half-turned towards the other man. 'Human Resources have devoted a considerable amount of time to planning your career path within the group. There was a strategy for you, Dillon. At a personal level, I regret that you have been unable to fulfil the hopes we had of you.'

'Huh?' said Dillon, not sure he had grasped her meaning. She handed him a thin white envelope.

'We have carried out an internal investigation as is required by the group employment directive in the case of a breach

249

of contract.' Human Resources stepped forward to assure him of this. The movement seemed threatening. 'We have worked out a package for you in line with the circumstances.'

Dillon got it. They were firing him and trying to give him the bum's rush on compensation. Now it was happening, it did not seem such a bad thing.

'Well, goodbye then,' he said cheerfully, shaking Donna's hand. She seemed a mite wrong-footed for long enough to return his matey squeeze.

'My colleague will see you out,' she told him, indicating Human Resources.

'Very kind of you,' Dillon assured them.

At his desk, he found cables disconnected and a new anorak busy with a screwdriver. 'Any files in the system are the property of the company,' Human Resources mentioned. Dillon took his gym bag, his picture of Flora and Merita Halili's catalogue. As he left the building a flush of pure delight spread out from underneath his tie.

Dillon pulled off the tie and stuffed it in his jacket pocket. He took off his jacket and let it hang over one shoulder from one finger. He felt like lunch, a sort of flashy Italian, posh pizza lunch with a lot of rocket and Montepulciano. Flora was not answering her phone as usual. Des was showing properties all day. His mother was girlishly flattered but on her way to a hair appointment with a stylist who had a three-month waiting list. The man in the gallery was delighted. Dangerously close to that dangerous woman, of course, but the best offer Dillon could get. Anyway, he would have masses of time now to give Flora all his attention.

*   *   *

'There is nothing to worry about,' the secretary of the Sir Rudolph Trippitt Retirement Home told Georgie. 'Your father is absolutely fine this morning. But he had a little fall in the night and the doctor wants him to go to hospital for an X-ray to make sure that everything's all right. They'll keep him overnight.'

'Is he in pain?' she asked. The home never called her unless there was at least a 5–1 chance of her father dying.

'Doctor gave him a little something for it,' she was told.

'How did he manage to fall?' Her father's condition made it very difficult for him to move about in bed. Two nurses went in to his room twice a night to turn him from one side to the other and make sure that he did not develop bed sores.

'We don't know,' the secretary admitted.

Georgie loaded a couple of days' work on to Great Lats and called Felix. 'You'll need the

251

car then,' he said magnanimously. 'I'll leave the keys at reception for you.'

Flora seemed to have gone quiet for a few days, but Georgie felt she ought to call her again. 'My father's had a fall,' her message said. 'He'll be in hospital for a couple of days. Seems like a good reason to take some time off. Be in touch when I get back.'

'Of coursh they don't know. Who knowsh anything?' Her father was looking radiantly unconcerned. He had been propped precariously against his pillows, wearing new navy-blue pyjamas with white piping and his initials monogrammed on the breast pocket. Georgie thought he sounded drunk, but alcohol made him pink in the face; his skin was very white and it seemed to have thinned to the point where it was almost translucent. In the veins on the inside of his bad arm the blood showed blue.

'What are you on?' She looked at his chart but could not understand it.

'I don't know, but itsh wonderful,' he giggled. 'Shall I ask for shome for you? She's a shweetie, the little nursh. A poppet. Do anything for me. And they've going to shend me a massheushe.' He turned his head to wink at Linnet, who sat regally at the other side of the bed, fingering her graduated pearls.

'A masseuse?'

'For his bad arm,' Linnet explained. 'Help the circulation. He was getting himself a drink,

252

if you ask me.'

'Why shouldn't I have a drink?' her father asked in a rhetorical tone. 'Doctor hashn't told me I can't. It helpsh me shleep.'

'I didn't know you were having trouble sleeping.'

In his glory days, her father had been said to have the most eloquent eyes in the British cinema. The lids were now wrinkled and the corners red, but they were still the rich, sincere, spaniel-brown that had melted the hearts of the girls who had gone reluctantly to the flicks with their boyfriends in the fifties to see the films full of gunfire and heroics. He turned his eyes on her and let them say that he had trouble doing everything, that every normal process of living was a struggle and on top he made the effort not to let her be aware of that, because he loved her and there was nothing anyone could do about it.

She squeezed his good hand, gently. It felt fragile.

'I bet this is costing you an arm and a leg,' he cackled, nodding at the calm, sweet-smelling room, the professional flower arrangement and the reproduction Regency chairs and table. He had made this joke at six-month intervals ever since she had taken out private health insurance for him, but it always made her laugh.

'I must be getting on. Bye, bye, Georgie. See you later, Alligator,' said Linnet, not without jealousy. She stood up on her stiletto heels, gave the patient a sloppy kiss and tip-tapped out of the ward.

'Read me shomething, shweetheart. They let me bring the book but we sheem to have forgotten the paraphernalia.' At the home, her father had a silver-handled page-turner and a book rest, which made it possible for him to read a book by himself. He still had a taste for the history of the war he had fought with exuberance in real life and a grave face on the screen. The book on his table was two inches thick and probably too heavy for him to lift by himself with his useful hand.

For some years, Georgie had been aware that her father's insouciant take on life was camouflage for the unglamorous qualities of foresight and practicality. The thick book said that he had expected to be in the hospital for some time.

'After the failure of the harvests in the Ukraine in the summer of nineteen-forty . . .' she began. The memory of reading with him in her childhood rushed upon them both. He had worked less and less as he grew older and there was less call for heroes, so every script had been an excitement. Playing opposite his characters, Georgie had read the parts of generals, spymasters and master criminals. It had been a real bore to take drama at school and be simpering Cordelia or idiotic Gwendolyn.

The masseuse bustled in half an hour later. As Georgie left the ward, a nurse called to her and she found herself smoothly ushered into the office of a doctor on the floor above.

'I wanted to have a word with you about your father,' the doctor said, covertly checking the file that lay open on her desk. 'We haven't seen him here for a year or two so I thought it would be a good opportunity to assess his condition.' She paused, searching for words.

'It's not good.' Georgie helped her, wondering how long her father was expected to live.

'No fracture, he was lucky there. But I am concerned about his heart,' the doctor continued, looking at her warily. 'It has had more work to do since . . .'

'Since he's been paralysed.' Because her father's tragedy had probably been the result of medical negligence, no doctor ever liked to talk about it.

'Yes, since then. The arteries can't help so much in moving the blood around the body. There is no real disease, as such, but there are signs that his heart is—wearing out.'

'He's very brave, but he is seventy-nine,' Georgie said, hoping to put over her father's belief that he owed God a death and would be happy to settle up soon.

'In the absence of an actual illness, people can go on like this for a year. Sometimes even two years. You would probably be safe to make plans for Christmas, anyway. All our results will be copied to the matron at . . .' She sneaked another look at the file. 'The Rudolph Trippitt Home. I'll recommend that we see him every month from now on so we can monitor his condition.'

Two years, tops, Georgie translated to herself as she searched for Flat Eric in the car park. Felix had not yet met her father. She told herself that Felix had been too busy to take out the time while he was getting his project up and running. In fact, that was what Felix had told her when she suggested it.

*   *   *

The sun slanted through the windows at 17A and warmed Flora's back while she was meditating. She noticed it and allowed the sensation to slip away like blossom petals falling on a river. It was great to get her head back. Dillon had been crowding her ever since the end of the Heartswap affair. She needed to get away from everybody and be with herself for a while. That insight also was released and allowed to float away.

Serendipity was just your karma working and wishing to remain anonymous. Flora found she had a client to see in the afternoon in Notting Hill. Before she left she checked her messages just in case the client had cancelled. Her meeting was confirmed and

Georgie was going to be away overnight. One should learn to honour the workings of circumstance.

The client was a sensible woman who understood that she could transform her life if she employed Flora to transform her house. Her husband had recently left her. She had already thought of a water feature for the front garden and a lighting scheme for the back. Flora gave her a rhodochrosite crystal to start the healing process and recommended demolishing the utility room in her marriage area and replacing it with a mirrored alcove displaying paired objects. The washing machine was to be moved to the bathroom, which would be painted red to mitigate its tendency to wash helpful people out of the owner's life. The client was delighted with all these ideas and gave Flora a cash deposit on the spot.

Cash made Flora think of shopping. The sun made her think of a new dress, a frivolous flowery sort of dress. Precisely the kind of dress she had in mind was displayed in the window of a boutique which she had to pass on her way home. The shop was quite near Georgie's flat. Very near it, in fact. It was late in the afternoon. Flora went into the shop and asked if they had the dress in her size. They did not, but their sister establishment in Chelsea did and the manageress was eager to keep the shop open until it could be sent over

257

by taxi. Flora accepted a cup of strawberry tea and sat down to wait for her dress to arrive.

Her energy had definitely changed. Events just fitted themselves together as sweetly as the stars fitted into the sky. It was very bad karma to resist the flow of life when it was so strong. One had to learn to accept the lessons that the universe offered.

The dress arrived and fitted perfectly. She couldn't resist trying the pink sandals that matched it. While she was standing in the body of the shop doing a twirl in front of the long mirror, she absolutely felt Felix walk past in the direction of the flat, but she was very good, she did not look up or try to catch his eye. Although she did see a fragment of his head reflected in the corner of the mirror. But there were lots of blond men on the street, it could really have been anyone.

It was when he walked back a few minutes later, while she was seeing how the sandals would look with a much shorter skirt, because she had shorter skirts and she liked to be sure that she could get good value out of her clothes, that she got a really good look at him. He could have seen her looking, that was possible. Flora decided that the sandals would be too much of an extravagance. She kept the dress on and had the happy manageress fold up her old one and put it in a bag.

And there he was, sitting outside the Brazilian café, reading some American newspaper. There was no getting away, he saw her as soon as she stepped out of the shop.

'Hello,' he said.

'Well, hell-*o*,' she said.

'This is a surprise,' he suggested.

'Isn't it?' she agreed.

'Have you got time for a coffee?'

'Why not?' she asked.

The man was suave, 22-carat suave. He could have written the book on suave, which Flora found somehow natural, right and relaxing. She realised that Dillon was suave only occasionally. Felix, despite the debacle of the previous Saturday morning and the fact that she hadn't called him since, was utterly cool, and acting as if he had never even noticed her in that shop. He was behaving, in fact, as if meeting her was nothing more than divine serendipity. Which of course was all that it was.

He said he owed her dinner, which was only the truth, and suggested a charming little restaurant around the corner. He knew the designer of her dress, which was understandable since he had probably walked past it in the shop window every day for a week, but flattering all the same. He never made her feel that he needed any money from Pforza Pharmaceuticals; in fact, he was perfectly comfortable talking about personal things all evening. Flora's personal things, her spiritual beliefs and her love of travel. He knew a lot about Hinduism. He wanted to go to Barcelona to see an exhibition of sculpture from Kerala.

In truth, she did not intend to go back to the flat with him, and when she got there she really did intend to leave. But she liked being there. There was nothing of Georgie in it to feel discordant. It was quiet, it reminded her of Donna's living space. The token resistance was something she sort of fell into once he made his move. They performed the whole thing as exquisitely and with as much respect for tradition as a pair of Thai temple dancers. Then he swept her off her feet and carried her into the bedroom. It was all just perfect. She adored linen sheets.

In the morning he made her an espresso with lemon zest. The way he pared off the skin of the lemon, the precision with which he twisted it and sent a little spray of citrus oil over the black surface of the coffee, the whiteness of his impeccable hands. It was exquisite, a ritual to welcome the new day.

As if preordained they returned to the shop where she had bought her dress and he insisted that she try on the pink leather sandals, for, he implied without the slightest hint of sleaze, his own pleasure as well as hers. And then he bought them for her. Flora felt for the first time in her life that her special unique individuality had been recognised.

CHAPTER SEVENTEEN

MAY 6–8

The goat stood in the centre of the lane, chewing on a hank of vegetation. It was a young one, its white sides contrasting smartly with its brown back, its muzzle a fresh, pale pink. The spiky horns looked as if they had never been used. Beneath its dainty hooves a ridge of grass grew up the centre of the crumbling Tarmac, showing that very few vehicles ventured up this gentle Somerset hillside.

'Shoo! Piss off!' Des suggested, leaning out of the window of his car and waving his arm.

He sounded his horn, an effete, urban bleat which disappeared in the wild hedges that enclosed the narrow track in walls of blackthorn and foxgloves. The goat cantered a few paces uphill, away from the car, then turned around and lowered its horns.

'Oh, for Christ's sake.' The goat appeared to change its mind, pulled up its head and resumed chewing. It was still dead-centre in the lane. Des sounded his horn again. The goat lowered its head again and made a practice run at the car.

'Stupid fucking animal.' Des stopped the car and opened his door. The bitter wind from the downs stung his cheeks. It was a tempestuous day. Huge clouds bowled across the sky, randomly threatening a storm.

The goat skipped sideways and butted the car door with all its weight and the advantage of the slope. There was a loud bang as its skull rammed the coachwork and a squeal from Des as the edge of the door slammed into his leg.

'You STUPID fucking animal,' he repeated, in pain. The car door was dented. The goat tripped around in a circle and resumed its stance in the centre of the road. 'Fuck off! Just fuck off!' He clapped his hands, another sound that was instantly muffled by the surrounding plant life and whipped away by the wind. The goat put its head on one side and appraised him with its diabolical yellow eyes.

Des knew more about goats than most people imagined. The more he advanced on this one, the more aggressive it was likely to become. He was not at all sure that his insurance covered the car for assaults by ungulates. As it was probably his parents' goat, the best thing to do would be to catch it and take it home with him. Most goats were principally interested in eating. He had half a giant chocolate chip cookie in the car.

'Here, have some choccy bikkie,' he tempted the animal, holding out the cookie. The goat rushed forward, snatched the biscuit, made a pass at him with its horns and retreated to its original position before he could make a move to grab it.

'Sod you!' said Des, losing his temper. He made a run at the goat, a move that it had not anticipated. Alarmed, it bounded sideways to the left. He leaped forward, holding the middle of the road, his arms widespread. In panic, the goat jumped as high as it could to the right and tangled itself in the hedge.

'Gotcha!' Dodging the horns, Des embraced the goat around the top of its legs and dragged it triumphantly out of the blackthorn. In the process of climbing out of the hedge he fell straight into the ditch but kept hold of his prize. The goat, which had consumed the half-cookie in one gulp, snatched a good mouthful of grass as he staggered to his feet, causing him to fall over again. The animal struggled and tried to stab him with its horns.

'Make my day,' he growled, heaving them both back on to the road. Which was empty. His car was not where he had left it. It had rolled back down the slope and run into the ditch on the corner, somehow breaking off the driver's door as it went.

'Buggeration.' Keeping a firm grip on the goat, Des turned around and walked the remaining fifty yards to his parents' farm, following the clashing of windchimes and the smell of the herd. What exactly was supposed to be so restful about a weekend in the country he did not understand.

'Wowie!' his father called out from the

smithy as Des shouldered through the dilapidated gate and into the farmyard. This was not an exclamation but his family name. At a dewpond on the downs twenty-five years earlier, Des had been baptised Worldpeace. They called his sister Endofhunger. Growing up, they had been known as Wowie and Endie.

'Love, son.' Des put down the goat and tried not to flinch at the smell as his father gave him a hug and a kiss. 'Wowie's come home for Beltane,' his father called joyfully into the barn where Des saw his mother and sister were standing by a row of aluminium vats.

'Beltane? I thought that was last week.'

'Only in the Anglo-Saxon calendar,' reasoned his father earnestly. 'When they invaded Wessex they tried to stamp out the Druidic religion by imposing their own Germanic names on the ancient Celtic festivals. So Beltane became May Day.'

'Beltane will be a little late this year,' his sister quipped, giving him a resigned smile. 'Dad forgot to cover the bonfire and it rained.'

'Better celebrate Beltane a couple of weeks late than have polythene stuffing up the ditches.' His father started blustering. 'Do you know how long it takes for polythene to biodegrade?'

The women finished their work in embarrassed silence. In the close air of the barn the general stench of goat was almost smothered by the rancid smell of fermenting milk. His mother lifted a plastic crate on to a stack already loaded on their lopsided cart. The crates contained cartons labelled: 'Unpasteurised Organic Goat's Milk from Sanctuary Farm, Somerset. Please dispose of this Container without harming Our Planet.'

'Like the technology,' he complimented his family, indicating the assembly of silver pipes and apparatus that spread over the bare earth floor randomly littered with old goat shit and broken flower pots.

His mother rolled her eyes in exasperation. 'They made us buy it, the drongos at Min of Ag. Or they were going to take away our licence. Bastards. What a rip-off.'

'I've knackered my car,' he told them, not wanting to get her started on one of her rants about the Ministry of Agriculture.

'Cosmic! So have we,' said his father jovially, indicating the aged Land Rover propped against the old oak tree on its jack and a pile of firewood. The goat was now on top of the vehicle, poised on its hind legs, trying to reach the tree's leaves. 'I'm just about to see what I can do with it.' As far as Des could make out, his father was proposing to weld a broken axle.

His parents looked more weather-beaten every time he saw them. Their bodies, bundled in thick clothing from the charity shop in the nearest town and tied around the vanished sites of their waists with short lengths of twine knotted together, grew thicker as their cheeks became more deeply lined. Each year their hair moved more towards salt than pepper and it curled wildly from their foreheads, tied down with headbands that his mother wove from the sheep's wool that she collected from the hedgerows and coloured with herbal dyes. His sister looked nearly as old as their parents. She had some children, who were usually somewhere about the place, and a partner, who divided his time between this homestead and his own commune.

In addition to the goats, there were about three dogs, a family of feral cats, various poultry and a visiting population of convalescent wildlife foisted on the household by a neighbouring vet. The horse, a survivor of their original intention to work the land without machinery, completed the farm's livestock. His mother coaxed it into its bridle and collar and they set off down the lane. As they approached the gate the goat saw its opportunity, leaped from the Land Rover and sprang in front of them to freedom.

'Don't worry about it,' his mother advised. 'It's a billy, isn't it? I expect it was one we liberated.'

'Liberated?'

'They're no use, they don't give milk. We might keep one for stud every now and then but the rest had to go to the abattoir. We

266

couldn't get our head round it really. And we had to pay and they kept putting up the price. And then we'd have to sell the meat. So we liberate them now. It's much nicer. They just run away and live wild.'

'Oh.' Des made a sincere effort not to sound judgemental, although he thought it was most likely that the neighbouring farmers, who were inclined to regard his parents as two-legged vermin, shot the liberated billy goats on sight and fed them to their dogs.

When they reached the car his mother looped a chain from the horse's collar around the front bumper and suggested that he get in and steer while she led the horse forward. It began to rain, heavy drops thudding on the car roof. They had an argument while Des undid the chain and fixed it to a part of the car that he felt was more capable of bearing the full weight of the vehicle.

'You always have to know best,' his mother snapped.

'It is my car,' he insisted.

To his surprise, his mother leaned against the horse's shoulder and burst into tears. As if in sympathy, the rain began pelting down in sheets from the blackened heavens.

'Mum?' Yelling into the tempest, he put his arms around her then remembered she did not like to be called by any variation on the word Mother. 'Sarah? What is it? I didn't mean to upset you.'

267

'It isn't me,' she shouted. 'It's your father. You're breaking his heart.'

'Not this again,' muttered Des, feeling wretched. Rain was streaming down the back of his neck and funnelling down his backbone. His T-shirt was soaked.

'Of course you have the right to live your own life,' his mother wailed, wiping her nose on her sleeve. 'You were brought up to believe in the beauty of individual freedom. He has tried to accept it, he really has. But he can't help it.'

'Neither can I,' Des bawled in reply. The ditch was filling rapidly with muddy water. 'I am the way I am, I can't change. I don't want to change, I'm happy.'

'But what about us? Your father can't see any justification for the way you live. It's completely against his morality.'

'I'm sorry if I've hurt you, really I am. But it is my life, I have to make my own choices.'

'You seem so different. We look at the pictures of you and Endie and we can't see you any more. You're so profit-oriented, such a bread-head. Like all you care about is your car and your clothes, you know. How can we feel proud of you, knowing what you're doing in London?'

'I know you don't like me being an estate agent.' Des made a supreme effort of tolerance and prayed that the car was still driveable and would take him back to the city in time to go out that evening and forget this nightmare. The ditch was gurgling and gushing; water swirled up to the sills of his car. 'But it's all I can do. You didn't want me to get any exams . . .'

'Indoctrination! Thought control! You learned things at home they'd never teach you in school.'

'Yes I did,' Des assured her, thinking of the night of the magic mushroom harvest when he was eight years old and had to call ambulances for eleven people before hitching a ride to school. 'But I haven't got any straight qualifications so I have to earn a living somehow. People do need places to live, you know.'

'You were taught that property is theft,' wailed his mother.

The horse sighed, straddled its back legs and pissed lengthily, adding its steaming puddle to the flood spreading over the road. Ditch water eddied into the back of the car. Des was soaked to the skin. He observed that his Diesel jeans were ripped and the goat had bitten a chunk out of his T-shirt. Both he and the car were covered in mud and would smell terrible when they were dry.

His mother was now going to guilt-trip him silently for hours and there would be lentil soup and goat's cheese for lunch. He wanted a hot bath and a strawberry Martini. He had a song on the brain; a loop tape of it was running in his head: *Beltane will be a little slow to start, a little slow reviving the music it made in my heart.*

*   *   *

'It's eight o'clock, sweetheart.' Felix prepared to get out of bed. Georgie had rolled to the far edge of the mattress. Lying face-down, she was idly drawing patterns on the carpet with one finger.

'I don't like Mondays,' she said. 'I'm going to chuck a sickle.'

'You had a day off last week,' he reminded her, heading for the bathroom.

'That was for my father.' Georgie waited for him to ask how her father was. Felix had been aware of his illness for more than three days and she was still waiting for the question. She had chosen to wait, rather than do what she usually did and run the basic emotional scenario past him so he knew that she expected him to respond. She was curious to know how long it would take before Felix picked up that she was feeling sad because her father was going to die. Her curiosity was not innocent. She was feeling some pain.

From the bathroom came the noise of Felix's electric toothbrush. Then the noise of the shower. He reappeared in a bathrobe, scrubbing his hair with a towel. 'Employers don't like family problems,' he pointed out.

270

'Or illness. They like people they can trust.'

'People without lives,' Georgie agreed. 'They like robots. Or zombies. And if you aren't a zombie or a robot when you start work, they get you modified. They should hire your toothbrush, it would be kinder.'

'That's childish,' he told her, pulling open his wardrobe and looking at his clothes. 'You're very highly paid. They have a right to expect a high level of commitment.'

'So because you're not very highly paid, the hospital shouldn't expect a lot of commitment from you?'

'It doesn't work like that. You know it doesn't. This isn't like you, Georgina.' He pulled out a new shirt and some trousers still in the dry cleaners' bag, then selected underwear from a drawer.

'I don't feel like me,' she hinted.

'If you're having motivation issues, you should handle them.' This instruction was issued from inside his shirt as he was pulling it over his head. Felix was unstoppable when he felt that his security was threatened.

'They told me my father was going to die. Two years, tops; that's what the consultant said.'

Felix's head emerged indignantly from the shirt and he flicked the soft collar into its place. 'And you're reacting by withdrawal? You always do that, you know. Any little stress and you just throw in your cards and resign. You put the pillow over your head and hope it will all go away. That's not the right way to deal with life. It doesn't solve any problems.'

Georgie discovered that she really despised the way he stepped into his trousers. First one leg, then the other. Always the same. It was gross. 'I'm sorry,' she said sarcastically. 'All these years I've been doing life wrong. Thank you so much for showing me that. I really didn't know. I didn't even realise that my father dying was a problem. Of course, it makes it much worse that I love him and he's always been there for me. How could I have messed up like that?'

'This isn't about your father,' Felix informed her. Her sarcasm had floated over his head. Georgie thought that the way he buckled his belt was just repulsive. 'It's about your mother. Everything about you is to do with your mother abandoning you. I can't believe you're still in denial about it. You're nearly thirty, you should get a grip.'

'OK. I'll work on that,' she assured him. Again her irony missed by a mile. It was as if he was operating inside some force-field that repelled all criticism.

'Enjoy your day,' he advised her, bending down to give her a dry kiss. 'If you insist on putting your whole career on the line, it might as well be worth it.'

When she was alone, Georgie got up and wandered around the flat, breathing the

272

untainted air. To some degree, Felix was right. She was in cocoon mode, she didn't even want to get dressed. From the Brazilian café she ordered in a large filter coffee with cinnamon toast. When she had finished that, she ran a deep bath and wallowed in it for half an hour, reading some ridiculous book she'd bought at the airport in Chicago and had to hide from Felix's scorn ever since. Her toenails needed painting. She violated his hi-fi and found a classical music station. Thinking of Chicago, she decided to e-mail some old friends and sat down at the computer.

The receipts were on the keyboard. The large bill from the boutique, with the details hand-written in lime green ink and the small credit card slip with Felix's signature etched with the same pen. '1 pr pink strap Joan & David sandals, size 6.' The price was impressive. The date was Saturday. The credit card slip even noted the time, 11.37 a.m. Joan & David size 6 was just about big enough for Flora. She had dear little feet.

So that was why he was acting weird. More weird than usual. Or perhaps, in her vulnerable condition, Felix just seemed to her to be weirder than he normally was. Something was different, that was certain. Georgie was accustomed to Felix being mentally absent for much of the time. She had always assumed that he was preoccupied with his work, and resisted her unworthy instinct to feel hurt. Since her father, since Friday, she had sensed a change. He had been getting to her. Was it him? Was it her? Was it fallout from the Heartswap foolishness? Whatever the reason, it was nothing to get out of proportion.

The morning had been lazed away most effectively. It was nearly one o'clock, the hour of the clinic lunch break.

'Darling, I'm sorry I was so ratty this morning,' she told him on the phone. 'You're right, I'm having to deal with all kinds of stuff that I don't want to know about. Forgive me for stressing you out at the start of the week like that. I will get a grip on it, I promise.'

'OK.' He sounded bewildered, as well he might. 'What are you doing?'

'Just catching up,' she reassured him. 'Filing our receipts, great world-changing stuff like that.'

'Oh.' Now he was disappointed. Well, Georgie said to herself, how about that? He actually wanted me to find that bill. Men are such martyrs to their guilt.

'Flora,' she giggled into the inevitable voicemail. 'I hope those sandals give you blisters.'

*   *   *

'I'm looking for a woman with a metallic blue Audi coupé,' Dillon told the man who was the

274

brother of a mate of the man he had met in the J Bar a couple of days earlier.

'Aren't we all?' the man said, winking at him.

'It's not what you think. It's business.' God, I sound pathetic, Dillon told himself.

'Of course it is.' The man winked again. He was undersized all round, short, thin and small-featured. Only his teeth were large, and they seemed about to crowd each other out of his undershot jaw. His leather jacket had more presence than he had but it looked too large for him and flapped from the shoulders.

'Your brother's friend said . . .'

'We have the exclusive dealership in London. There's a waiting list for 'em. So we keep the book. With the names in. Names of people who're waiting.'

'So her name might be in the book?'

'Her name, her address and her phone number.' The man winked again, then half-turned away from Dillon and looked out over the river. They were drinking in some faux-naval place on the South Bank that was done up with fluttering yacht pennants, white rope knots displayed in mahogany-veneer frames and a gratuitous quantity of brass fittings.

The man turned back to him. 'So what are you? City bonus type?'

'You could say that.'

'Wondrous with wonga, eh?'

'I guess.'

'You in a hurry for this?'

'I've been trying to get hold of her for days. She's disconnected her mobile and I haven't got an address.'

The narrow eyes appraised him expertly. 'I'd have to do it after the boss went home. Have to change my plans for the evening.'

'That would be extremely kind.'

'Extremely dodgy, more like. I'm not supposed to mess around with his paperwork. It's confidential.'

Dillon nodded his appreciation and tried to make the job seem less demanding. 'It's this year's registration.'

'It would have to be. This year's car, innit? But this year is almost over as far as the motor trade goes. This year's reg could be any time in the past ten months.'

Dillon ceased to struggle and waited to hear the price.

'A monkey'd do it. Half a ton,' the man said. 'And half up front.'

Important not to agree too fast, in case the man deduced that he could have asked more and therefore started to resent the whole deal. Dillon drained his glass before he said, 'OK. Don't go away.'

He walked around the corner to an ATM machine, withdrew £250 and returned with a spring in his steps.

'Cheers,' the man said, stowing the notes in the inner pocket of his jacket. 'A bit of a babe, is she?'

'Yes she is,' Dillon told him, thinking of how the blue of the car picked up the grey of her eyes, and the extraordinarily lovely movement she made when she put her arm on the window sill. 'She's a sculptor,' he continued in self-justification. 'I want to commission something from her.'

'She should be pleased to hear from you, then,' the man observed with a smirk. Something pinched and bitter had come into his face. He was fishing for information so that he could have more grounds for envy. While he was finishing his drink Dillon thought about offering him another. It would be courteous but it would commit him to spending more time with someone who wanted to be able to resent him mainly for knowing a woman with a new Audi coupé. There would be no point in explaining that he had just lost his job, that his girlfriend was turning moody, his flat was a rat-hole and he had no friends. In this man's eyes he was guilty of being an overprivileged arsehole and nothing would change that.

Dillon had become accustomed to being envied. There was nothing rational about it. Kids at school who had slagged him off for doing his homework then envied his exam results. People at university whose goal was to get wasted whenever possible envied him his degree. His father envied him because his mother was proud of him. All those goons at

Direct Warranty had envied him because he was Donna's golden boy. Even Donna had envied him when he pulled the Marmeduke Whiskers project out of the hat; any demonstration of creativity made her jealous. As if the Whiskers project was the Sistine Chapel.

'I've got to go,' he told the man, implying that a deal was a deal, a drink was a drink and real men were always moving on. 'I'll give you a phone tonight, yeah?'

Driving towards his home was difficult. He did not want to get there. A single day spent alone in the place had been a revelation. It was a pit, a tip, a hole. He hated it. Walking up the stairs was going to be like walking into hell. The stain on the bathroom wall oppressed him every time he saw it. The kitchen was like the cave of some loathsome mythical monster waiting to choke him with its poisonous breath. The living room was a wasteland. The bedroom was a swamp of despair ready to engulf him. Extraordinary that he had needed Flora to rescue him from the place. She would probably say she had put him in touch with his feelings about it.

He turned towards Des's office, parked illegally and strode to the door with a resolute face.

'Des is out with some buyers. I'm the senior negotiator, can I help you?'

She was a rounded, pleasant woman in her

late thirties, wearing several Victorian rings on her left hand with a wide wedding band. He trusted her.

'I've been on the market two weeks and haven't had a single viewing. I'm getting married and I want to find a place for both of us. I was thinking perhaps the price was a problem.'

'It's a seller's market at the moment.' The senior negotiator frowned and went to the old-fashioned filing cabinet at the back of the office. He gave her his address. Finding nothing in the files, she went back to her desk.

'I'll have to search the database,' she told him. 'I'm sorry about this. It looks as though your details may have been mislaid.' Hesitantly, she pecked at the keyboard with one finger. 'Ah! Here you are! You're under offer.'

'No I'm not. I can't be. Nobody's been round. Des hasn't spoken to me. It's wrong. It's a mistake.'

'Well, then it must be,' the woman agreed in a stricken voice. 'I'm terribly sorry. Des has so much on his plate at the moment. You poor man, you must have been wondering what on earth was going on. The price looks fine to me. We had someone in this morning looking for two double beds and a balcony. Thank goodness you came in. Let me make some calls. Have we got your keys? Are you in this evening?'

'I can be,' Dillon assured her. He went back to his car like a new man.

At seven, he called the man, who sounded embarrassed.

'You sure it was blue?' He phrased the question so that it sounded as if Dillon was entirely responsible for his own disappointment. 'There was only one blue coupé sold this year and that was to a leasing company. She married, this sculptor?'

'Maybe she is, I don't know.'

'Well, if you really want to go there, the blue coupé belongs to Eon Leasing. Part of the Eon Group. They probably have a couple of thousand cars in London.'

The idea that Merita Halili might be married was troublesome. Dillon decided he wanted to go there, if only for peace of mind.

'They wouldn't tell me who had the car, would they?' he hazarded.

'If I was you, I'd give 'em a call and say you're Customer Services at Audi and you gotta do a product recall.' The man had seen a way to deserve the balance of his five-hundred-pound fee. 'It's almost new, the blue one. Couple of months, that's all. Say it's the steering. That'll be a safety issue. Ask if you can send a mechanic round to check it. They'll probably give you the driver's address.'

'You think so?' Dillon was not convinced. He had never been a good liar.

'Yeah, no worries. Tell you what, I've got a

contact at Audi. I'll get you an ID.'

'Really?'

'A carpet'll do it,' the man proposed.

'A carpet instead of half the monkey?' said Dillon quickly, seeing an opportunity to be £50 ahead of the game.

'Awright. It's a deal.' Since the man had been expecting him to renege on the half-monkey, he reckoned that this would put him up £200.

'Brilliant. Cheers.' Dillon's heart suddenly soared. Then his doorbell rang and a shamefaced Des appeared with the first of a procession of potential buyers for his flat.

CHAPTER EIGHTEEN

MAY 9

The Eon Group occupied the upper half of a steel-coloured tower that dominated the award-winning Caraway Spit development on the north bank of the Thames. The original Spit was a flat headland that stuck out into the river. Building was only just beginning on the remainder of its land mass so the Eon Tower stuck up like a single fang in a monstrous jaw.

The sky was a solid grey, reflected darkly from the tower's colourless cladding. The river lapped inkily at its stone-built banks. A violent wind scoured the Spit, lashing the new trees planted in the concrete until it seemed inevitable that their trunks would snap.

Against the force of the blast, Dillon pushed the car door open and felt his hair whipped back from his forehead. The building's car park was full. The streets were empty, waiting for the cars that would be driven by the people who would be working by next year in the towers that would have been raised from the surrounding clay. At that point, all that Dillon could see were cranes delving in the clay, a few trucks growling to and fro, and double red lines at the roadside that claimed that this was an important arterial route prioritised for buses and through traffic on which no decent citizen would even think of leaving a car.

A notice attached to a pole and anchored in a block of concrete had blown over. Lying on the pavement, it informed him that the patch of road on which he had stopped had been designated for the use of motor-cycle couriers only. Inappropriately parked vehicles would be clamped and ransomed only for a release fee of £90. Dillon refused to care. Rules were made to be broken. He saw no couriers. He saw no traffic wardens. He was on a mission.

As he struggled to the doors, leaning forwards into the wind, a train was gliding to a halt at the far side of the building. The Docklands Light Railway stopped at Caraway Spit only for the benefit of Eon Group employees. Several hundred of them stepped from the carriages and shuffled towards their workplace like a nation of the undead, ready to take over the mid-morning shifts.

'I'd like to see someone in Eon Leasing,' he informed the desk guard.

'You don't have an appointment,' the guard deduced.

'I'm from Audi,' he responded, flashing his pirated ID card at a safe distance from the man's bi-focals. 'We're doing an urgent product recall. It's a safety issue.'

'Give me a minute,' the guard requested, picking up one of his telephones.

The Eon Tower was a small town on its

own. Two floors of commercial units began at ground level, offering food, painkillers, print media, lavatory paper, cards, dry-cleaning, a nail bar and a flower shop—essentials only, no purchasing decisions tempting enough to distract the workers and waste their time. Above these was a floor of eating options— fast food, bistro, gourmet, coffee shop. Next came the clinic, the beauty spa and the fitness suite. The conference facility took floors six and seven. Above that, the offices began.

The air was soft and silent. The thrashing trees outside the glass walls looked absurd because they made no noise. The sky might have been cheap wallpaper. A pair of geese flew past as if they were part of a rudimentary early animation. The river was invisible, sunk below the concrete horizon.

From the rear doors the silent crowd of mid-morning shift workers entered and made towards the doors of the lifts, which hissed apart to swallow them. A single figure emerged from the last doors to open and battled upstream against the flood of bodies until she stood alone and dazed in the middle of the floor.

She looked a little like someone Dillon thought he knew. Afraid of staring, he turned away and checked her image on the security monitor above the desk. With a hurried stride, she marched off towards the shopping mall. No, nobody he knew.

Georgie fled to the back of the corner shop. From there she could peek around the news stand without looking too obvious. Yes, it was Dillon. What the hell was he doing here?

Looking for you, said her instinct.

As if, she retorted. No way.

Yes way, her instinct insisted.

Why? she asked, feeling the onset of panic. Since you know so much, what's he looking for me for?

What do men usually go on mad quests for women for? It's the mojo working. The old rock'n'roll. That old black magic. The same old voodoo.

Crap! Georgie had to put her hand to her mouth to stop herself speaking aloud.

I didn't deserve that, her instinct argued. You started it. You and Flora. You women always start it. You let the genie out of the bottle. You open the box. You picked the bloody apple.

Get out, Georgie warned it. If you're trying to lumber me with five thousand years of sexual guilt, you've picked the wrong girl.

All the same, her instinct said craftily, that's what he's here for.

No it isn't. It's business, it must be, pleaded Georgie. He's come to see somebody else in the building on business.

And I'm the queen of Romania, suggested her instinct. As if you weren't hoping he'd come after you.

I was not!

You were too. Ever since you changed your phone number. You can't fool me, I'm your instinct. I know what goes on in that woman's heart of yours.

I am not a woman, I am a person, Georgie informed her instinct sternly. My brain does the thinking. My heart is just a pump. And you are nothing but a disgusting bag of hormones and cultural conditioning, so don't you tell me who I am and what I'm feeling.

It's a tough job but somebody's got to do it, her instinct sniggered.

Right. That's enough. I'm way too busy to waste time arguing with you. I'm going over there and I'm going to ask him what he's doing here. That'll sort this out.

You're right there.

It was maddening the way her instinct always thought it knew everything. It was as bad as Felix sometimes.

That wasn't me! I didn't say anything! Her instinct was laughing.

As she approached the reception desk the guard put down his telephone and said to Dillon, 'Can you take a seat, sir? Someone's coming down to see you but they're tied up for a few more minutes.'

Taking a deep breath, Georgie stepped in front of Dillon as he turned away towards the black leather couches by the glass wall. 'Are you looking for me?' she asked simply. It

286

didn't seem too political to smile. In fact, it was impossible not to smile. She could almost have danced as well.

'Uh?' He was looking puzzled. 'I'm sorry, I . . . oh. Oh! Oh, my goodness! Is that you? Merita Halili?'

'Yes.' Georgie found that her mouth would not behave. 'Yes and no,' she managed eventually.

'I was looking for you,' Dillon told her.

You see? Was I right or was I right? demanded Georgie's instinct.

'This is great!' he continued.

You see! You see! Georgie decided that it was time to be brave and deal with both of them.

'No it isn't. Not really,' she announced. 'Look, we should talk.'

'Oh, yes,' Dillon agreed. If anything, she looked even more exciting in this smootheddown disguise. He found that he was clasping one of his hands with the other to stop himself ruffling her hair.

'It's complicated,' she promised him. 'Maybe we should sit down.'

'OK.' They moved to the benches and sat. The way it worked out, they were sitting so close that their knees nearly touched. Georgie thought of moving back but did not want to seem rejecting. Dillon thought of moving back but did not want to acknowledge that there was any reason why they should not have been

287

sitting close together in the first place. So they stayed put.

Georgie took a deep breath and began. 'Your fiancée . . .'

'Yes. Yes. Flora.' For a moment there, while he was stopping himself noticing the way the deep breath caused movement under her silk blouse, Flora's name had slipped away like a frightened fish. Very strange.

'Flora. She's got a friend, hasn't she? Called Georgina?'

'Why, yes she has. How do you know that?'

'Because I'm Georgina.' OK, this was it. Time to get real, finally. 'And we were . . . we had . . . it was . . . it was a sort of a game.'

'You mean you're not Merita Halili?'

'No. She's a real person, a real sculptor . . .'

'I know, I saw her things. In that exhibition in that gallery.'

'Flora and I went there. I had the invitation in my bag. My other bag. And when I ran my car into yours I kind of lost it and her name was there so I used it.'

Dillon's mind was reluctant to scale the necessary height of fantasy. 'So she really doesn't want to make another blue glass thing?'

'I don't know what she wants. I don't know her. She's not part of this.'

'Oh.'

'Flora and I had a bet.' A bet was a recognisable concept. He'd be able to get his

288

mind around that, surely? 'With Donna. You know Donna?'

'Oh yes. She introduced us. I used to work for her. Donna the prima donna.' Dillon felt a shiver of foreboding. If Donna was mixed up in this, it was probably bad.

'You *used* to work for her?' It was off-topic, but Georgie had to know.

'I got fired last week.'

'I'm sorry.'

'I'm not. Go on, you and Flora had a bet with Donna?'

'When she found out we were getting married . . . because, I was engaged too, you see.'

'You were engaged?' Really bad. He was never wrong where Donna was concerned.

'I am engaged, what am I saying? Flora and I are both engaged, you see . . .'

Badder than bad. Dillon found himself suddenly up to his neck in gloom. While Georgie expounded the basics of the Heartswap adventure, putting much emphasis on Flora's belief that he was a loving and faithful partner, he heard her as if from the next room.

'So you see,' she concluded, 'it was a game. I was pretending to be Merita Halili. I'm really just a fund manager. You did everything absolutely right. You were great, really. And it's over now, we called it off.'

'That's awful,' he said in a mild voice. His

289

face was white and his eyes were black.

'That's what we thought. So we decided to stop.'

'Well,' he got up without warning, wavering a little as if his knees were weak. 'Thanks for putting me straight.'

'I'm sorry,' she told him. 'I really am sorry.' At that instant, there was no one in the world she would have wanted to hurt less.

'Yes. Well. I'd better go.'

He stumbled as he turned, then got control of his legs and walked to the revolving door. Georgie thought he was about to be sick.

Outside the building, a pair of overweight, shaggy-haired men in jeans were fixing a wheel clamp to the Saab. When he saw them, Dillon instantly lost the desire to throw up. His yell was loud enough to be heard over the wind and through the thick glazing of the hallway. The revolving door spun violently as he jumped out to save his car. Behind the desk, the reception guards looked up and watched the ensuing argument with one hand poised over the alarm button.

Faced with the force of Dillon's rage, the clampers soon decided that they were not paid enough to be heroes and drove away in an old white van. The door whirred again and ejected Dillon in the hallway. His face was now white with rage.

'Let me get this straight,' he said to Georgie, who had been sitting on the bench without moving, paralysed by self-inflicted shock. 'You and Flora decided to run some kind of fidelity test on me? Because that's the most disgusting, the most cynical . . .'

I told you, Georgie's instinct reminded her. I told you someone was going to get hurt. I told you, but you never listen.

*   *   *

'They pick the grapes by night, so that they're cool, and then let them ferment at a really low temperature to keep that almost-scented taste. The vineyards are in a region that is also famous for its almond orchards. I always think there's a hint of the almond blossom in there.' Felix gazed at his glass, then at Flora, implying that she was as exquisite as all the almond orchards of Catalonia.

Rain was spotting the windows of 'their' restaurant, just a few steps away from the flat where the linen sheets were smooth and fresh and waiting for them.

'You are involved, aren't you?' Flora asked him, pulling in her hands and feet before he could make contact with any of them.

'Not really,' he replied.

'Felix,' she said sternly, 'I know you are involved.'

'You're an intelligent woman,' he told her. 'You must have noticed that someone had left her things in my flat. I noticed you didn't leave

291

anything. Anything tangible, at least.'

'The Epilady in the shower was a bit of a giveaway,' she assured him with an impish grin. 'And I couldn't really see you painting your nails Kensington Rose every weekend. Chelsea Red is more your colour. But the fact is, Felix, I've always known what your situation is.'

'I'm intrigued,' he admitted, deciding that since she did not seem to be taking a judgmental tone he was already home and dry, and this part of the conversation was therefore just a formality. Some women liked to invent a little emotional complexity just to add spice. He appreciated that. 'How do you know what you say you know?'

'Your fiancée. Georgie.'

'Georgina,' he corrected her. It was no part of the strategy to go into a new relationship with a carry-over of gender issues from the old one.

'I call her Georgie. We're friends. Been friends for ages.' And she zipped through the edited highlights of the Heartswap affair, glossing over the unladylike question of a wager and implying that it had been all one to Georgie whether Felix cheated on her or not. She chose to leave the question of her real-life occupation for later. When he was in deeper. Just in case he was not comfortable with a woman who ran her own business.

'Clever,' he said when he had the picture. He did not seem deeply moved, only amused.

292

'And whose idea was it? This other friend? Donna?'

'Georgie, mostly,' Flora asserted. 'Do you ever think she has a kind of obsession about fidelity? It seems like it's a really big issue for her. We decided it was some kind of revenge trip. Did she ever talk to you about her history with men?'

'Not really,' he said sadly. 'She was always withholding, it seemed to me.'

'Well, it wasn't good.' Flora admitted this as if it were a great wrench to her loyalty. 'It wasn't just one Mr Wrong. It was Mr Bad, Mr Worse and Mr You-Must-Be-Fucking-Joking. Before she went to Chicago, she was getting dumped more often than nuclear waste.'

'That's so sad,' he commented, concealing the opinion that he was enjoying a lucky escape. 'She's really a wonderful person.'

'And she was strange about the man I was with. Maybe she was jealous of me and wanted some rationale for coming on to him. It was all getting much too weird. I had to get out of it, I was going crazy.'

'And where does that leave you?'

'Me? Me and Dillon, you mean. Oh, we were over anyway. It was a mistake, we both knew that. I think maybe this was something we had to go through to find that out, you know?'

'That's how I feel about Georgina. She's changed since we've been back in London.'

'She'll never change,' Flora assured him. 'But I have hopes of Dillon. He's dealing with his own stuff now. I must have been put in his life to show him that he needed to do that. We'll always be friends, I know we will. I think that's important, don't you?'

'Not always,' said Felix sagely. The baggage issue was an important one on his negotiating agenda for a new relationship. 'Sometimes you need to move on. It's not healthy to hold on to something that doesn't nourish you any more.'

Doesn't like baggage, Flora noted, therefore jealous of old boyfriends. Plenty of them around, thank goodness.

Felix decided that the whole affair was rather piquant. It recalled *Les Liaisons Dangereuses*. It made him think of whispers by candlelight, stockings rolled over the knee and breasts swelling over the rim of a tight satin corset. Flora would be one of those delicious little maids. There was definitely something below-stairs about her kind of appeal. He needed to be back at the clinic by half past two. It was time to move the discussion on to the next item on the agenda.

Felix captured one of Flora's hands and applied it to the part of his body that required her attention.

*   *   *

It had stopped raining by the time Flora got

home. Drops sparkled on the wild flowers in the front garden—they were not really weeds and she saw no reason to pull up living things that wanted to share her life. The moss that crusted the drainpipes was a lovely fresh green. Her body had all kinds of souvenirs of Felix, exciting tastes, spots of fresh tenderness, places that felt deliciously stretched, or crushed or excited. As she tripped up to the front door she was conscious of the wonderful, optimistic energy in all her movements. It was a time of renewal, of rebirth, of awakening.

'Hello,' said Georgie.

'Hello,' Flora answered in surprise. Her friend seemed to be anxious, guilty and elated all at the same time. If Flora had been able to read auras, there would have been a halo of electric mauve all around Georgie's head. 'What's up?' she asked, opening the door.

'I've been with Dillon half the day.' Georgie followed her into the familiar hallway, remembering the choking weekend she had spent sanding the floorboards and the logistical nightmare of getting the essential six coats of varnish applied while Flora complained about the smell and her boyfriend of the moment climbed in and out of the front window getting their shopping. The boards looked as if they had been neglected ever since. She stumbled over Des's trainers.

'Oh,' said Flora, a touch of acid in her voice. 'Why's that, exactly?'

'He turned up at work.' Georgie noticed that Flora did not seem to be deeply concerned. Her inward smile was almost radiant. When she moved there was a languorous elasticity about it and when she was still she seemed wrapped in cat-like self-satisfaction. Georgie knew the signs, she had seen them many times. Flora had a new man. An unworthy feeling of annoyance presented itself in Georgie's mind. She had been scourging herself with guilt for hours, and all for nothing.

'Whatever for?' Flora demanded, reaching into the fridge and pouring herself a tall glass of elderflower cooler. 'D'you want some of this?'

'No thanks. It tastes of cat's piss. He was looking for me.'

'Go, Georgie!' Flora raised her glass with an ironic gesture. 'She moves, she shoots, she scores. Congratulations.'

'You don't care, do you?' Georgie leaned against the worktop, contemplating this friend who was so familiar and yet so distant.

'Donna fired him, you know that? He hasn't got a job any more.'

'Yes, I know.'

'You mean he told you?'

'We told each other pretty much everything. He was pissed at Donna.'

'He doesn't like her. Never has. Dillon resented all my friends.'

'Especially me,' said Georgie morosely. 'He hated the job, anyway.'

'Bollocks.' Flora slammed the fridge so hard it rocked. 'He was doing great until he had to screw up.'

'What do you mean, had to screw up?'

'Donna only fired him to turn up the heat. So he'd lose it, break up with me and start running after you.'

'She what?' Georgie felt outraged, whether on Dillon's behalf or her own she was not sure.

'If he'd come on to you in the first place, she wouldn't have had to do anything. She was gutted, believe me. He was her golden boy.'

'That's just sick,' said Georgie, feeling her skin turn cold as if the temperature had suddenly dropped. 'You've betrayed him. You've betrayed me. You could have ruined his life.'

'Oh come on,' Flora exhorted her. 'Don't you start with that crap. He can get a job anywhere. You and Felix would have broken up anyway. I was trapped. He wouldn't give me any space, he was all over me all the time. What else could I do? You didn't really expect me to marry him, did you?'

'Flora!'

'What?'

'Are you telling me you started the whole Heartswap thing just because you wanted to break up with Dillon?'

'Well, not exactly. But it was fun, you've got

to admit. Much more fun than sitting around in some poxy flat doing all the it-isn't-you-it's-me routine. I do despise that, you know. It totally sucks.'

'But he trusted you. He believed in you. He really loved you. And now he hates both of us.' Georgie was too distraught to register the slam of the front door.

'You had to tell him this "pretty much" everything, didn't you? You might as well have gone for the whole nine yards. You're such a pair of idiots, you deserve each other.'

'He's chucked it all in. Cancelled all his interviews. He wants to get out of London. Travel or something. Go to Australia. As soon as he's sold his flat.'

'Not long to wait then,' predicted Des, coming into the kitchen in bare feet, carrying his trainers in one hand and his boots in the other.

'Ugh!' Flora held her nose and opened the kitchen window with a violent shove which splintered the frame. 'Now look what you've made me do.'

'What do you mean?' Georgie demanded.

'I mean I got three offers on that rat-hole today. All cash, all keen, all looking to move in as soon as they can. We're going to sealed bids tomorrow. He could go Waltzing Matilda by Friday if he really wants. My feet are in agony.'

'Oh,' said Georgie.

'Way to go,' Flora commented. 'If you don't

get those filthy boots out of here I'll kill you.'

'Unless they kill me first. I need a vodka-cranberry before I take one more step,' insisted Des.

Georgie's attention suddenly switched to herself, a new and unaccustomed focus. 'And what do you mean, Felix and I were going to break up anyway?' she challenged Flora.

'I thought so,' Flora defended herself. 'Didn't you think so?' Georgie shook her head. 'Des?'

Des was now at the sink assaulting an ice tray. 'He had his feet well under the table there,' he paused to gesture at Georgie. 'What would he want to spoil that for?'

Georgie thought about the clean sheets, the *New York Review of Books* and the dog-eared edition of the *Neurological Digest*. 'You're having an affair with Felix,' she told Flora.

Flora shrugged her shoulders and walked out of the room.

Georgie followed her. 'Answer me,' she asked in a calm voice. 'You owe me that.'

'You see everything in terms of money,' Flora said. 'I don't owe you anything. I am not responsible for your choices. Or Felix's choices. Or for your anger.'

'I don't seem to be angry,' Georgie pointed out, surprised herself. 'I'm quite relieved, I think. I might even be pleased.'

'Answer the question, wickedness.' Des followed them, pulling ghoulish faces at Flora, who was sorting through the vials of aromatherapy oil which she kept in a Thai basket on the bookcase. 'Have you been shagging him?'

'Let's just say Donna's bought the tickets and we're all going to Bali, shall we?'

'You and Donna can go to Bali,' Georgie told her. 'I'm out of the deal. You're too much for me; I can't compete at your level. I'm just a mushy little bunny looking for someone to love me and I'll get run over on the Road Less Travelled. Roadkill in the gutter, that's my destiny in your world. And don't start in with a load of junk about how I'm just withdrawing and stuffing my energies.'

Flora shut her mouth on that precise observation. She took a deep breath to keep her own chakras aligned and clear out the negativity. 'Whatever,' she allowed, graciously, and began mixing a new euphoric blend for the Environmental Aroma Harmoniser. Ylang-Ylang, Lemongrass and Red Cedar seemed right for Felix.

'We were friends. I trusted you.'

'Trust is a delusion,' Flora instructed her. 'If you learned to live in balance with your energies you wouldn't need to manipulate people that way in order to feel secure. You should relax, Georgie. Learn to let go. Stop resisting change. Be more accepting.'

'I feel sick.' Georgie's mood suddenly flipped into sadness. She had lost it, the warm, nourishing closeness of a woman friend. The shelter of their intimacy, which they had cooperated to build carefully, year after year, had collapsed. She was alone on a cold mountain top and night was falling.

'You see,' Flora argued. 'Even your body is stuck in rejection.'

'My body is right. You're always telling me I should listen to my instincts more. How come now my instincts are telling me all this is vomit-making you've changed your opinion?'

'Can't you see? This is all your pattern of resistance, Georgie.'

'You're welcome to Felix. He's a control freak. A closet Nazi. You really suit each other.'

'Don't try to fix your pain, Georgie. Just be still and experience it. Be with it. Pain teaches us what we need to learn.'

'I think I need to learn to get out of here.' Georgie lunged for the door, her stomach heaving.

'Stop!' Des implored her. 'This is such a bummer. You can't do this, you're friends. You love each other.'

Georgie paused in the doorway and turned back. Flora looked up from her oils. They spoke as one woman. 'Love? What the fuck does that mean?'

The door slammed and Georgie was gone. Des pulled it open and ran after her. 'And as for you,' she said, stepping out into the street,

301

'let this be a lesson to you too, Bright Eyes. Wise up. Don't freeze in the headlights. Run like hell.'

CHAPTER NINETEEN

MAY 12–13

'Can I store my stuff in the garage?' Dillon asked his mother. 'I've taken an offer on the flat. They're desperate. They want to move in as soon as they can. It's a seller's market at the moment.'

'So I've heard,' said his mother drily. 'If it's a seller's market, you can tell them to wait. And where are you proposing to live?'

'I'm not going to live anywhere. Anywhere I know about. I need to sort my head out. I want to pack everything up, stick it in the garage and take off for the summer. Doesn't matter where. I thought I'd take the ferry to Spain and keep driving until I found a reason to stop.'

'Oh,' she said, making a superhuman effort to be tactful.

'You mean, "Oh dear,"' he told her. In a woman, his tone would have been called feisty.

'Do I? As bad as that? Is it that job?'

'Sort of,' he conceded.

'You weren't happy,' she told him.

'How did you know?'

'It was obvious. You looked like a dying dog whenever you talked about it. And you never talked about it unless I asked you. And then all you did was tell me how much your next bonus was going to be.'

'I thought you liked me making money,' he said in an aggrieved tone.

'I didn't know it was going to make you miserable,' she explained.

'Anyway, the money was stupid. The more I earned the worse I felt about it. I felt pathetic getting paid so much for inventing things nobody needed.'

'Money isn't everything.' She tried hard not to sound knowing. He did so hate it when she was right about things. 'So it isn't the job. Is it that girl?'

'It's all girls,' he confided, against his better judgement. It was usually a major mistake, confiding in La Mère.

'Worse than that, then? Worse than "Oh dear" is serious. Is the engagement off?'

'You needn't sound so pleased about it.'

'Darling, I am pleased, what can I do? Everything you told me about her sounded ghastly. We'd have fought like cats. I'm glad I never met her.'

'I wish you had met her. You could have scared her off and saved me from being miserable.'

'Would you like lunch?'

'Haven't you got a hairdresser?'

'I can cancel him. He's not the most important man in my life.' And what was a blow-dry when her boy was growing up?

'All right then,' Dillon agreed. His wounds were beyond the help of TCP and Elastoplast now, but at least someone cared that he was bleeding. Flora, for all she was so proud of her intuition, had never even noticed when he was hurt.

*   *   *

Georgie walked to the tube station and began to battle through the rush-hour crowd towards the platform marked Westbound. It was solidly packed with people. The atmosphere was a miasma of dirt and the stink of sweat.

A train hurtled in, the doors opened and more people burst out of the crammed carriages into the crowd. People fought past each other with shoulders and elbows, dragging bags of work and small children behind them. Georgie found herself backing away from the train until she was flattened against the wall. The stampede of feet trampled her toes.

She waited until the train had moved on, then made a break for the stairs. While I'm in rejection mode, I reject this, she decided. I will not be a zombie; I will not shuffle through my life as if I were already dead. I want a life, and I want to be awake to enjoy it.

Diving out of the populous main street, she stepped into a derelict doorway in an alley. In this sanctuary she pulled out her mobile, ignored her messages and called her bank, patiently keying in the numbers to activate the automatic information system. Her reserve was healthy. Her savings were handsome. She could afford to take some risks. She went through to an operator and withdrew from the joint account, leaving it in Felix's name alone.

Next she called the office. 'Where the fuck are you?' Great Lats hissed in her ear.

'Doesn't matter,' she told him. 'Can I see you tomorrow?'

'Uh . . .'

'It's business and it will be to your advantage,' she prompted him. Sex was such perverse stuff. Months of lusting after him and he'd never noticed; now she didn't care he was quivering with the fear that she was planning to make a move.

'I have plans,' he asserted nervously.

'It's like this,' she explained. 'I'm going to leave. I can fix it so you can have my job, or I can just bugger off and leave you to scrap for it with everyone else who thinks they can stand the pace. Now, can you get to the J Bar tomorrow at six or can't you?'

'I'll be there,' he agreed, with proper humility.

Georgie turned off her phone. Back on the street, she gulped down some filthy air and decided to find a coffee shop and wait until the rush was over. Her stomach actually rumbled. Gastric juices were churning around looking

306

for trouble. She had eaten nothing all day.

The nearest coffee place was To Bean Or Not To Bean, just off Hoxton Square. She awarded herself a large filter with biscotti and wondered what she had been in such a hurry to get home for anyway. Responding with its usual efficiency, her mind put up a menu of tasks. Dump Felix. Change the locks. Fix your nails. Get back the keys to Flat Eric. Throw out Felix's stuff.

She re-prioritised the list. Get back the keys to Flat Eric became number one. No change with change the locks, still in second place. Dump Felix at third, fixing her nails was at four because it took hours to strip off a power manicure, which left throwing out his stuff trailing the leaders at number five. She started to daydream pleasantly about life without Felix.

'Good evening,' said Smiley-and-Beefy, looming over her with a double-almond-mocha and a chocolate muffin. 'May I join you?'

'You certainly may,' she told him. This was a good omen.

'Weather's picking up,' he suggested as he squeezed on to the chair. It was a neo-Starck chair, the kind of thing Felix would have loved. No more of that rubbish, Georgie promised herself. I fancy something with silly gilded legs. Four legs, one at each corner, no cheating. After Fragonard, that's me.

307

'Is it?' she replied in an absent voice.

He bit off a hunk of muffin. 'Pity about Flora and that chap of hers. Whatsisname.'

'Dillon. No it isn't. She didn't deserve him.'

'No, she didn't. Bloody good bloke. Knew his art. He was going to commission something from one of my artists, you know. Wedding present for her. Hell of a lot of money. Artist wouldn't do it, so it's all one in the end.'

'You know I know about that,' she said, merrily slurping the last of her coffee. An idea had come to her. A scenario was taking shape. Certain material facts were becoming clear. If money was power, she might as well enjoy it.

'Oh yes. I forgot you were in on it all.' His vigorous brows twitched as he remembered some bizarre conversation about the price of 'River Number Four'. Something going on there he hadn't quite fathomed. She was like that, this one with the hips. Mysterious. 'How's that boyfriend of yours?' he enquired, in what he seriously thought was a casual tone.

'Fine.' Cautious but honest. Georgie congratulated herself. Of course Felix was fine. He wouldn't be leaving her until he was sure of Flora. He was just clearing his way out. He had never been to 17A. He didn't know that Flora was an environmental consultant with an ethereal cashflow and a burning ambition to jack it all in. He was still working on her as the killer bimbo from the drug company who was going to fund the next phase of his research.

Georgie crunched her biscotti; the crumbs met a giggle and she had to cough.

'That good, eh?' said Smiley-and-Beefy regretfully, slapping her on the back. 'You'll let me know if things change, won't you?'

She reached over and squeezed his huge arm. 'You'll be the first.'

'And who was that Scary Power Woman who came along with Flora to my opening?'

'Donna. Donna the prima donna. Head of New Business at Direct Warranty. Dillon's boss until she fired him. Why?'

'She needs some art,' he said, sounding as if he'd been talking himself into this opinion for days. Which he had. 'The walls of her soul are bare.'

'If that's the criterion, art is what she needs,' Georgie agreed. 'I could give you her number. Tell me, have you got a man with a van?'

'Eh?' He spluttered into his foam, perplexed.

'A man with a van. When you crate up stuff at the end of a show and get it moved. Not a specialist fine art remover. Just a man with a van who owes you a favour. I need some stuff moved tomorrow morning.'

'You'll put in a word for me?' negotiated Smiley-and-Beefy eagerly.

'For what it's worth. I'll give you Donna's direct line, mobile, home number and e-mail. And I'll throw in dinner because I haven't eaten all day and everyone's been dumping their stuff on me and one biscotti doesn't go far and I may shortly faint from hunger. You can choose the restaurant. How about it? Do we have a deal?'

'Absolutely,' promised Smiley-and-Beefy, pulling out his phone. 'Let's see if Momo can give us a table.'

*   *   *

Georgie got home late. Felix was already asleep but, wary of his morning habits, she chose to sleep on the sofa. She woke up early, copied some files from the computer then went out for more coffee. At eight-thirty, she was at her door to meet the locksmith.

'Hello, darling,' said Felix sleepily, when the drilling had woken him. 'What's going on? Did you lose your keys? I wondered where you were.'

'I need the car,' she said, holding out her hand. Felix stumbled back to the bedroom and returned a few seconds later with his own keys, which Georgie handed to the locksmith.

'Would you mind taking this one off?' she asked him, indicating the sliver of metal that would animate Flat Eric. How much better life would be when she had time to get rid of the power manicure.

Georgie threw the rest of the keys back to Felix, who muffed the catch and had to scoop them off the floor, dragging his bathrobe around his chicken knees. 'You're out of here,' she told him.

'Huh?'

'You'd better get dressed. In about ten minutes a man with a van is coming round to move you out. You and your stupid furniture, your crap music, your espresso machine, your clothes, your books and your wine.'

'Way to go!' muttered the locksmith admiringly, through a mouthful of screws.

'Don't be ridiculous,' Felix retorted. 'You're just being childish.'

'Maybe,' Georgie agreed. 'I missed out on some of my childhood, remember? There are things I had to skip. Now I'd like to catch up.' To the locksmith's regret, she pushed Felix into the kitchen and shut the door. 'All those vital developmental stages I need to complete. Like name-calling. You're an arsehole. You're a pretentious ass. You're a control freak. You'd make Himmler look *laissez-faire*—'

'Who?'

'Himmler. The one who ran the SS. The one with two balls but very small.'

'That was Goebbels.'

'I think not. You're a cultural illiterate. You're a fuckwit. You're a seam-head. You've got legs like a chicken and you make me sick.'

Felix folded his arms to stop his bathrobe gaping and assumed a superior smile. 'Have you been talking to your friend Flora?'

'Probably for the last time.'

'Because I think she has some problems. She came to the clinic yesterday. She seems to have trouble dealing with reality.'

'You may be right.' Georgie enjoyed that idea for the first time. 'I think she's been claiming she works for some drug company and earns a lot of money. Because you know she has this environmental aromatherapy business. If you can call it a business.'

'You mean she's completely delusional?' Felix struggled between hope and despair.

'I know you two will be just perfect together. I've given the van driver her address.'

'She was trying to suggest that you and she had been in some conspiracy to seduce me.' Felix deployed his piercing look. 'I mean, I know you, Georgina. I just couldn't see it. I thought you understood how important it is to have trust in a relationship. You have your own problems, of course, we all do, but I've always thought that it was basically important to you to live with integrity.'

'That's why I'm throwing you out,' she told him, as if explaining to a five-year-old child. 'Now go and get dressed before the driver gets here.'

*   *   *

Felix looked at the seating arrangement in the living room at 17A. The choice was a rather passé purple futon which was losing stuffing

312

from all its corners, a beanbag with a dark stain in its hollow and an old pine carver chair with a broken arm. There was a peculiar smell in the air. He picked the chair.

'So,' he said to Flora, trying a feel for the situation. 'This is where you live?'

'For the moment,' she told him with a meaningful sigh.

'And you work . . .'

'Over there.' She pointed to her desk, a sagging trestle table whose paint-splattered legs emerged below a makeshift covering of torn oilcloth. A cardboard box contained some papers. To the side of the box was pinned a yellow note with a smiley face and the announcement, 'I AM A MONEY MAGNET,' printed in green ink. Another note was stuck to the grubby white wall and it read, 'I WELCOME WEALTH INTO MY LIFE.' The third one, taped to the front of Flora's dog-eared Filofax, said, 'I ACCEPT THE ABUNDANCE OF THE UNIVERSE.'

'This is my product,' she told him with pride, unplugging the Harmoniser. 'It releases aromatherapy scents into the atmosphere. I get my oils from this little firm that imports high-grade organic . . .'

Felix felt faint. Georgina had been right. He had been conned. He was a victim. The impossible had happened.

He thought fast. Felix hated to look helpless. Women hated men to look helpless

313

also. To a woman, neediness was a turnoff. It had never been his way to appeal directly to a woman's generosity at the start of a relationship. Therefore he had not told Flora that he was looking urgently for a home. The van containing his possessions was parked around the corner and the driver was enjoying a pint and a pie in a pub at Felix's expense.

Felix adjusted his perception of Flora. She was definitely not an attractive potential partner. She might be a passable prospect for sex. Apart from that, she had only one thing that he wanted.

'Darling, are you OK?' Flora sensed some turbulence in his aura. The aura that was normally as cool and unruffled as an alpine pool. Also, his skin tone seemed almost green.

'I think my blood sugar's a little low this morning.'

'Let me get you some lemon tea with honey,' she offered sweetly.

'Yes,' said Felix, massaging his forehead with his fingertips. 'Perhaps that would help.'

As soon as he heard her enter the kitchen, he reached for her Filofax and extracted Donna's home address and telephone number.

'So what made you decide to drop by?' Flora enquired, trying to walk provocatively without spilling the tea.

'I'm seeing a colleague in the Paediatric Department at Bart's' he improvised, taking the mug from her and putting it down. 'It

314

seemed a good opportunity. Good heavens, is that the time? I'm sorry, sweetheart. I can't be late. I'll have to run.'

At the door he made himself kiss her. 'I'll call you,' he promised. 'Very soon.'

Flora knew exactly what that meant. She would never hear from him again unless he hit a dry weekend and was desperate enough to try it on for a shag. She had to stop herself from slamming the door behind him.

'Fuck you!' she muttered. 'Fuck Georgie. Fuck everything.'

*   *   *

'What a mare's nest,' said Georgie's father sadly. 'It sounds like *Love's Labour's Lost* in modern dress. I do despise modern dress.'

Flat Eric was carrying them smoothly along the leafy lane which led to the Sir Rudolph Trippitt Retirement Home for Actors. Her father's new wheelchair rattled elaborately in the boot.

'I thought something would have to give,' he continued, watching the trees flash past. 'You didn't have as much fun as you deserved, did you? All work and no play, that was your story.

'Are you saying I'm dull?' she demanded, touching the gas to flash past the car in front. Her father also despised fast driving, because it scared him.

'You're a dangerous woman,' he chuckled,

315

gripping the dashboard. 'The best sort.'

'So what am I going to do?'

'Slow down,' he advised firmly.

'No, I mean about Dillon?'

'I like the sound of him,' said her father in a reflective tone. 'He is the only character who comes out of this affair with any honour in the last act. I suppose he's crawled away to lick his wounds?'

'He isn't answering his messages.'

'Well, you'll have to go and see him, won't you? PDQ. None of this letting "I dare not" wait upon "I would". You know that's the right line? But it always sounds the wrong way round to me. Anyway, go to it, girl.'

CHAPTER TWENTY

MAY 14–28

Dillon looked around his flat. From the wreck of his life he had salvaged two suitcases of clothes, seven crates of books, five crates of music, one TV, a bag of stuff from the kitchen and his coffee table. The rest was to be consigned to the sea of fate. The new owner was buying the dining table, the chairs, the bookcases and the sofa.

He had refused to sell the bed. That deserved to be burned, infested as it was with bad memories. After considering the matter longer than it deserved, Dillon had resolved that to burn the bed would be giving Flora too much importance. A banal last journey to the public rubbish dump would be more fitting. He would throw it into the jaws of a municipal digger and with it ditch a major mistake and whatever weakness had led him to it. When he had sorted his head out, his heart would be clad in steel and he would never open it again to any female. Shag 'em and dump 'em, that would be his style. Rock till you drop. By the time he was fifty he would have been on a triumphant sex-binge for twenty years. He would be as sleazy as Rod Stewart and damn proud of it.

His car was not big enough to take the whole bed. It would need two trips. Today, Sunday, he would take the base, which had been made in two halves and was easy to dismantle. On Monday he would roll up the mattress and take that. Then he would dump the rest of his worldly goods in his mother's garage and begin a new life.

The table, now revealed in its full glory, ought to be polished before it was stored. Dillon went out to buy polish, and was forced to travel to the supermarket a mile away.

While he was out, Georgie arrived in her car. The row of bulging black bin bags outside the door told her which building housed Dillon. She consulted the names on the state-of-the-art security system and tried his bell. There was no answer.

'You want him?' The owner of the kebab shop paused in the middle of cranking up his shutters and indicated the bin bags. 'He just left. I see him. He moving out, you know.'

'I know,' she said.

'Please, come in. Have a drink,' he invited her. Stale kebab fumes at ambient temperature gushed into the street as he opened the door.

'Maybe later,' Georgie promised him, and drove away to find somewhere more inviting to kill time.

When Dillon returned, the shop owner intercepted him. 'Someone looking for you,' he announced. 'I know you not be long. I ask her to come in but she say maybe come back later.'

'What was she like?' Dillon asked, telling himself he didn't want to know and it couldn't possibly matter.

'Nice girl,' said the owner appreciatively.

'Dark hair?' Dillon suggested.

'I don't know. Maybe. Nice car.'

'Oh right. I know who that is. Thanks,' said Dillon. He decided to buy a Coke. Packing up your life was thirsty work.

Back in the flat, he polished his table until it gleamed like gold. It was a satisfying thing to do. He remembered the pleasure it had given him to make it, the excellent smell of the wood, the fun of drawing the design, the fascination of finishing every tiny sliver of ebony for the inlaying to the precise size it needed to be. Perhaps he had taken a wrong turning after that. Hell, the country was crawling with design millionaires. Why shouldn't he be one of them? People would always need chairs.

He spun out the polishing as long as he dared, until a bare quarter of an hour before the dump closed. The owner helped him to carry the bed base down the stairs and load it into his car. Dillon found himself glancing apprehensively up the street. Did he want her to turn up or not? He wasn't sure.

'I'm going to the dump with this,' he told his

malodorous neighbour. 'I'll be about an hour.'

'OK,' the man assured him.

Ten minutes after he had gone, Georgie came back. She tried the bell once more. No answer.

A train began roaring over the railway bridge, drowning the street in noise. The shop owner shouted to Georgie, but she could not hear him. As he ran across the road to speak to her, she drove away without seeing him.

'She was here!' the man said indignantly when Dillon returned. 'The same woman, here again! I say her to wait but she don't hear me!'

'Thanks.' Dillon tried to sound as if he didn't care. He tried to feel as if he didn't care. Neither of these pretences was successful.

He cracked a beer and flopped down on the sofa. The television offered him a depressing game of cricket, the mating of the loggerhead turtle and two hundred Seventh Day Adventists singing spirituals in Bradford. He picked the turtles, killed the sound and decided to check his messages. There were five.

'Um, this is Georgie,' said the first one. 'I know you may not want to hear from me, but I was wondering how you are.'

'Me again,' said the second. 'I realised you don't have my number any more.' She repeated it twice.

'Only Georgie again,' said the third message.

320

'God, this is embarrassing,' sighed the fourth.

The fifth message was the longest. 'Look, if you're not answering, I don't blame you. I can't believe I got into anything so bad. I am sorry. I know it's pointless me saying that. I just don't want to leave it here. Look, I'm going to come over. See you if I see you.'

He decided to leave his phone on. He got a call from Des, ostensibly to confirm that he would come round for the keys at ten the next morning.

'How are you?' Des asked in a tentative voice.

'Not too bad, thanks. I'm all packed.'

Hopefully, he mentioned, 'Madam's here.'

'Did she ask you to tell me that?' Dillon found he was snarling.

'No, no. I just thought . . .'

'I don't care where she is. Anywhere she can eat shit and die would be fine by me.'

'Why are you taking this so seriously?' Des asked. It puzzled him that straights got so screwed up about sex. 'It was only a bit of fun.'

'Not for me,' said Dillon. 'I'll see you in the morning.'

He played his messages again. In the misty blue of the coral sea, the turtles paddled lustfully around each other, getting washed apart by the swell every time they made flipper contact. His thoughts swirled elusively, refusing to settle into a recognisable shape. He was hurt. He had been badly treated. They were all bad people. The future was exciting. The future was frightening. He wanted to see her. He did not want to see her. She had behaved the best of them. They had all behaved badly. He felt bad.

Eventually, he recalled a half-empty bottle of whisky in one of the crates and decided to drink enough of it to stop himself dreaming of Georgie. Just before he went to bed he decided to erase his messages.

*   *   *

At first, Dillon's morning went exactly according to plan. At nine a removal van arrived and a disappointed pair of moving men loaded up his modest household and set off for his mother's house in Hampshire. When Des arrived at ten, the mattress was squashed in the boot of the Saab and Dillon's travelling bag was on the back seat.

'That's it then,' Des observed, taking the keys which Dillon had ready for him. 'So what's next for you now? Where are you going?'

'To the tip with that,' Dillon told him, indicating the mattress, 'and then to Spain.'

'Have we got a forwarding address?' Des's pen was poised over his jotter. Dillon gave him his mother's address.

'Well, I'll say, *"hasta llego"*,' said Des,

shaking his hand, 'and good luck.'

Dillon drove away. Des, who expected the new owners of the flat in half an hour, bought himself a kebab and posed, leaning against the door, while he ate it.

Flat Eric glided to a halt in front of him. Des's first thought was that Georgie's haircut was still looking good and he had done a great job with it. Then he deduced that if Georgie was here, she was looking for Dillon. Which had to mean that she hadn't scored with the bloke with great lats he'd seen her with in the J Bar on Saturday. Who had to be gay anyway. So something could come of the Heartswap madness after all. Des had never quite rejected the theory that all you needed was love.

'Brilliant stuff!' he shouted at Georgie as she opened the car door. 'But you've missed him. He's gone off to the tip. And here's his address. Go get him girl!'

Georgie thought of being reserved and enigmatic, then thought again. 'But where's the tip?' she squeaked in alarm.

He drew her a map and she roared away.

On his way to the tip, Dillon's thoughts finally took shape. Georgie was an amazing woman. He wanted to see her. If he had to choose between being irredeemably wronged without her and magnanimously forgiving with her, he'd go for the second one. Which meant that he might be going through some temporary love thing for her. So the Rod

Stewart plan was on hold. She seemed to like him. In fact, she must like him a lot. He had erased her telephone number. At least he could stop by and say goodbye. He drove to the Eon Tower.

Georgie drove to the tip but did not meet Dillon. The supervisor was positive that nobody with an old black Saab 900 had been there all morning.

The reception guard at the Eon Tower recognised Dillon and told him regretfully that Ms Lambton had not yet arrived. Great Lats, grand with his new responsibilities as acting senior fund manager, came down to assure him of this personally. Dillon extracted the information that Ms Lambton was on extended leave and was not expected to return. Great Lats, wondering if this fazed-looking bloke with good thighs could possibly be a stalker, refused to give Dillon any more information.

When he had returned to his office the reception guard, who had seen the way this man and Ms Lambton had looked at each other, rang through to Human Resources, gave them a story about redirecting a courier, and obtained Georgie's address.

Dillon drove to Notting Hill Gate and found no one at home.

Georgie threw Flat Eric on to the M25, hurtled off on the M3, whistled off on the A339, zipped around Alton and found herself skidding to a standstill in front of a small but elegant Regency house. A cuckoo was calling. The blooms of a wisteria dripped from the front wall. At the side of the house was a spacious Regency-style garage, into which the two moving men were carrying Dillon's coffee table.

'Excuse me,' she said to the woman who was watching them, 'are you Mrs MacGuire?'

'Not any more,' said the woman brightly, 'but I am Dillon's mother. You aren't Flora, are you?'

'No way,' Georgie assured her.

'Then you must be the other one,' Dillon's mother concluded. 'I liked the sound of you. You'd better hurry, dear. He's getting the ferry at one. Portsmouth to Bilbao. Get back on the A339 then take the A3. Fast as you can! Not a moment to lose!'

'Thank you!' called Georgie, jumping back into her car.

'See you again!' Dillon's mother waved energetically.

Flat Eric ate the rest of the route, zipped through the back streets of Portsmouth and got her to the docks at 12.23. The woman on the gate sent her to the ticket office, where another woman listened to her story and suggested her best bet was to buy a day ticket for Le Havre. 'You won't need your passport for a day trip. The ticket'll get you through the barrier to the embarkation area. The Le Havre boat is that one.' She pointed with her biro through the office window. 'And that's the Bilbao boat on the next quay. So what you do on the embarkation side is up to you.'

As if it was advising her to chill out, a light drizzle began to fall. Georgie put Flat Eric at the end of a queue of cars waiting for the Le Havre boat, got out and ran across the quay. She checked every vehicle queuing for the *Pride of Galicia*. She looked behind the caravans. The truckers whistled appreciatively as she made sure there was no black Saab on the far side of their rigs.

At 12.35, the queue of trucks began to move. In distraction, Georgie dashed to the edge of the water and watched them rolling aboard the ferry.

When the last truck had rumbled up the gangway, the caravans began to follow. Georgie stood on tiptoe to see the entrance to the quay. Nothing. No black Saab. No Dillon. He had changed his mind. She tried his phone one last time, but only the voicemail answered.

The cars fired up and followed the caravans. At three minutes to one a platoon of Hell's Angels swooped through the entrance gate and spluttered aboard.

The stewards who had directed the drivers conferred in a group, their collars turned up against the dropping wet. Finally, the senior steward broke away and walked over to Georgie. 'Excuse me, miss, are you booked on

326

this crossing?' He nodded behind her.

Georgie turned around to see Flat Eric all on his own in the middle of the empty quay. The boat for Le Havre had loaded up and sailed. She had never even noticed.

'I'm afraid not,' she told the steward.

'Well, do you want to be? Because there's one berth left.'

'Oh.' Georgie's instinct told her that it would be a really good idea to get on the boat. It mentioned that she had never been to Spain, that she had nothing better to do, that if she couldn't have Dillon she could at least have an adventure and that recklessness always worked.

'Are you waiting for someone? Because we can't hold the boat more than five minutes.'

'I'll get on,' she agreed.

When Flat Eric's front tyres were six inches from the gangway, Dillon's old black Saab hurtled through the entrance and drew up beside him.

Dillon got out of his car. Georgie got out of her car. The stewards exchanged anxious glances. The *Pride of Galicia* sounded its siren. A group of truckers gathered around the entrance to the hold, watching the action.

'My God, you're here!' Dillon's mind broke up. Things like this did not happen to him. 'I went to your place to find you.'

'I went to your place to find you.'

The truckers started cheering. It seemed

best to go for a kiss.

The senior steward assumed all the authority of his position and went to have a word. 'I don't want to break this up, but the boat is ready to sail and I've only got one berth.'

'We can take mine,' Georgie offered.

'The long-term car park is just over there,' prompted the steward.

'OK. Give me one minute.' Dillon took another kiss to be going on with and prepared to leave his car.

*   *   *

After ten days in Bali, Donna, Flora and Des felt they had done justice to the island's culture, that they were bored with the beach and deserved a full day by the pool. They lay side by side in the soft, fierce heat and watched the humming birds visiting the hibiscus.

'Do you think they get bored, flitting from one flower to another?' Des drained the last of his vodka-cranberry and wondered how many calories there would be in another. He didn't want to go home looking like a blimp. Especially since he'd got a date with that boy with the great lats.

'Their brains are too small,' Flora murmured. It was the right day to get her back brown. Bali was so spiritual. She was really inspired by the way the people lived, in harmony with nature. Perhaps Donna would lend her the money to take home some batiks.

'What am I going to do? Speaking of small-brained creatures.' Donna snapped shut her PowerBook.

'Checking your e-mails?' Des suddenly felt weary.

Donna had messages from Smiley-and-Beefy and from Felix. She had no intention of letting Flora know these identities. It wouldn't be important once they got home. Flora was on the way out with Donna. She had realised in Bali that Flora was never going to be a fast-track woman. All right for a holiday, but a waste of time in real life.

Blissfully unaware, Flora murmured, 'What's the problem?'

'Sex,' hazarded Des. 'Is there anything else worth worrying about?'

'I've got two blokes on the scene,' Donna told them complacently. 'I can't decide which one to go with.'

'What's the choice?' Des propped himself up on one elbow. He was interested.

'The arty shagmeister or the guy next door. Actually, the guy three floors down. New neighbour.'

'Could be embarrassing if it all goes horribly wrong,' Flora suggested. She was glad to have been able to master the concept of relationships going horribly wrong. Every day she gained in wisdom.

'Yeah, but he's kinda suave.' Donna gave a wistful sigh. 'And the other one's a business contact. That could be difficult.'

'Have they got any money? That's the real question.'

'Of course they haven't got any money. They're as broke as each other. Like I care. I mean, what's the point of having money if it can't get you what you want?'

'Right,' agreed Flora.

'Then why do you have to make a choice?' Des asked what he considered the obvious question.

'That's true.' Donna rubbed some SPF30 with aloe vera into her lips to keep them kissable. 'Why am I obsessing about this? It doesn't matter, does it? They're all the same.'